TERROR ILLUSION

With best wishes to
John & Hazel Armstrong

James R. Conway

James R. Conway

Published 2012 by Island Publishers
Haying Island PO110EL

www.islandpublishers.co.uk

ISBN 978-0-9573732-1-1

British Library Cataloguing in Publication Data
A catalogue record for this book is available from the British Library

Printed and bound in the UK by Biddles, part of the MPG Books Group, Bodmin and King's Lynn

Prologue

There was a bridge, of course, at Ravensgill Bridge, but not much else. There was a railway line that saw a few trains each day. There was a railway station, where the paint looked fresh and bright and well tended flowers grew in boxes beneath the windows and along the platforms. That was pretty much all there was to Ravensgill Bridge.

Except for the noise. There was always noise at Ravensgill Bridge, always the noise of flowing water draining off the fells and always the vocal accompaniment of sheep. Peace and quiet? There was a great deal of peace at Ravensgill Bridge, but it was not actually so quiet.

Chapter 1

Jonathan Long needed a project. He was supposed to be enjoying his retirement but idle retirement did not suit Jonathan. He had spent most of his life as a creative problem solver and his retirement had been unexpectedly forced upon him at the relatively young age of forty-eight.

So, Jonathan had taken himself off on one of his occasional trips to London. Perhaps, he thought, a change of scene would provide some mental stimulation.

He was not really a "city man", having spent years in the busy, noisy, bright lights of Los Angeles and the Hollywood movie industry. He was happy and somewhat content to be living in the place he had selected to enjoy his retirement, high in the Pennine hills in northwest England. However, occasionally he needed a change of scenery to get his brain back into gear, so he had left his Pennine idyll and taken the train to London for a three day midweek trip. One of the things that Jonathan loved about England was the railway system. From Ravensgill Bridge, the train would take him two hundred miles, right into the heart of London in a little under four hours. Of course, he could drive himself but why bother facing all that traffic and once in London he would have to find somewhere to park, probably paying an outrageous parking charge and a good chance that someone would steal his car or at least kick in the door or break the window. The train fast clean and comfortable, was a much better way to travel, especially at this time of year. Early December brought rain, ice and all sorts of other challenges to drivers.

Jonathan had checked into a small hotel in South Kensington. He had planned to spend most of his time in London visiting the museums. He particularly enjoyed the museum district of London. As a college student in London many years ago, he had found that the museums offered a cheap way to occupy a Saturday or Sunday when his meagre student finances were running low. His favourite was the Science Museum with its fascinating working models of all sorts of inventions and machines.

The problem with being a tourist in London in December was that outdoor activities were rather limited both by the weather, which was often windy and rainy, and by the short winter days. The sun would rise at about eight in the morning and would set again by four in the afternoon. However, to Jonathan these were not so much limitations as charming quirks of English life. The early darkness of the evening meant that the London streets and shops, decorated for Christmas, looked bright and cheerful, as did the London pubs.

To Jonathan, there was nothing in the world that even came close to an English pub, whether it was a charming old country pub with flagstone floors and oak beams or a typical Victorian London pub such as the one he was in this evening. It was very different from his local pub back in the Pennine village of Ravensgill Bridge. This London pub looked like something from the Hollywood set of a Sherlock Holmes mystery but it was a genuine pub, probably here more than a hundred years. Away from the brightly lit bar area, each table had an old fashioned oil lamp which provided a warm glow, illuminating photographs of Victorian London on the wall, street markets, railway locomotives, horse-drawn brewery wagons carrying casks of beer. Outside, a steady drizzle spattered against the window as office workers headed home.

It was early evening and Jonathan had enjoyed a delightful afternoon in the Science Museum, studying the history of film special effects. He planned to travel back home to Ravensgill Bridge tomorrow. He thought he might get a train late morning so that he could have lunch on the train and complete most of the journey in daylight. Tonight he was going to enjoy a couple of beers and a pub meal, then take a cab back to his hotel. Maybe if the rain stopped he might walk.

Jonathan ordered a pint of beer at the bar, paid for it, and took it over to a table by the window. He watched the pedestrians rushing by outside, under a forest of umbrellas, watched the raindrops trickling down the window and he had a feeling of warmth and security. He had lived in California for nearly twenty years but he had never truly felt that he belonged there. But here, tonight, he had a strong sense of peace with the world.

He had brought a book into the pub with him. When he visited museums, he always stopped by the museum bookshop and picked up something related to what he had been studying. Jonathan was not an idle browser when he visited a museum. He would pick a subject and seek out all the information that he could. This particular afternoon he had decided to study special effects in films.

As Jonathan enjoyed his beer and got absorbed in his book, the pub started to fill up with people, mostly commuters who had decided to shelter from the rain and wait for the rush hour to die down. Jonathan mused that his retirement had allowed him to escape from the workday rat race but in the back of his mind, he also envied these people their sense of identity, their sense of purpose. Since he retired these were things that he had come to value. There was no way that he wanted to get back into the rough and tumble of the corporate world but he still needed to find some sense of purpose and direction in his life.

The pub had become considerably more crowded by the time Jonathan was ready for his next pint of beer. When he looked over towards the bar, he saw that it was packed two or three deep with customers holding up empty glasses and waving five or ten pound notes, trying to attract the attention of the one overworked barmaid who was rushed off her feet.

Leaving his book on the table and his overcoat over a chair, Jonathan stood up and walked over towards the bar. He saw that there was slightly less of a crowd at the one end of the bar so he positioned himself there to wait for his fresh pint. Sarina, the barmaid, always got stressed at this time of day, the evening rush hour. The wet weather made it even busier as more commuters dropped into the pub to escape the rain for an hour. She tried to remember who the next customer was among the sea of faces, money and empty beer glasses. Her eyes fell on Jonathan who was quietly waiting at the end of the bar with his empty glass.

"I'm next!" shouted a man over near the middle of the bar. "A pint of bitter, please!"

Sarina turn round to collect a clean pint glass from a shelf behind the bar. When she turned back, she could see no one at the bar except Jonathan. She shook her head and walked over to him.

"What can I get you, luv?"

"A pint of Best Bitter, please," said Jonathan.

Sarina turned around to get a fresh glass for Jonathan's pint. When she turned back, she saw the crowd of faces again. Confused, she drew Jonathan's pint and passed it across the bar to him, then went on to serve the next customer without even asking Jonathan for the money for his drink. Jonathan, being a generally honest soul, placed the money on the bar and carried his pint of beer back to his table.

His ability to produce hallucinations in people could prove very useful at times.

Chapter 2

The rain had cleared by the time Jonathan woke up next morning and the London streets had a freshness in the wintry morning sunshine. Jonathan thought that it would be a great day for travelling. He got showered and dressed and packed his suitcase, and then he left his hotel room and went downstairs to the small dining room where the smell of breakfast bacon and sausages persuaded him to indulge himself in a full English breakfast.

After breakfast, he collected his suitcase from the room and checked out of the hotel. He planned to catch the train that left King's Cross at noon. It was only just gone ten o'clock so, rather than call a cab he went down into the London Underground station at South Kensington. From his college days, Jonathan knew the main routes of the London Underground system like the back of his hand and he caught a Piccadilly line train, which would take him directly to King's Cross.

As Jonathan stood on the platform at South Kensington station, his mind went back again to his college days in London, years before his American adventure and it seemed almost as if he had never been away. Superficially, many things had changed in Britain while he was gone. Everybody seemed to be constantly chattering on their mobile phones or pecking away typing text messages with their thumbs. How had we organized our lives back then? Perhaps we planned our days better in those days or maybe we weren't so spontaneous. Maybe life was slower, maybe we thought more about things. Was it better then, is it better now? Who knows?

Jonathan's' musing was suddenly interrupted by the rush of air from the tunnel to his right and the roar of the train as it pulled into the station three hundred and fifty feet below the streets of South Kensington.

He boarded the train, the automatic doors hissed shut and with a jolt and an electrical hum, the train plunged into the tunnel at the end of the station.

The train worked its way through the tunnels deep under central London. Knightsbridge. Hyde Park Corner. Green Park. Piccadilly Circus. Leicester Square. Covent Garden. The names sounded romantic to Jonathan, probably because he didn't have to struggle through the rush hour every morning and evening. It was mid morning now and even though it was a weekday, there were few passengers in his car. A lady got on at Knightsbridge carrying a large green Harrods bag stuffed with purchases, presumably Christmas presents. A couple of teenage girls got off at Covent Garden, giggling irritatingly. Covent Garden had been a flower and vegetable market in Jonathan's college years but now it had been converted to trendy boutiques and bistros.

Finally, the tube train pulled into Kings Cross and Jonathan picked up his suitcase and got off the train. As he navigated his way through the station and up the long escalators to the street level, he started thinking once more about his difficulty in finding a mental challenge to occupy him in his retirement. He had hoped that a few days away from his usual surroundings might help but he felt no clearer in his mind now than when he had arrived in London a few days ago. If anything, he felt even more at a loss. Still, he had a few hours train journey through the English countryside, it was a cold, clear, sunny day and perhaps inspiration would strike before he got home.

Jonathan checked the departure board at the Kings Cross main line station concourse and saw that his train was scheduled to leave on time at noon from platform seven. He had about twenty minutes before the train was due to leave so he made his way to platform seven and walked alongside the train until he found a fairly empty coach just ahead of the buffet car. He climbed aboard, put his suitcase into the overhead rack together with his overcoat and settled comfortably into his seat. He placed his book on the table in front of him and checked his watch against the digital clock above the platform outside his window.

Twelve minutes to departure. The train had been fairly empty when Jonathan came aboard but as he waited for departure, the carriage that he was in began to fill up. He stood up, pulled his overcoat from the luggage rack and placed it folded on the empty seat beside him to discourage anyone from sitting right next to him. This lunchtime departure was popular on a Friday, because it was the last departure that would finish its run in daylight. The later Friday departures would probably be standing room only as long distance commuters finished their workweek and headed back to their homes in towns like Peterborough and Grantham for the weekend. Jonathan looked around and felt guilty as he sat next to his folded overcoat, but apart from one old woman across the aisle who gave him a strange look, everyone else seemed preoccupied with his or her own affairs. They were reading newspapers, calling and texting on their mobile phones, an elderly couple were nodding off to sleep. Jonathan decided to bury his nose in his book.

Three minutes to departure. Jonathan had barely finished reading the table of contents when he heard a crashing and banging coming from the far end of the carriage. He looked up and saw a woman struggling into the carriage, carrying two suitcases. They were not unusually large but from the way that the woman was struggling with them, they were clearly quite heavy.

"Excuse me!"

"Oops!"

"Sorry!"

The woman made her way down the carriage with her suitcases, bumping into people on the way. Jonathan shrugged his shoulders and went back to his book.

"Excuse me."

"Excuse me."

The woman's voice was louder and when Jonathan looked up, he could see that she was talking to him.

"Excuse me."

"Yes," said Jonathan.

"Could you help me, please?"

Realizing that he was cornered, the courteous side of Jonathan's nature kicked in.

"Sure," he said and he stood up.

"Could you help me get these suitcases up onto the luggage rack, please? I'm afraid they're a bit heavy!"

Jonathan lifted one of the suitcases and quickly put it down again.

"I see what you mean!"

"Sorry!"

He tried again, grabbing the handle of the suitcase with both hands and with a grunt, he managed to lift it onto the table. It must have weighed fifty pounds. He paused for a moment to catch his breath then lifted the suitcase over his head and managed to slide it onto the luggage rack next to his own suitcase. Red faced from exertion he looked around at the woman who was still standing in the aisle of the carriage.

"You're so kind," she said and her face had a look of gratitude and embarrassment all at the same time. "The other one is not quite so heavy"

Jonathan managed a smile and lifted the second suitcase onto the rack.

"Thank you so much. You are so kind"

Now it was Jonathan's turn to feel embarrassed. "No problem," he mumbled and he sat back down in is seat.

At that moment, the train started to move out of the station and the woman, who was still standing in the aisle half slid, half fell into the seat opposite Jonathan, facing him across the table.

"Phew! Just made it!" she gasped.

Jonathan grunted and picked up his book.

"Thank you so much," the woman said again.

She did not seem to expect a reply so Jonathan shrugged his shoulders and turned his attention back to his book.

The inside of the carriage was briefly illuminated by the bright winter sunshine as the train rolled slowly out from the shade of the station canopy but almost immediately the carriage was back in dim light again as the train accelerated into the tunnel which carried the tracks beneath the houses just to the north of the station. A minute later and the carriage was brightly lit again as the train emerged from the tunnel and picked up speed through the northern suburbs of London. Jonathan checked his watch. As usual, an on-time departure. Jonathan smiled. The train was now at its cruising speed of one hundred and twenty five miles an hour.

"It's Karen, by the way. Karen Wilson," said the woman with a smile as she extended a hand across the table towards him.

Jonathan looked up from his book.

"Jonathan," he said, lightly shaking her hand and then withdrawing his hand as quickly but politely as he could. He thought that Karen had a pleasant mature voice. He usually didn't like engaging in conversation while travelling but Karen seemed pleasant enough and she seemed to want to talk.

"Are you going all the way through to Leeds?" said Jonathan, trying to make polite small talk and secretly hoping that she might be getting off at the next stop in just over half an hour.

"Yes. You too?"

"Yes," he replied, then after a short pause he continued.

"Yes, I change trains there. I get the train over the Pennines."

Jonathan looked out at the wintry sunshine, bright but cold and the sun was low in the south western sky as the train sped on through the most flat countryside to the north of London. They had been running for about fifteen minutes but they were already about thirty miles out and were well clear of the northern suburbs of London.

The doors at the end of the carriage hissed open and an attendant in uniform came in and started taking passengers orders for snacks and drinks. There were a couple of menu cards lying on the table and Jonathan picked up one. Karen picked up the other and they studied their lunch choices.

After a few moments, Karen looked up from her menu and said, "Could I buy you lunch? It's the least I can do after the way that you helped me."

"There's really no need," said Jonathan.

"It's the least I can do."

Jonathan thought that one refusal was polite but two would be churlish.

"OK," he said, "I'll probably just have a sandwich and a beer. Thank you."

"Oh good!" she said.

The attendant arrived at their table and looked at Karen, waiting for her order. She waved him over to take Jonathan's order first and the attendant turned to face Jonathan.

"Sir?"

"I'll have a toasted ham and cheese sandwich please. And a lager." He put down his menu and smiled at Karen, nodded towards her partly as a way of indicating his appreciation and partly to invite her to place her own order.

"I'll have a Chicken Caesar Salad." She paused for a moment. "And a glass of white wine, please."

The attendant moved on to the next pair of seats and, unsure of what to say next, Jonathan picked up his book again and started reading.

"That book looks very interesting," said Karen.

Jonathan looked up. "Excuse me?"

"Strange title."

He turned the book over and looked at the cover.

"From Méliès to CGI?""

"Who or what are Méliès and CGI"

Jonathan chuckled.

"It's a book about special effects in the movies. Méliès was Georges Méliès, a French filmmaker in the late nineteenth century who practically invented movie special effects. CGI is Computer Generated Imagery, which is how most special effects are produced now. Actually it's a fascinating subject."

Jonathan could see from the doubtful look on her face that Karen was not entirely convinced.

This will bore her to tears and maybe she will leave me alone.

The attendant arrived with their lunch, breaking what Jonathan thought was a rather tense moment. Jonathan smiled as he unfolded his napkin and placed it on his lap and Karen smiled back rather sweetly.

Jonathan put his book aside, opened his can of beer and poured it into a glass. Karen picked up her glass of wine, raised it and said, “Cheers!”.

“Cheers!” said Jonathan and he took a sip of his beer.

“If you don’t mind me asking,” said Jonathan, “what on earth was in that suitcase that made it so heavy?”

“Books,” said Karen.

”You must do a lot of reading.”

“Actually, I do,” said Karen. “It’s part of my job.”

“Really? What kind of job is that?”

“I work for a publisher in London.”

“You have to proof read the books, or something?”

“Yes, that’s part of it. I read the stuff that writers send in to see if it might be worth publishing.”

“Always looking for the next Harry Potter, right?”

“There’s always a chance. You never know. But the part of the job that I enjoy the most is working with the writers.”

“Do you have to travel round to see them?”

“Sometimes. That’s what I really enjoy. Of course, sometimes I have to meet them in the London office but if I can I’d much rather meet them at their homes, where they write.”

“It sounds very interesting,” said Jonathan.

Jonathan took a bite of his sandwich. Karen took the cue and started on her salad. They sat in silence for a few minutes, eating their lunches and looking out at the scenery as it flashed past the window. The countryside for this part of the journey was mostly flat farming country. The winter sun was getting lower in the sky to the southwest, illuminating the carriage brightly. In winter in England, the sun didn’t rise very far above the horizon because of the northern latitude at which Britain lay. As a result, it shone through the window very brightly, making the most of the limited winter daylight.

Karen paused from her salad and looked over at Jonathan. He rather nervously swallowed the piece of toasted sandwich he was working on.

"What do you do for a living, Jonathan?"

"I don't," said Jonathan. "I'm retired."

"Retired?" said Karen, a hint of disbelief in her voice. "You look a bit young to be retired."

Jonathan could see from the quizzical look on her face that she wanted to know more but he did not feel at all sure about how much he wanted to tell her.

"I was fortunate to be in a position to retire early. I don't really look on it as retirement., more as an opportunity for a second career. You know, do something different for a few years."

Jonathan took a sip of his beer and nervously looked out of the window as the train started slowing down for Peterborough, its first stop since leaving London.

"I'd love to have the chance," said Karen.

"Well, I thought I would too and I really enjoyed it to start with but I must admit that I sometimes have difficulty keeping my mind occupied."

This was getting a bit deeper than Jonathan wanted to go but Karen seemed to be genuinely interested and one of Jonathan's problems was that he rarely got the opportunity to bounce ideas off other people. He suddenly realised that he was sounding sorry for himself.

"Don't get me wrong," he said, "life is pretty good. It's just..."

"You're stuck in a rut?"

"Sort of."

"I see writers all the time who are stuck like that. They call it 'writer's block' but it's just that they can't get their minds focused on finishing their stories. What I try to do is to get them to focus and finish the job."

"Does it work?" said Jonathan, "I mean, do they get their books finished?"

"Most of the time. Sometimes I get cursed at and sworn at and there's often a lot of screaming and shouting but we usually struggle through!"

"Sounds like an ugly business."

"It can be. But the sense of satisfaction that I get when I see the finished book on the shelves of a bookshop makes it worth all the trouble." Karen had a genuine sound of pride in her voice.

"I think I know what you mean," said Jonathan.

The conversation paused for a few minutes. The train was back up to speed now, after its stop in Peterborough and Jonathan checked his watch. The train was due to arrive at Leeds at two thirty in the afternoon and Jonathan had about twenty minutes to make the connection with his train through the Pennines to Ravensgill Bridge. This train to Leeds had left the previous station exactly on time so he thought that he would make his connection without much problem. If he missed the connection, he would be stuck in Leeds for three hours waiting for the next train.

"Do you think we'll be in Leeds on time?" said Karen.

"I think so. We seem to be keeping pretty much on schedule."

Jonathan saw that Karen had finished her glass of wine.

"Can I get you another one?"

"No, I'm fine thank you, but I wouldn't say no to a cup of tea."

Jonathan waved to the attendant who was standing at the end of the carriage and the attendant walked over to their table.

"Pot of tea for two, please?", said Jonathan.

The attendant went off to get the order.

"Do you live in Leeds?" said Jonathan.

"No, I live in London but I'm visiting my mother for a couple of weeks. She lives in Leeds. I'll probably take time to visit two or three of our writers who live in Yorkshire and I'll probably pop down to the London office for a day sometime before Christmas."

The attendant brought the tea.

Jonathan could see that Karen was about to say something but she quickly diverted her gaze and looked out of the window.

"Shall I pour our tea?"

"Oh! Yes, please."

Jonathan poured out two cups of tea and passed one over to Karen.

"Thank you," said Karen. She was biting her bottom lip and looking pensive. After a few moments she spoke. "You know, I think I might be able to help you, help you get focused and all. After all, it's what I do for a living. I suppose you could call me a motivator, or something like that."

Jonathan felt slightly awkward but this was too good an opportunity to pass up.

"I could use all the help I can get," he said and he laughed nervously.

"I can't make any promises, but we'll see what we can come up with," said Karen.

"I would really appreciate your advice. It's very kind of you to offer."

"Not at all," said Karen with a smile. "Tell you what, why don't we get together for lunch one day next week. Do you live far from Leeds?"

"It's about fifty miles. About an hour on the train. In a lovely Pennine village called Ravensgill Bridge. I'm amazed it still has a train service, actually."

"It sounds delightful," said Karen, "Would you mind if I came out there for lunch? After a few days with my mother I could use a day out in the country!"

"Are you sure you want to come out all that way?"

"I spend too much of my time in the city," said Karen.

"Well, my local pub, The Ravensgill Arms, is a lovely old country pub and they do great pub lunches."

"That settles it then!" said Karen with a laugh.

She pulled a business card out of her purse and passed it over to Jonathan.

"That's got my mobile number on it. And my office number in London. But of course I won't be there very much."

Jonathan pulled out his wallet and passed one of his own cards to Karen.

Karen looked at the card.

"The Old Station, Ravensgill Bridge," she said. "You actually live in a railway station? Really?"

"Actually, yes. Really!"

"Oh! My God! Tell me about it! How do you come to be living in a railway station?"

"It's a very long story and we'll be getting into Leeds in a few minutes," said Jonathan, looking at his watch. "I promise I'll tell you the whole story next week over lunch."

"Well, that will guarantee that I'll show up. It sounds fascinating."

Karen sounded excited.

"How do I get there?" she said.

"There's a train about every three hours from Leeds. It takes about an hour. Ravensgill Bridge is a request stop so make sure you tell the ticket collector on board, otherwise the train will roll straight on through!"

"You actually mean to tell me that you have trains running through your house?"

"Well, yes, but you get used to it."

The train slowed as it made the big curve into Leeds station.

"I can't wait to see this station of yours," said Karen.

Jonathan smiled and stood up to pull on his overcoat. The train came to a halt in Leeds station and Karen stood up. She looked up sheepishly at the overhead luggage rack.

"Would you mind?"

"Of course not."

He carefully lifted each of her suitcases down, grunting slightly as he got the heavy one.

"I'll take this one out to the platform for you," he said.

"Thank you so much," said Karen as she picked up her other suitcase and they made their way down the aisle and out onto the platform.

Karen walked over and retrieved an empty luggage cart then Jonathan loaded both of her cases onto it.

"There you go," said Jonathan.

"Thank you so much," said Karen. "How about next Thursday for lunch?"

"That will be fine," said Jonathan. "Give me a call on Wednesday just to confirm that we are still on."

"I'll do that," said Karen.

"I need to go back aboard and get my own suitcase," said Jonathan.

"Yes, of course. Well, my sister will be meeting me outside the station so I'd better go. See you on Thursday!" and, with a jaunty wave, Karen pushed her loaded luggage cart off in the direction of the ticket barrier.

By the time Jonathan emerged from the train with his own suitcase, there was no sign of Karen.

Jonathan looked at his watch. Ten minutes before his next train was due to leave. He started walking slowly to the footbridge that spanned the platform and shook his head. He muttered quietly to himself, “What have I let myself in for?” then he chuckled and started climbing the stairs.

Chapter 3

Karen Wilson had been born and raised in the area around Leeds.

Her father and mother had owned and run a bookshop in the city for many years and Karen, with her older sister Jane, used to help their parents in the shop after school, unpacking boxes of new books, stacking the shelves, dusting off the books and generally helping around the shop. As a result, both girls had grown up with a love of books.

The Wilson girls' parents, Fred and Barbara, had encouraged their daughters' interest in reading, which they saw as critical to a proper education. Both girls had gone on to university. Jane, who was four years older than Karen, had gone to the University of Durham to study Graphic Design and now ran a successful design practice in Leeds. Karen, on the other hand, pursued her love of books and did a degree in Publishing at the University of Birmingham.

While Jane had returned to the Leeds area after university, Karen had found that most of the good jobs in publishing were in London and had moved to the Big City when she landed a job with one of the major London publishing firms.

On Thursday morning, Karen set off from her mother's house in a pleasant suburb of Leeds and caught a bus to the railway station in the city centre. It had been overcast when she had left home and by the time the bus reached the railway station, it had started to rain. She pulled up the collar of her raincoat and dashed into the station buildings.

Karen had promised Jonathan that she would think up some ideas about his retirement to talk about over lunch but up to now, she had drawn a blank.

Perhaps she would come up with some ideas during the train journey.

She bought a day return ticket to Ravensgill Bridge and looked at the departures board for details of her train. There it was, the train to Carlisle, stopping at about seven stations before Ravensgill Bridge. She had never been on this line before although she had heard that many people considered it to be one of the most picturesque railway lines in England.

She checked her watch, ten minutes until departure. She made her way to the platform where the train was waiting. The train consisted of just two carriages with a driver's cab at each end. The diesel engine was idling quietly as she got aboard. She was travelling lightly this time, just a small briefcase that she placed on the table in front of her.

She was surprised to see that she was the only person in the carriage, in fact the only person on the train and that made her a little nervous. She decided to stand by the open door and watch the people on the platform and the other trains pulling in and out of the station.

A uniformed conductor walked up the platform, a ticket machine on a strap over his shoulder.

"Mornin' ma'am," he said as he stepped aboard Karen's carriage at the door where she was standing.

"Good morning."

Karen felt more comfortable now there was someone else in her carriage and she returned to her seat. A few minutes later the carriage doors hissed shut and the train pulled out of the station.

Karen watched the station buildings slide away as the train gathered speed.

"Ticket please!" said the conductor.

Karen reached into her purse, pulled out her ticket for Ravensgill Bridge, and handed it to the conductor. The conductor looked at the ticket.

"Ravensgill Bridge, eh?"

"Yes, I'm going to have lunch with a friend who lives there."

"It's about an hour to Ravensgill," said the conductor, "about six stops before then. I'll tell you when we are getting close. Are you coming back today?"

"Yes, later this afternoon."

"I might see you again, then. We take this train up to Carlisle then bring it back again. Now, Ravensgill Bridge is what we call a request stop so when you get on the platform to come back you'll see a phone. You just pick it up and tell the dispatcher where you are and he will call the driver and tell him to stop and pick you up. You got that?"

"Yes. Thank you very much."

The conductor clipped the edge of Karen's ticket and handed it back to her. Then he walked though the connecting door to the next carriage.

When Karen looked out of the window again, the train had cleared the urban sprawl of Leeds and was now travelling alongside a river through a hilly wooded area. Karen's thoughts turned to her lunch meeting with Jonathan and what she might discuss with him. Of course, the problem was that Karen did not really know anything about Jonathan except that he was retired and he lived in an old railway station - the railway station where she would be meeting him in less than an hour. She was puzzled as to why he was retired at such a young age – there had to be a story behind that. He was obviously struggling to find something to challenge him in his retirement and he seemed to be especially interested in movie special effects. She didn't have much to work with but what she had was interesting. This could be quite a challenge, thought Karen.

Karen realised that, as she had been lost in her thoughts the train had now emerged from the wooded valley and was now travelling through open moorland. In the distance, the hills were shrouded in low cloud. Everything around looked very green as a result of the rain. She thought that the train might have stopped in a couple of stations while she had been lost in thought and now the train was slowing down for another stop. It looked like a small market town, a river or canal running alongside the tracks as the train pulled into a very old fashioned looking station, obviously dating from the Victorian era. This was Skipton. After a short stop, the train started again. Karen checked her watch – about half an hour until the train reached Ravensgill Bridge.

The train continued to wind its way through the magnificent, rugged scenery, moorland split by valleys with streams running off the hills, sheep feeding on the sparse vegetation. Karen found it a very stimulating but relaxing ride. After about three more stops, the conductor came back into the carriage.

"Ravensgill Bridge next stop, miss," he said.

"Oh! Thank you!" said Karen and she picked up her briefcase from the table in front of her. The train started to slow down as it approached the station and Karen stood up and waited for the automatic doors to open.

The train came to a halt, the doors opened and Karen stepped out onto the platform. She looked along the platform and saw Jonathan waving to her. Behind her, the doors of the train hissed shut and with a roar of its diesel engine, the train pulled out of the station.

Karen walked along the platform towards Jonathan and he walked to meet her. As he reached her, he smiled and extended his hand.

"Karen, thank you so much for coming," he said and they shook hands. "Did you have a good journey?"

"Yes. It's such beautiful countryside once you get out of Leeds".

"It gets even better north of here, further up the line."

They were walking towards the main station building.

"This is my house," said Jonathan. Karen smiled.

They walked into a room which had doors on each side, one set of doors leading in from the platform and the doors on the opposite side of the room leading out onto a road. This was the public part of the station where passengers purchased tickets for their journeys at a small ticket window. These days the small window was boarded up and there was an impersonal electronic machine on the wall of the ticket hall, which accepted cash and credit cards and spat out tickets according to the buttons that passengers pushed.

"My part of the station is through here," said Jonathan, unlocking a door at the side of the ticket hall. He pushed open the door and Karen stepped into a living room.

"Would you like a cup of tea?" said Jonathan.

"Yes, please."

"Take a seat."

Karen sat on the sofa and Jonathan walked through to a small kitchen area and put a kettle of water on to boil. Then he walked back into the living room and sat down in an easy chair opposite Karen.

"This is a fascinating place," said Karen.

"I'll show you around when we've had a cup of tea," said Jonathan. "So, have you had any thoughts since last week?"

"Actually, I haven't been able to think very clearly this last week. I was hoping a day out in the country might help to clear my mind."

"That's exactly why I moved here," said Jonathan. "I find it very inspiring."

The whistle on the spout of the kettle began to sound and Jonathan got up to make the tea. He returned with a tray containing the teapot, cups and saucers, a milk jug and a plate of biscuits.

"You know, I don't really know much about you," said Karen as Jonathan poured the tea. "What did you do before you retired? Why did you retire so young? I don't want to pry into your personal affairs but I need a bit more information if I am going to be able to help."

Jonathan passed over a cup of tea to Karen, sat down in his easy chair and stared out of the window towards the hills. He sat in silence for a minute or two.

Karen could see that he was gathering his thoughts and she decided to give him time to think. She sipped her tea.

Eventually Jonathan spoke.

"It's difficult to know where to start."

"Do you mind if I make a few notes?" said Karen, pulling a pencil and notepad out of her briefcase.

"No, of course, no problem, go ahead."

Karen could see that Jonathan needed some encouragement.

"Quite often, my writers get overwhelmed by the idea of having to lay everything out in sequence from start to finish so they don't try to write that way. They just pick a starting point and work from there. Sometimes they work forwards, sometimes they work backwards from where they started. Eventually they pull it all together. Why don't you try that?"

Jonathan appeared to relax and started to talk. Karen discreetly made notes as he talked.

"Well, I'm not actually retired, strictly speaking. I'm disabled, although you probably wouldn't notice. A few years ago, I was in a pretty bad car crash. I was quite badly injured and I was in a coma for three months. The broken bones healed fairly quickly but I had a head injury and that's what caused me the biggest problem."

"How so?" said Karen.

"Well, I had some brain injury and it really slowed me down. I get tired very easily and I think and move more slowly than I should at my age."

Jonathan paused for a second or two, then continued.

"You know, a head injury is one of the most difficult disabilities to live with because you look so normal on the outside, but inside you're struggling."

"You look and sound pretty normal to me," said Karen and she immediately realised that she sounded crass. She continued quickly, "But it must be very hard."

Karen felt that she sounded so lame. She was feeling really awkward and embarrassed. Jonathan smiled and reassured her.

"Don't worry! Don't feel bad! I could be in a wheelchair. I could be in a vegetative state or still in a coma. I'm really quite lucky. But I could not keep going with my career. I went back to it after I recovered but I couldn't keep up with the pace. I tried to work part time but in the end it became too hard."

Karen felt relieved. Perhaps getting Jonathan to talk about his former career might throw up a few ideas.

"What type of work did you do before you retired?" said Karen.

"I was in the movie business."

"A film actor?"

"No! I worked in the technical side, special effects. I worked on quite a few films. My name was pretty much the last one on the credits, at the end of the movie after everyone had left the theatre."

Karen laughed. Jonathan seemed to be much more relaxed now.

"Where were you working? At Pinewood Studios?"

"Actually I did start my career there and I went back a few times to do special projects, but I spent most of my time in California. You know, Hollywood, Los Angeles, around there."

"How long did you live there?"

"Twenty years, roughly."

Images of sunny California beaches, palm trees, surfboards danced through Karen's mind and then she looked out of the windows towards the hills, shrouded in low cloud."

"And you came back to this?" she said, nodding towards the window.

"It would probably take me a very long time to explain all the reasons that I came back, but I can tell you that the weather was not one of them!"

Jonathan thought for a few moments, then said, "Do you mind if we go for a walk while we talk? If we walk across the bridge, there's a path that leads to the stream and then down to the village. Maybe we can get some of lunch there."

"Is it very far?"

"Not really. About a mile to the village. We can come back along the road. It's shorter"

Karen sensed that Jonathan had something important to say and she thought that perhaps walking and talking might make it easier for him.

"That would be a great idea," she said.

"I've got a spare pair of Wellington boots that should fit you," said Jonathan. "The path can sometimes be a bit muddy in winter."

Jonathan went into a back room to get the boots and Karen pulled on her overcoat. After a few moments, Jonathan returned wearing an overcoat and wellington boots carrying a spare pair of boots for Karen.

"Try these on for size. I've got another pair in the back room if they don't fit."

Karen grunted as she pulled on the boots and then stood up and stamped her feet on the carpet.

"These will do just fine," she said. "Let's go! Lead the way!"

They walked out onto the platform, which was empty of people. The next train was not due for a couple of hours.

"The path is this way," said Jonathan, pointing to the north end of the platform.

They started off at a brisk pace.

Chapter 4

As they approached the end of the platform, it sloped down to the ground and a path ran northwards along the left side of the tracks. The path was just wide enough for them to walk side by side. Leaving the station, the tracks curved to the right through a narrow, steep-sided valley. Jonathan and Karen walked on together in silence and as they followed the curve of the path, Karen could see the tracks straightening out again and the valley falling away. The tracks pushed on straight ahead onto a stone viaduct across a wide valley.

"Is that the actual Ravensgill Bridge?" said Karen.

"Yes, that's it."

"Wow! It looks high!"

"Two hundred and fifty feet above the valley right in the middle."

"Can we walk across it?"

"Sure, there's a path down to the village on the far side."

"What if a train comes?"

"There are no trains due for a couple of hours, but even if an unscheduled goods train comes through, there's enough space for it to pass."

As they walked up onto the bridge, the wind picked up slightly and the clouds skimmed across the hills around them. Karen thrust her hands into her overcoat pocket to keep them warm. She looked at Jonathan and smiled.

"It's great to get out of the city for a while," she said.

Jonathan smiled and nodded.

As they got to the centre of the bridge, Jonathan paused and pointed down the valley to their left. There below, a stream flowed quickly over rocks and boulders down the centre of the valley. Gently rising moorland rose on either side of the stream then steep crags rose up, enclosing the valley on either side. However, only a few hundred feet high, the crags gave the impression of great mountains.

"That's Raven's Gill," said Jonathan. "Gill is an old word meaning 'ravine'. It's pronounced with a hard G as in 'girl' rather than a soft G as in 'generous'."

"Well, thank you for expanding my vocabulary this morning," said Karen, and they both laughed.

At the far end of the valley, Karen could see a small village, occasionally obscured by patches of cloud being blown up the valley and beneath the bridge.

"Is that where we are going for lunch?" she said.

"Yes. The path at the other end of the bridge runs right into the village. Or we could walk back to the station and walk along the road to the village."

"Let's walk along the path. We can come back along the road."

They continued on across the bridge. Karen really wanted to continue her interrupted conversation with Jonathan but the cold wind across the bridge made serious conversation difficult and Jonathan did not seem to be particularly anxious to engage in conversation. Karen decided to wait for a better opportunity and they walked on in silence.

As they reached the far end of the bridge, the path became sheltered by the crags on the north side of the valley as the tracks entered a rocky cutting, and the wind died down. Karen could not immediately see how she and Jonathan were going to get down to the valley floor from the high bridge.

"This way!" said Jonathan as he opened a gate in the bridge parapet and Karen saw a long steep flight of stone steps going down the outside wall of the bridge to the valley. Karen thought it all looked rather dangerous but she did not want to show her nervousness to Jonathan and there was a fairly solid-looking handrail on the outside edge of the steps. So she looked at Jonathan, smiled weakly, and started down.

There was a landing on the steps about every thirty feet down and Karen stopped at the first landing to let Jonathan catch up. She had been concentrating hard on keeping her footing as she came down the steps but now she felt a bit more secure and she looked around. Ahead to her left she now saw the great bulk of the bridge, made of stone blocks that must be very old because they were covered in moss and lichen. Now that she was below the top of the bridge she could look up and see that it was built in a series of tall narrow arches, each arch taller as the ground sloped down towards the centre of the valley then the arches getting shorter as the ground sloped up towards the station on the far side of the valley.

Jonathan joined Karen on the landing and paused.

"Pretty dramatic, isn't it?" he said.

"It looks very old," said Karen.

"Built in 1870, I think."

"Very solid looking."

"It's had to stand against the wind blowing up this valley for more than a hundred years!"

A gust of wind tugged at Karen's overcoat and she laughed.

"I see what you mean!"

With that, she started off down the steps again. When they reached the bottom of the steps, Jonathan and Karen turned right and began to follow the path as it ran just below the crags on the north side of the valley. Karen stopped and looked up at the bridge where she could now see the whole span across the valley.

"How much further to the village?" said Karen.

"About ten minutes walk."

"Let's go then! I'm getting hungry!"

The path ran alongside a grassy field, where cows were grazing then joined a paved road. Walking was much easier now and Karen thought that she could perhaps continue the conversation that she and Jonathan had started earlier back in his living room at the station. She decided that it was time to throw caution to the wind and dive right in.

"So Jonathan, you were going to tell me the reasons that you came back from California," she said. "I think I can see one of the reasons," she added as she swept her arm across the view of the valley climbing up toward the bridge in the distance.

"I have a sense of belonging here," said Jonathan.

"Here in Ravensgill Bridge?"

"Here in England. But Ravensgill Bridge is also a very special place to me that encapsulates a lot of what is good about England."

"Did you have that sense of belonging when you lived in California?"

"Not really. I was happy enough, especially when my career was going well. But after the accident..."

Jonathan paused. Karen waited for a few moments to see if he would continue but he seemed to have stalled again.

"The accident?" said Karen. She noticed that Jonathan's eyes were getting moist.

"Yes," he said. "It was a car crash. Jill and I had taken a weekend trip up the California coast north of Los Angeles and we were on our way home. It was just getting dark, on the Sunday evening. The coast highway is just a two-lane road with a lot of bends. A beautiful drive, really."

Jonathan paused again.

"Jill was driving. As we came round a bend, a car coming the other way took the bend too fast and swung out toward us. Jill couldn't really avoid the other car because the edge of the road drops away a hundred feet down a cliff to the ocean."

Karen was about to ask who Jill was but she felt that it would interrupt Jonathan's account so she just looked at Jonathan and waited for him to start again.

Jonathan cleared his throat.

"The other car hit us on Jill's side, you know, driver to driver. The next thing I remember was waking up in a Los Angeles hospital three months later."

"Oh my God!" was about all that Karen could manage. She could tell that she had not yet heard the worst of the story.

"Tell you what, Jonathan, it looks like we're nearly at the village now. Why don't we get inside out of this cold wind and get warm and perhaps we can talk about this some more."

"Yes," said Jonathan. "The Ravensgill Arms pub is just down the road. Let's get in there and get warm."

Karen smiled and picked up the pace. In a few minutes, they were in the middle of the village. Three roads came together and there was a small grassy area in the middle of the intersection with a war memorial on it. There were still several wreaths of poppies around the base of the memorial from the Armistice Day service that had been held there a few weeks ago. One of the streets was lined with shops and curved away to the left. Another street was mostly houses and cottages and the road they had walked in on stretched out behind them, mostly bounded by fields.

On one side of the green stood a very old church with a square tower. On the other side stood a magnificent building, built of the local stone with small windows looking in through thick walls. Outside a sign swung in the wind with a coat of arms painted on it and across the front wall of the pub in large wrought iron letters, was the name Ravensgill Arms.

Jonathan pointed to the front door of the pub and said “Behold! Lunch!”

“It’s lovely!” said Karen. “Let’s go in.”

Jonathan led the way, up a couple of stone steps and in through a heavy wooden door. Inside there was a patterned carpet on the floor and the ceiling had wooden beams running across the width of the room. Most of the back of the room was taken up with the bar along which several bar stools stood. On the right hand wall was a huge fireplace in which a log fire was burning brightly. There were bench seats along the walls with wooden tables in front of them. The walls were stone blocks and they were adorned with pictures of the village from years gone by including pictures of the bridge when it was under construction. To the left of the bar was a separate area, which appeared to be a restaurant with tables set for lunch. A couple of the tables were occupied and a couple of people were sitting in the bar area.

The gentleman behind the bar was a middle-aged fellow, balding with a round face.

“Good morning, Jonathan!” he said as Jonathan and Karen walked in.

“Good morning, John!” said Jonathan, then he turned to Karen. “This is Karen Wilson, a friend of mine from Leeds.”

John reached across the bar to shake hands with Karen. “Very pleased to meet you, miss.”

“You’ve got a beautiful place here,” said Karen, returning John’s handshake.

“What would you like to drink, Karen?” said John.

“A glass of white wine, please.”

"Usual for you, Jonathan?"

"Thanks, John."

John poured a glass of white wine and handed it to Karen, then drew a pint of Best Bitter and handed it to Jonathan who pulled out his wallet to pay for the drinks but John said "No, Jonathan. First one's on me today!"

"Thank you, John," said Jonathan. "We're planning to have lunch today but we would like to have a quiet drink and chat first, if that's all right."

"Of course, I'll just put a sign on the table by the window to reserve it and you just let me know when you're ready to order."

Jonathan and Karen walked over to the corner beside the fire and sat on the bench seat, placing their drinks on the table in front of them.

Karen looked around the room,

"This is a lovely place," she said, "especially with the nice warm fire on a cold grey day like today."

Jonathan took a sip of his beer and smiled. "Yes, this is what I missed about England during my twenty years away. There really is nothing else in the world quite that same as a traditional English country pub."

Karen was anxious to steer the conversation back to the car accident so after a short pause while she sipped some of her wine she turned to Jonathan and said "You said that after the car crash the next thing you remember was waking up in the hospital three months later."

Jonathan took a sip of his beer and waited for a few moments before responding. "I'm told the crash was pretty bad. When they pulled me out, I had hit my head on something and I was unconscious. I also broke a few bones but they mostly fixed those before I woke up. I was pretty much torn up, so they tell me. It was just as well that I was out cold!"

"And Jill?" Karen knew what the answer was going to be even as the words left her mouth. Jonathan paused again, his eyes moist. He cleared his throat and looked down, avoiding eye contact.

"She...she didn't make it"

This time it was Karen who tried to avoid eye contact

"The police said that she was killed instantly. Most of the damage was on her side of the car, see. They were surprised that I made it out alive."

"I am so sorry," said Karen quietly. It seemed a very weak thing to say in the circumstances.

"You never really get over things like that," said Jonathan, "but time does soften things and it was nearly three years ago now."

Karen could not think of anything to say and they sat in silence for a couple of minutes. Finally, Jonathan spoke.

"It really changed my life, losing Jill like that. And my disability. I had some brain damage in the accident. We were both wearing seat belts but the car was so badly damaged. I was in hospital for about five months, altogether. For the first three months I was in a coma, then a couple of months of rehab, learning to walk again, learning to look after myself."

Jonathan paused and sipped his beer. Karen felt that he was glad to be able to talk about this to someone.

"I suppose they told you about Jill when you came out of the coma," said Karen.

"Actually no, not straight away. I suspected something when Jill wasn't there at the hospital. At first, they said that she was very badly injured in the accident and was unable to visit, but after a few days, Jill's parents came to visit me and they told me the real story. That must have been very difficult for them."

Jonathan paused again.

"Well, anyway, I gradually got better and started to try to put my life back together again."

"Isn't medical care expensive in America?" said Karen.

"Yes it is, but I had medical insurance from my job and Jill had life insurance so money was never really an issue."

"Were you and Jill married?"

"Yes. We'd met while we were both working on a movie where I'd been doing the special effects. She was an assistant director. We'd been married about two years. We had a small flat in Santa Monica, out near the coast."

Karen wanted to ask about where they had lived but she needed to keep the conversation on track. "Did you manage to go back to your old job?" she said.

"I did for a while. The company was very good to me. I couldn't drive for the first few months, so the company sent a car for me every day to take me into work and they let me work part time. But eventually I had to quit. You see, the problem with brain damage is that it slows you down. You can't think as fast and you get tired very easily. I was really lucky that I could function at all. You see, a lot of people who have brain injuries or strokes do actually look and behave quite normally. Because we're not in wheelchairs or lying in bed unable to move or speak, folks don't realise how much damage there is on the inside." There was certain sharpness in Jonathan's voice as he said this.

"I think I understand your difficulties, Jonathan," said Karen, "and I would truly like to understand more. It must take a great deal of effort to try to live a normal life."

"Well, the problem that I have is that, although I move and think more slowly, and I get tired easily, the brain damage did not affect my cognitive ability."

"Cognitive ability?"

"Yes, my intellect if you like. I may think a bit more slowly than I used to, but my actual intelligence is not damaged. The problem is that I cannot compete in the big bad world out there. It makes me feel a bit like I am on the scrap heap and I still have so much to offer the world."

"Idle retirement is not for you?"

""No way!" Jonathan laughed. "And that is why I wanted to talk to you, see if we can come up with some ideas. Do you want another drink?"

"Yes please, and then perhaps we can order some lunch."

Chapter 5

Jonathan approached the bar carrying the empty glasses.

"Same again, Jonathan?", said John from behind the bar, an empty pint glass in his hand.

"Yes, please, and can we have a couple of menus?"

John placed the drinks on the bar. "I'll bring your menus over to your table. I'll put the drinks on your food bill if you like."

"Thank you," said Jonathan as he picked up the drinks and carried them back to where Karen was sitting. Karen took a sip of her wine and started to speak as Jonathan sat down.

"So, your retirement. What do you want from it? Fame? Fortune?"

"Well, I'm living on the insurance money for the now but that will probably run out one day. I'm in reasonable shape for money for the moment and I can probably live the way I am doing for a few years. I would like to think that I had the ability to make some money to supplement my investments. It feels a bit strange, not going out to a job every day."

"So money is not your main concern, " said Karen, "at least for the moment."

"No, not my main concern."

John walked over to their table and handed them each a menu. "I'll take your orders when you're ready."

Karen placed her menu unopened on the table. She didn't want to interrupt Jonathan's train of thought.

Jonathan continued, "I feel like I need some purpose in life." He emphasized the word "purpose" noticeably. "I've spent most of my working life solving problems and inventing solutions and things. I need a mental challenge. I need a direction in life. It's very easy to feel you have been put on the scrap heap of life when you are disabled and I don't like feeling that way."

"You've got a few physical limitations but you don't have any mental limitations, right?" said Karen.

"Exactly!" said Jonathan. "I just have to work at my own speed and not try to move at the speed of the world around me."

"Let's order lunch, then talk about it some more," said Karen and she picked up her menu and started to study it.

"I'm going to have a Ploughman's Lunch," Karen announced after studying the menu for a few minutes, "with Stilton Cheese and a pickled onion."

"I'll have the same thing," said Jonathan, "but I think I prefer mature Cheddar."

"Could we eat here, at this table, rather than moving into the restaurant?" said Karen.

"I'll ask John to serve us over here," said Jonathan as he picked up the menus and walked over to the bar to place the order for lunch.

When Jonathan returned to the table, Karen spoke. "Jonathan, tell me some more about the work you used to do, before the accident."

"Well, I did special effects for the movies...sorry, films. All sorts of things. Simple flashes and bangs. Models. Green screen. All that kind of stuff."

"What's green screen?"

"That's where you film the actors in front of a green background. Then later you replace the green background with a different scene."

"Like when they're playing Quidditch in the Harry Potter films, flying around on broomsticks?" said Karen.

"Exactly!" said Jonathan. "The actors were suspended on wires on a stage in front of a green screen. The Quidditch field was set up in a meadow in

Scotland and filmed from a helicopter. Even the crowds of cheering supporters were put in afterwards."

"Fascinating!" said Karen.

"Well, when you know how it's all done, it does take some of the magic away," said Jonathan, "but I like watching films that I haven't worked on."

"Yes," said Karen. "I've often wondered how actors feel when they watch their own films and remember all the effort that went into them."

Karen could see that Jonathan had an enthusiastic demeanour, talking about his previous work.

"I think the best special effects are the ones that you don't even notice in the film," said Jonathan.

"Such as?"

"Let me see...sometimes a scene will be filmed in the winter, when the trees are bare, but the script calls for it to be spring or summer, so we use special effects to put leaves and blossoms on the trees."

"I would never have thought of such a thing!" said Karen.

"Things in the movies are never quite what they seem," said Jonathan. "That was my job, fooling you into believing that something was there when it really wasn't."

Their lunch arrived, each plate carrying a generous serving of cheese, crusty bread, pickle and butter.

"I'm quite hungry after our walk this morning," said Karen.

"Me too!" said Jonathan.

They ate in silence for a few minutes. Then Karen spoke.

"I'm not sure what it is, but something that you said has triggered a thought in my head. It's floating around in there but I can't quite grab hold of it yet."

"What was it that I said?" asked Jonathan.

"You said something about things in the movies never being quite what they seem. I need to mull that one around for a bit."

"Has it given you some ideas?"

"Well, it's triggered something. Maybe a walk after lunch will get my brain cells working."

"It's an easy walk back up the road, or we could get a taxi if you want."

"No, I would prefer to walk," said Karen. "I need to walk off this lunch!"

They finished lunch, Jonathan settled the bill and he and Karen pulled on their overcoats and stepped outside. It was still cloudy but the wind had died down while they had been inside.

"Are you sure that you want to walk back?" asked Jonathan.

"Yes. The fresh air will do us good!"

Jonathan led the way and they headed off on the road out of town. A signpost in the centre of the village showed that the road led to the railway station a mile away.

Karen walked alongside Jonathan. After a while, she spoke.

"Have you ever thought about writing, Jonathan?"

"What sort of writing?"

"Magazine articles, books, novels, all sorts of things."

"I've thought about it, but I'm not sure that's really what I want to do with my time. At least not just that. I really need some outlet for my inventiveness, my problem solving skills."

"You're a tough nut to crack, Jonathan!" said Karen, and they both laughed and walked on together.

Chapter 6

As they rounded a corner, Karen could see the Ravensgill railway station about a hundred yards ahead. Jonathan looked at his watch.

"The next train back to Leeds is in about ten minutes, or there's another one in about three hours."

"If it's all right with you I would like to get the later train," said Karen.

"That would be great! I can show you some more of the station and we could talk a bit more."

They walked across the car park in front of the station and walked into the booking hall. Jonathan got out his keys and opened the door to his private quarters. When they got inside, they removed their overcoats and hung them up. Then Karen sat down on the sofa and pulled off her boots. Jonathan took the boots into a back room as Karen slipped on her own shoes.

"I'll brew another pot of tea, if you like," said Jonathan, "and then we can go and take a look at my study."

Karen stood up. "That will be nice," she said.

"Come into the kitchen while I make the tea."

Karen followed Jonathan into the kitchen and sat at the kitchen table while Jonathan filled the kettle and put it on the gas stove to heat up. As Jonathan started setting up a tea tray with mugs, spoons and a teapot, Karen started to speak.

"Jonathan, do you have any interest in politics?"

Jonathan looked up from his tea preparations and in a tone that was somewhere between surprised and defensive he said, "Why do you ask?"

Karen felt that she had to be careful how she pursued this line of questioning. She did not want

Jonathan to feel he was being interrogated but on the other hand, she was still having trouble coming up with ideas to suggest to Jonathan.

"The way that you talk about things," said Karen, "your experience living and working in America, the reasons that you came back to England. I'm trying to establish how you think, your view of the world."

Jonathan smiled. Karen relaxed. It seemed to her that Jonathan had a pretty good attitude to life and that helped to build her confidence in talking with him and asking him sensitive questions.

"I don't mind admitting that my time in America pushed my political views to the left," said Jonathan.

"To the left?" said Karen. "Frankly, I'm surprised!"

"Yes, to the left," said Jonathan. "What's the saying? ' If you're not a liberal when you are young, you have no heart; if you're not a conservative when you are older, you have no brain.' Well, I was exactly the opposite way round. When I was at university, I was absolutely the establishment man, pro-business, pro-government. But as I grew older, I became more and more cynical about that kind of thing, especially when I saw the effects of unbridled capitalism on the working people of America. I often say that when I arrived in America my politics were somewhere to the right of Attila the Hun; when I left they were somewhere to the left of Karl Marx!"

"Would you call yourself a communist?" said Karen.

"Not really. I suppose I would call myself a socialist."

Jonathan picked up the tea tray. "Would you like to carry on this discussion in my study?" he said, and without waiting for a reply, he went out of the back door of the kitchen, carrying the tea tray and turned right along the platform. Karen followed, closing the kitchen door behind her."

At the end of the platform, there was another building. It was two stories high. The lower storey was made of brick with a door and a couple of windows. The upper storey had wood-framed windows all the way round the building. There was a metal staircase leading up the outside of the building to the upper storey.

Jonathan paused at the bottom of the stairs.

"This used to be the old signal box," he said. "It controlled the trains coming through Ravensgill Bridge. They are all controlled electronically now, from control rooms in Leeds and Carlisle, so I converted it into my study."

Jonathan looked up the stairs then turned to Karen.

"Go on up and open the door. I'll bring the tea."

Karen climbed the stairs, opened the door and stepped inside. She held the door open as Jonathan came in and put the tea tray down on a desk just inside the door.

"What a delightful office," said Karen.

It was a bright room, with windows all around. There was a polished hardwood floor and the room itself was a mixture of Victorian engineering and high technology. Along the side of the room nearest the tracks was a large metal frame with about ten long metal handles. On the wall next to the frame, there were several very old looking polished wood cabinets with dials and brass bells and clocks on them. On the other side of the room, where the view from the windows looked west down the valley towards the village, was a long low workbench on which was a desktop computer with a flat-screen monitor, a laptop computer, a television, a phone, a stereo unit and several books.

"Actually, I don't call it an office," said Jonathan. "Now I'm retired, I call it a study!"

"Oops, sorry!" said Karen, with a giggle.

"When the weather is clear there are beautiful views from up here," said Jonathan. "On a clear day you can see Morecambe Bay and the mountains in the Lake District."

Jonathan pointed to the old Victorian ironwork on the other side of the room.

"Those are the levers that controlled the signals and points for the trains in the old days. I decided to leave them in to add to the atmosphere."

"It's perfect!" said Karen, clapping her hands together.

Jonathan poured two cups of tea and handed one to Karen.

"Let's go and sit down," he said.

They walked over to the workbench and sat in the two high backed office chairs there. They swivelled to face each other.

They sat in silence for a while and Karen thought it best to let Jonathan set the pace of the conversation. She could see very clearly that Jonathan was a complex person, a person with a great deal of mental energy. But right now, he was really struggling to apply that energy to something that he thought useful. Karen was not sure about Jonathan's real motivation. Was it fame, fortune or fulfilment that Jonathan was looking for? She suspected that it was a little of all three, with fulfilment being the most important to him.

Jonathan swivelled his chair to look out of the window, smiling at Karen as he did so. He put down his cup of teas, picked up a pen and started to chew the end of it. His face tightened up into a frown. Karen suspected that Jonathan had something that he wanted to tell her but he seemed to be having difficulty knowing what to say. Though she felt rather awkward at the silence between them, she resisted the temptation to interrupt Jonathan's thinking.

Suddenly, Jonathan turned back to face Karen.

"You work with a lot of authors, don't you Karen?"

"Yes," said Karen, "that's the main part of my job."

"I suppose you see a lot of stuff that is...well...confidential?"

"Of course, all the time. When an author is working on a new book, a new idea, we usually want to keep it under wraps. Quite often, I don't even tell the London office what is going on. There are so many false starts and twists and turns when you are creating a book. It can be quite an ugly process, sometimes."

Karen laughed. She felt a bit more relaxed now that Jonathan had started to talk, but Jonathan still had rather a tortured look on his face.

"If I told you something," said Jonathan, "or showed you something, you could keep quiet about it, then? Not tell anybody else?"

"Absolutely!"

She wondered what on earth Jonathan wanted to tell her. Was it some dark secret from his past?

"Do you remember how I told you about the car crash? How I was in a coma for three months?"

"Yes, I do. As I said, you seem to have made a remarkable recovery."

"Well, once you damage your brain, things are never quite the same again."

Jonathan paused for a moment.

"Don't worry!" he said quickly, "I didn't turn into a monster!"

Karen was feeling rather edgy about how the conversation was going and Jonathan seemed to have noticed her nervousness. Here she was, miles out in the country, alone with this person that she had only known for a few hours. She scanned the room, looking for possible escape routes but trying not to make it obvious to Jonathan.

"No, Karen! Don't be alarmed."

Jonathan's voice was calming and Karen felt slightly reassured. It was probably best to get whatever this was out into the open and deal with it.

OK," said Karen, "Go ahead."

Jonathan smiled and beckoned to Karen.

"Move your chair a bit closer."

Karen had lost a lot of her apprehension and it had been replaced with curiosity. She rolled her chair over so she was face to face with Jonathan.

"Now," said Jonathan, "I need you to just relax in your chair and look at my face. Try to empty your mind of thoughts. Don't worry about me. I'll be quite all right. This will only take a few minutes. Don't worry if you feel a bit drowsy."

"What happens if something goes wrong?"

"I promise you, nothing will go wrong. Trust me. You ready?"

Karen had no idea what was about to happen but there was only one way to find out. Nothing ventured, nothing gained. Or something like that. She nodded towards Jonathan, leaned back in her chair and looked at Jonathan, noticing how his blue eyes were so bright, almost intense. Almost immediately, Karen started to feel rather sleepy. What was happening? Was Jonathan trying to hypnotise her? She did not really want to close her eyes. She wanted to see what was going on. But she did feel very drowsy. Perhaps she could just close her eyes for a moment. No! The curiosity to see what was going on overpowered her need to nap and she forced herself to open her eyes again.

But something had changed. Jonathan wasn't there.

Gone were all the computers and screens, to be replaced with several big books, which were full of hand written entries. Karen leaned forward in her chair. The books seemed to be records of train arrivals and departures at Ravensgill Bridge station. Karen stood up and looked through the window above the books. She could see the view of the valley with the village in the distance.

Behind her, Karen heard a bell ring three times, followed by a clacking sound, like a two blocks of wood being clapped together. She turned around to face the other way, towards the side of the signal box that faced the tracks. She could see the row of old iron handles that were used to control the signals and the points at the station.

She saw a man wearing a peaked cap and dressed in dark blue trousers and a white shirt with braces and rolled up shirt sleeves, revealing muscular arms. He reached over to one of the large iron handles and pulled it towards him, grunting with effort as he did so.

She thought she ought to introduce herself to this man, as he looked rather official.

"Hello," she said. "My name is Karen Wilson. I'm a friend of Jonathan Long."

The man in the peaked cap did not respond.

Karen heard the sound of a train whistle. She had seen steam trains in films and she recognized the high-pitched scream of the whistle. She turned round to look out of the windows on the south side of the signal box where the tracks curved away through the hills. In the distance, behind a hill, she could see white steam billowing up and in a few moments, she saw a train appear round the curve. It was an old steam locomotive hauling four carriages up the slope towards the station.

Karen knew that railway enthusiasts preserved old steam locomotives and occasionally took them out for a run. This must be one of those special railway enthusiast trains. She watched the train as it slowed down passing the signal box, preparing to stop at the station. She looked along the platform and towards the bridge beyond. A man in a dark blue uniform and wearing a peaked cap came out of the station buildings as, amid a great cloud of steam, the train pulled to a halt.

Several of the carriage doors swung open and passengers stepped down onto the platform. Two ladies dressed in 1940-style suit dresses got out, then two more ladies dressed in khaki army uniforms and wearing army caps stepped out. These ladies were followed by four young men in army battledress, each carrying a kitbag. All the passengers walked along the platform and turned into the booking hall in the middle of the main station building.

Karen hear the sound of an engine and she saw an ancient motor bus pulling up on the road outside the station The passengers from the train climbed aboard and the bus chugged away down the hill towards the village.

Karen turned her attention back to the window above the workbench. There was an old style calendar hanging there with large squares for each day. At the top of the page, Karen could see the month and year:

December 1943

Karen sat down in her chair and rubbed he eyes, then she looked up. The study had been restored to the way it was with all the computers and screens and with

Jonathan sitting there grinning. Karen didn't really understand what she had just seen. She would like a few answers.

"What did you think of that?" said Jonathan

Karen did not know how to respond. She sat for a few moments, alternately looking around the signal box and at Jonathan. Jonathan's grin changed into a quizzical look. He was clearly looking for some kind of response from Karen.

"Well?" said Jonathan.

"I'm not sure that I really understand what I was seeing. There was something about it that didn't quite fit. Something I can't quite put my finger on."

"I suppose the easiest way of putting it is that you were looking at a dream," said Jonathan. "Well, an hallucination actually, but in my book an hallucination is just a more realistic dream."

Karen shook her head. Either this was a very clever trick using some kind of special effects or it was the most amazing thing that she had ever seen.

"Does anyone else know about this?"

"Just the doctors."

"Are you kidding me Jonathan? I mean, is this one of your special effects, like you used to do in Hollywood?"

"I swear there is no trickery, no special effects. What you just saw was absolutely real."

"But it was me that was having the dream or hallucination or whatever you call it."

"Remember I told you about that car crash in California and how I was in a coma for three months."

Karen nodded.

"I had quite a lot of damage deep inside my brain. When I came out of the coma, I started to get hallucinations. What I call waking dreams. Really, the only difference between an hallucination and a dream is that you are actually awake during an hallucination, although like in a dream your physical body is more or less paralyzed. But to your brain, it seems very real. I'm sure that you've had dreams that seemed very real to you?"

"Yes, of course."

"Hallucinations are just more intense dreams because your brain is awake."

"So how did you make me dream. Did you hypnotise me?"

"Not exactly," said Jonathan. "I'll try to describe to you how it works, if you're interested."

"Yes, I'm fascinated!"

"When I was in hospital I was actually blind and deaf. The brain injuries had broken some of the connections inside my brain. There was nothing wrong with my eyes or my ears, it was just that the signals were not getting through. They used a new experimental treatment where they implanted an electronic device in my head to restore the connections. It worked perfectly. I'm not familiar with all the neurological stuff that the scientists and doctors talk about so I use an analogy to help me understand it. It's all to do with memory. Do you realize that we humans remember everything that we experience?"

"Yes, I had heard that before."

"We never forget what we experience, it's just a question of being able to recall the memory. My analogy is that there is a video recorder continuously running in our head, recording all our thoughts and experiences in a continuous memory stream. Everything we see or hear is recorded. As more stuff is recorded, the older stuff is pushed further back into our memory. As this memory is written our brain attaches "hooks" or "keywords" to the recording to help with our recall. Are you with me so far?"

“”I think so.”

“There is a special part of this memory stream, right at the beginning of the stream, which handles our short term memory. That’s the memory that you keep in your head for just a few seconds, like when you look up a phone number and then punch it into the phone. You remember it just long enough to punch it in and then you probably forget it. Another example is when we are talking, like right now. We both have to keep the last one or two sentences in our short term memory so that we can keep track of what we are saying and make sense of what we are hearing. Anyway, short term memory is very limited so it has to be written out to the memory stream to make way for more.”

“So our current experience, our here and now, that’s what’s going into our short term memory?”

“Exactly! But also it goes into short term memory for a fraction of a second before it is passed on into our consciousness.”

“I see where this is going. You get into my short term memory before it reaches my consciousness and you put thoughts and images in there that are not real? You build an hallucination.”

“You’ve got it in one, Karen. But anyway, after the doctors in California put that electronic gizmo in my head I found that I could see people’s memory streams in my own mind’s eye.”

Jonathan paused. “Does all this sound too crazy to you?”

“Not at all! Carry on, it’s fascinating.”

“To start with I noticed that if people were near me and I could look into their eyes, you know, make eye contact with them, I could see their memory stream. Of course, things were a bit fuzzy, a bit cloudy at first. I had vague images but gradually the images in my mind became clearer and eventually I found that if I concentrated heavily I could pick up quite a lot. I discovered that I could actually influence the information I picked up by thinking about the information I wanted, such as "What did you watch on television last night?" or "Where did you go on your last vacation?"

"So how do you actually build an hallucination?"

"After the circuit had been inside my head for a year or so I discovered that I could plant thoughts in other people's heads. It was silly stuff at first, like attracting the attention of a barman or a waiter. I did not know what was happening at first. I would have in my mind a question for someone and they would answer before I had asked the question. Weird! It took me a few weeks before I figured out what was happening."

"You eventually found out what was happening?"

"Yes. I was hooking into their short term memory and feeding it with my thoughts before it was transferred into their consciousness or written out to the memory stream."

"So what they were experiencing were actually your thoughts and imagination?"

"Yes."

"I think I'm starting to get a grasp of this. If I have heard you right you can access people's memories and you can put your thoughts into their heads and make them think they are seeing and hearing things that aren't really happening."

"I think you've got that summed up pretty well."

"I've got a question, Jonathan. Can you see my memories and my thoughts right now?"

"Oh no! I have to be really concentrating for it to work. Otherwise I would be overwhelmed when I was surrounded by people."

"Thank goodness, it could be quite embarrassing!"

They both laughed.

Chapter 7

"I am truly amazed, Jonathan," said Karen. "When you were describing what you could do with your mind I was very sceptical. I really thought you were having me on. But you've shown me it's real!"

"It's an interesting trick to do at parties," said Jonathan.

"No! It's amazing! I am sure we can find a good use for your skills. In fact, I have an idea. Would you be prepared to go with me to visit a friend? He lives up in Scotland and I think he would be very interested in what you have to offer."

"How well do you know this guy?"

"He's one of my authors. I have been working with him for the last couple of years. We are publishing his memoirs. He's a great guy, lives in a castle near Fort William, lovely place."

Jonathan looked doubtful.

"Oh! Come on! It would be such fun! I'm off work between Christmas and New Year and we could go up then. Let me talk to him and at least sound him out."

"Go ahead, then. I'm up for it. To be honest I've not got much else planned after Christmas."

"Great! I need to see him about his memoirs, anyway. I can use that as an excuse. Can I use your phone, please?"

Jonathan gestured towards the phone and Karen picked up the handset. She pulled a notebook out of her briefcase, looked up the number then punched it in.

After a few rings, a gruff Scottish voice answered.

"This is Mac."

"Mac, this is Karen, from Greystones. Your publishers?"

"Oh yes! Karen. How the devil are you?"

"I'm doing great, Mac. Look, I've got a couple of things. I need to go over some changes we need in your manuscript and since our office is closed between Christmas and New Year I was wondering if I could come up to see you? You know how I love coming up to the Highlands."

"Of course. It would be great to see you. You could stay the night. I'll get one of the guest rooms ready for you. We could talk over dinner."

"Thank you, Mac."

"You said you had a couple of things?"

"Well, there was something else. I have a friend who I would like you to meet. I think you would find him very interesting."

"Bring him along."

"Thanks, Mac. I'm sure you'll like him. He's a really interesting person. How about we come up to see you a couple of days after Christmas? Say, the twenty-seventh?"

"I'll look forward to it. Are you coming up by train?"

"Yes."

"Let me know what time you'll be getting to Fort William and I'll come down and pick you up from the station."

"Thank you so much, Mac. See you on the twenty-seventh, then. Have a great Christmas!"

"Happy Christmas to you too, Karen!"

Karen put the phone down and looked across at Jonathan.

"Well, nothing ventured, nothing gained, I suppose," said Jonathan.

Karen clapped her hands with glee. "I can promise you, you will have a really interesting time there."

"I trust you, Karen. Actually, I need a project to get involved in. Thank you for setting that up."

"Can we go up by train?"

"Sure. We would have to change trains a couple of times but we could do it. We could go from here to Carlisle, then to Glasgow, then up to Fort William."

"Great! I can come up from Leeds and meet you here."

Jonathan looked at his watch. "Talking about Leeds, your next train is due in about ten minutes."

"We'd better get down to the platform then."

Karen closed up her briefcase and stood up.

"Jonathan, thank you so much for a great day. I am so glad we may have sorted out a project for you."

"I really enjoyed the day as well."

"It's time for my train!"

Jonathan walked over to the door and held it open for Karen. They walked down the outside stairs and onto the platform.

"We need to get across to the southbound side," said Jonathan and he led the way along the platform towards a footbridge that crossed over the line just south of the signal box. It was late afternoon and starting to get dark with just a few old-fashioned lamps casting pools of light on the platform. Karen and Jonathan walked over the bridge to the southbound platform.

"What are you doing for Christmas, Jonathan?"

"I've been invited for Christmas lunch by a family down in the village."

"Are you sure you'll be all right?"

"No problem!" Jonathan picked up the phone on the wall of the station building. "I'll just notify the dispatcher that we want the train to stop here." The dispatcher confirmed the request and Jonathan put down the phone. A few minutes later the two-tone horn of the train sounded and it pulled to a halt in the station. The doors hissed open.

"OK, Karen, off you go!"

Karen stepped into the carriage and turned round.

"Thanks again, Jonathan! See you after Christmas. Happy Christmas!"

"Happy Christmas, Karen! I'll call you."

The train doors hissed shut. Karen waved through the windows and blew a kiss as the train accelerated out of the station and disappeared into the night.

Jonathan watched the lights of the train disappear as it rounded the curve south of the station and then walked back over the footbridge.

Chapter 8

Christmas Eve dawned rather grey and cold at Ravensgill Bridge. As Jonathan sipped his morning tea and looked out across the hills, he thought that snow might be a possibility during the day. A white Christmas would be just perfect.

Jonathan dialled the number for Karen in Leeds.

"Karen, it's Jonathan."

"Jonathan! Happy Christmas Eve! How are things?"

"Pretty good! I'm meeting up with a few friends at the pub for drinks at lunchtime."

"Great! I'm helping my mother to prepare for lunch tomorrow. What are you doing for Christmas lunch?"

"I'm having lunch with a family in the village who I know quite well. But the main reason I wanted to call you was to finalize plans for our trip to Scotland. Is that all still on?"

"Yes. I called Mac yesterday to confirm."

"Well, if you want to get there before dark we'll need to get going early. There's a train from Leeds at six o'clock in the morning. Is that too early for you?"

"Not at all. I can make that train."

"I'll get on the train when it stops here, at about seven o'clock then we'll need to change trains at Carlisle and again at Glasgow. We should reach Fort William by about four in the afternoon."

"Great, we can get lunch on the journey."

"I don't suppose you want to tell me anything more about Mac, do you?"

"Honestly, Jonathan, I'm not being deliberately secretive. He's a bit of a mysterious character but very interesting to talk to. I've only just finished reading the first draft of his memoirs but I'll fill in a few more details for you on the train. It'll give us something to talk about on the journey."

"OK, Karen, I suppose it makes it all a bit more of an adventure. I guess I should pack for a couple of day's trip."

"Yes. I need to spend some time talking with Mac about his memoirs so I should think two or three nights. He's got plenty of spare guest rooms in the castle."

"I'll see you bright and early on the twenty seventh, then. Happy Christmas, Karen!"

"Happy Christmas, Jonathan! Have fun!"

Jonathan hung up the phone. He looked at his watch. Nearly lunchtime. A few snowflakes blew around outside the study windows.

"Time to start Christmas," he thought as he pulled on his coat and set off to walk to the Ravensgill Arms.

Chapter 9

It was still dark as Jonathan closed up and locked his house and walked out onto the northbound platform of Ravensgill Bridge station, wheeling along a black suitcase behind him. The Leeds to Carlisle train was due in a few minutes. He picked up the telephone on the wall of the station building and asked the dispatcher to have the northbound train stop at Ravensgill Bridge to pick him up. Jonathan had had a quick breakfast of tea and toast before leaving his house, but he was looking forward to getting something more substantial to eat on the hour's journey to Carlisle.

The cold light of dawn was just perceptible above the eastern hills as Jonathan heard the diesel engine of the train as it climbed the hill and approached the station. The train pulled to a halt with a squeal of brakes. The light from the carriages flooded onto the dark platform and the doors hissed open. Jonathan stepped inside and as the doors hissed shut, he heard Karen calling him from the carriage to his left.

"Hi, Jonathan!"

Jonathan turned and waved at Karen. Leaving his suitcase in the vestibule between the carriages, he walked down the carriage and sat down facing Karen.

"Good morning, sleepy head!"

"Hello Karen!" You seem to be full of energy at this early hour."

"Coffee," said Karen.

Jonathan noticed that they were the only passengers in the carriage.

"I took the liberty of picking up some breakfast in Leeds," said Karen as she pulled a thermos flask from her bag and placed it on the table between them. She also pulled out a couple of paper cups and a brown paper bag with sandwiches.

"Coffee and bacon and egg sandwiches," said Karen with a broad smile. "I hope you take your coffee with cream."

"Karen! You're a life saver!" said Jonathan.

"You're welcome! Dig in!"

Karen poured coffee into each of the paper cups and passed a package of sandwiches across to Jonathan.

Jonathan looked out of the windows of the carriage as he sipped his coffee. It was getting lighter outside. It was a cloudy morning and the train was rolling through hilly country at a moderate speed. There were sprinkles of snow on the distant hills but Jonathan felt warm.

"Thank you for breakfast," said Jonathan as he put down his coffee and picked up his bacon and egg sandwich. "How was your Christmas?"

"I stayed with my mum and dad and my sister came over for Christmas lunch. As usual we all ate too much and fell asleep in front of the television in the afternoon. How was yours?"

"I had lunch with a family in the village. I went back home in the afternoon to sleep it off and a friend stopped by in the evening and we made turkey sandwiches and had mince pies."

They finished their breakfast and Jonathan cleared away the wreckage and put it into a garbage can at the end of the carriage. When he returned to his seat, Karen had pulled out a thick sheaf of papers and placed them on the table.

"The Sir Fergus McKinnon Memoirs?" said Jonathan.

"The very same."

"So, are you going to tell me what I am letting myself in for?"

Karen laughed. "I really want to tell you what I know about Mac. We just ran out of time before Christmas."

"OK, but now it's time to spill the beans."

"Right. Well, I got to know Mac because our publishing house decided to buy his memoirs and he was assigned to me to look after."

"Have you visited the castle before?"

"Yes, just once. It's a fabulous place."

"Presumably I'll see that when we get there this evening, but what do I need to know about Mac before I meet him?"

"First of all, he is a very straight talking person but very polite, I would almost say gracious. I think he appreciates straight talk from the people he meets, too."

"Why do you think he will be interested in talking to me?"

"Jonathan, anyone would be interested in talking to you with what your mind is capable of. The thing is, I am fairly familiar with Mac's earlier life from reading his memoirs but I am not really sure what his current interests are. He claims that he's retired but, like you, he doesn't strike me as the kind of person who would be happy with a quiet retirement."

"Tell me his background as far as you know it from his memoirs."

"Right, there's a good idea. I think he will tell us more about what he's doing now when we meet him. But he is retired from an Army career and he is living in a castle in the hills near Fort William on the west coast of Scotland."

"Why a castle?"

"I think it's been in his family for many years. He doesn't have any close family these days though and he lives mostly on his own."

"Do you know what he did in the army?"

"Yes, and this is where it starts to get interesting. For a while, he worked in the Army Intelligence Corps but then he seems to have been posted to our Washington embassy as our military attaché. He was there for several years. He spent a lot of time travelling to our embassies in Central and South America. He speaks several languages including Spanish, Portuguese and Russian."

"Do you know what he was doing there?"

"Well, according to his memoirs, he was mostly working with the militaries of those other countries, liaison, training, that sort of thing."

"Was there more to it than he wrote in his memoirs?"

"I think there probably was. You see, when he came back to the UK he was eventually recruited by the security services."

"Security services?"

"You know? MI5, spies, spooks!"

"Good Lord!"

"Yes, I thought you might find that interesting! Look, why don't you read through the memoirs and they should fill in some of the blanks."

Karen pushed across the stack of papers and Jonathan started to read. He leafed through the first few chapters fairly quickly, covering Mac's childhood, his school days and his early days in the army. Then, about a third of the way through the book, Jonathan reached the part where Mac had been assigned to MI5 and he slowed down to take in the detail.

Apparently, it was not unusual for Army officers to be assigned for duty in the intelligence services because these officers had usually been subject to extensive security vetting and their loyalty had been proven in military service. As someone who had been involved with the Diplomatic Service and who spoke several languages, Sir Fergus was an obvious candidate for MI5. In his memoirs, Sir Fergus described the structure of the security services.

MI5 was the internal security service, responsible for security within the United Kingdom.

MI6 was the external security service responsible for ensuring Britain's security overseas. It was the "James Bond" side of the service and on the face of it more glamorous than MI5, but Sir Fergus felt that MI5 had a far more direct effect on the lives of British citizens and he was proud to serve the organization.

"Do we change trains here?"

Karen's voice jolted Jonathan from his reading and he looked up to see that the train had stopped at the station in Carlisle.

"Yes," said Jonathan, "we change trains here and we catch the train to Glasgow." He gathered up the manuscript and put it into his briefcase. "This is interesting stuff," he said.

They stepped off the train onto the platform and Jonathan looked up at the departures board.

"The Glasgow train is due in about ten minutes, a couple of platforms across," said Jonathan as he pointed across to the other platform and they set off together to walk.

Jonathan turned to Karen as they waited for the train. "I'm just getting to the interesting bit about MI5."

"Good, the manuscript is interesting but I think we will probably find out more about his work in MI5 when we meet him. I think you should go ahead and finish reading the manuscript before we get there. At least it will give you some good background information."

Their train pulled in and they stepped aboard. Karen went off to find a seat with a table while Jonathan stowed the suitcases. Then he went to join Karen.

"I think they have a buffet service on this train," said Karen.

"Yes, I could use another coffee," said Jonathan.

The train started to accelerate out of the station.

"I'll go and hunt down some coffee while you carry on reading the manuscript," said Karen.

Karen walked off in search of the buffet car while Jonathan found his place in the manuscript and settled down to continue reading. As he read, he learned that the MI5 mission was to protect the United Kingdom against forces that would seek to overthrow it politically or economically. Sir Fergus wrote about a few of the operations that he had been involved in during his time with MI5, where he had been involved in undercover work to infiltrate organizations and gain intelligence about their plans. However, much of the memoir discussed the relationship between MI5 and the government, including stories of intense arguments and mutual blame games when MI5 intelligence was ignored or misused by the government.

"Coffee break time!" said Karen as she sat down.

Jonathan looked up from the manuscript.

"What do you think?" said Karen.

"Interesting stuff, especially the power struggles within the service and between the service and the government."

Jonathan sipped his coffee.

"I think what he has left out of the memoirs is almost as informative as what he has included," said Karen. "I get the idea that there is some kind of subtext there."

"Yes," said Jonathan, "It looks to me as if he has some kind of resentment or bitterness about MI5. Tell me, why did he leave the service?"

"That's covered in the last couple of chapters. He is actually a bit vague about the details. He just says something about being offered early retirement and leaves it at that. He claims he was ready to retire to his castle in the highlands and spend his time hunting, shooting and fishing. It all sounds very plausible."

"That was his job," said Jonathan, "making weird things sound plausible."

"I expect we'll find out more when we meet him, " said Karen.

Chapter 10

As the train approached Fort William, the winter sun was getting low in the western sky, casting long shadows across the hills behind the town and reflecting brightly off the waters of the loch that stretched out towards the sea.

Karen and Jonathan collected their suitcases and stepped down onto the platform. Apart from a uniformed porter and a couple of other passengers there was no-one else on the platform so Karen and Jonathan walked through the ticket hall and onto the road outside the station.

"Karen!" a voice shouted. Karen looked around and recognized Mac walking towards them.

"How are you, Karen! How was Christmas?" he said as he gave Karen a hug.

"Just great!. This is Jonathan, who I told you about."

Mac gave Jonathan a vigorous handshake. "Welcome to the highlands, Jonathan."

Mac took Karen's suitcase and started off towards his green Range Rover. "We should be able to get home before dark. It's about seven miles."

He lifted the suitcases into the back of the Range Rover then directed Jonathan and Karen to get in. Karen got into the front passenger seat while Jonathan got into the back seat. Mac jumped into the driver's seat and started the engine. "How was the journey?"

"It was good," said Karen. "Took most of the day, though."

Mac drove out of the station forecourt and after threading through a few narrow streets, they were soon on a road out of town.

"Karen tells me you live in the Pennines, Jonathan."

"Yes, sir. A place called Ravensgill Bridge."

"Oh Mac!" said Karen, "It's fabulous! He actually lives in a railway station!"

"I want to hear all about it," said Mac as he swung the Range Rover round a corner. They were well out of the town now and travelling across a broad sweep of heather covered hills. Ahead was a valley and beyond, made just visible by the setting sun reflecting off its windows, was a large house.

Mac pointed ahead. "There's home sweet home."

In a few minutes, Mac pulled off the road and into a long curving driveway and drew to a halt outside a pair of huge oak doors.

"Here we are!" said Mac as he jumped out of the vehicle. He ran around to the back of the Range Rover and lifted out the suitcases then walked over to open the front door of the castle. Karen and Jonathan collected their suitcases and followed Mac into the house.

They found themselves standing in a large entrance hall with a magnificent stairway leading up to the next level. The floor of the entrance hall was polished wood, the walls were grey stone and the ceilings were supported by soaring wood beams.

"Come on, I'll show you where your rooms are. You can unpack and freshen up and then I'll see you in the Great Room and we can have drinks before dinner."

Mac started off up the stairs and Jonathan and Karen followed on behind. At the top of the stairs, they turned right into a long corridor with doors off both sides. Mac opened the first door on the right. "Here you are, Karen."

"Thank you, Mac. I'm going to get a quick shower and change."

"OK, I'll see you down in the Great Room in about half an hour. Turn right at the bottom of the stairs and the Great Room is through the door straight ahead of you. Dress casually!"

"I'll see you there, Jonathan," said Karen as Mac opened the next door along the corridor. Jonathan stepped into his room.

Chapter 11

Half an hour later, after unpacking, getting showered and changed into fresh clothes, Jonathan stepped out of his room, walked down the stairs, crossed the hall and opened the double doors into the Great Room. It was an enormous room. The floor, like that of the hall, was polished wood and the walls were grey stone. There were several pictures on the wall of highland warriors in kilts and there were several heads of deer mounted on the walls. The room was a full three stories high with arching beams across the ceiling high above. There were tall narrow windows along the right wall of the room and across the wall at the far end. There was an enormous fireplace on the left wall with a log fire burning brightly. Arranged in front of the fire were four luxurious high backed armchairs and a low table. There were several book cases along one wall and at the far end of the room was a large polished wood dining table with three places set and two candles, unlit.

The room was illuminated by soft lighting along the walls just above head height. The effect was to make the ceiling almost disappear in the darkness above. Jonathan noticed music playing softly in the background and he recognized it as music from The Phantom of the Opera. As the fire flickered, Jonathan thought it was an appropriate selection.

Jonathan heard a click of the door and turned to see Karen entering the room. She was smiling broadly.

"Isn't it fabulous?" she said.

"A bit overwhelming," said Jonathan.

"Come on! You saw how friendly Mac is. Relax! If he didn't like you he would probably have you hanging by your thumbs in the dungeons by now!"

Mac walked in from the far end of the Great Hall. "Hello guys!" he said cheerily. "I expect you could do with a drink of some sort, couldn't you? I have beer, wine, or a very nice selection of single malt whiskies.

"I'd like a glass of white wine, please," said Karen.

"And for you, Jonathan?" said Mac.

"I'd like to try one of your single malts, please."

"Right! You two take a seat by the fire and I'll bring the drinks. Ice in you whisky, Jonathan?"

"Oh no, sir! Never in a single malt!"

"Good man! Good man!" said Mac as he walked off to get the drinks.

Jonathan and Karen walked over to the chairs arranged in front of the fire and sank down into the luxurious leather.

Karen smiled at Jonathan. "Don't worry, you'll do great."

Mac arrived with a wheeled serving trolley on which he had placed a bottle of Chardonnay with a wine glass and a bottle of single malt scotch with two lead crystal tumblers. He poured the drinks, handed them out and sat down next to Karen, facing Jonathan.

"Well, cheers!" he said brightly, raising his glass and taking a sip of his malt whisky.

"Cheers!" echoed Jonathan and Karen as they each took a sip of their own drinks.

"I've got a joint of beef roasting in the oven but we can leave that for a while we have our drinks and a chat. Does that work for everyone?"

Karen and Jonathan both nodded.

"I want to talk to you about the book, Karen, but we can do that tomorrow. I want to find out about you Jonathan. What's your story?"

Jonathan sat a bit more upright in his chair, took a sip of his drink and started to tell his story. He told about his work for the film industry at Pinewood and his move to Hollywood. He talked about the road accident and how he had eventually moved back to England. He described Ravensgill Bridge and discussed his political views.

Mac listened intently, occasionally asking for clarification or explanation. When Jonathan finished his story, Mac said, "Wow! What a life you've had! I can see how you need some mental challenge in your life now. I'm exactly the same. When I retired, I had to find something to challenge my mind."

Mac refilled their drinks and said, "Look, I need to check on dinner. Why don't you kids relax for a few minutes while I serve up then come on over to the table? Wine with your dinner, Jonathan?"

"Yes please, Mac. I'll have the same Chardonnay that Karen is drinking."

"I'll put an extra bottle and glasses on the table."

Mac walked off to the kitchen, leaving Jonathan and Karen sitting by the fire.

"How are you feeling?" asked Karen.

"Much more relaxed," said Jonathan. "He is quite easy to talk to."

"When are you going to show him your tricks?" said Karen.

"Can you help me to introduce the subject over dinner?"

"Of course. What are trick are you thinking of doing?"

"How about the vanishing trick?"

"Yes, nice and simple. If that works maybe you can try the mind reading trick."

"I'm relying on you to help me out here, Karen."

"Stop worrying, you'll be great."

"Dinner's ready!" Mac called over from the dining table. Jonathan and Karen walked over. Mac had placed a large piece of roast beef on the table along with bowls of roast potatoes, Yorkshire puddings, peas and Brussels sprouts.

They all sat down, Mac at the head of the table, Jonathan and Karen at either side.

"Why don't you pour the wine while I carve the beef, Jonathan?"

Mac prepared three plates of beef. "Help yourselves to vegetables and gravy."

The group each made their plates and started to eat.

"Excellent dinner," said Karen between bites of food.

"Yes. Very good," said Jonathan and he took a sip of his wine.

"Well, you are very welcome. I rather enjoy having company for dinner. It gives me an excuse to have fun in the kitchen!"

Conversation within the group was suspended as they enjoyed their meal. One by one, they finished eating and sipped their glasses of wine. Mac was the last to finish and he leaned back in his seat, looking very satisfied. Karen was the first to speak.

"That was great, Mac. Thank you."

"Yes, I do rather like roast beef. Its Scottish Angus beef, you know. How were the Yorkshire puddings?"

"Better than I can do and I was born in Yorkshire!"

Mac laughed.

"Mac," Karen continued, "One of the reasons that I wanted to introduce you to Jonathan was that he has some skills which I think may be useful to you."

"Really? And what would those skills be?" said Mac.

"Well, would you mind a small demonstration?" said Karen.

Without waiting for Mac to respond, Jonathan focused on Mac's eyes to give him a temporary seizure. Mac froze, looking straight ahead, expressionless. Jonathan saw that the pupils of Mac's eyes had dilated, indicating that Mac was fully seized.

"Could you clear away the plates, please, Karen?" said Jonathan

Karen collected up the plates and the cutlery and took them out to the kitchen, then she quickly walked back to her seat.

"All set?" said Jonathan. Karen nodded.

Jonathan relaxed his concentration on Mac's eyes, which caused the temporary seizure to end. Mac blinked and shook his head. He looked down at the table and blinked again.

"OK, what's going on?"

Jonathan thought there was a touch of anger in Mac's voice but he also detected the hint of a smile.

"The plates. They just disappeared. What happened? They were here and then they were gone!"

Jonathan smiled, but it was Karen who spoke. "It's one of Jonathan's little tricks," she said.

"Is Jonathan some kind of magician? Is this a magic trick? I usually don't believe in magic but that was quite impressive."

"It's one of those skills that I was telling you about," said Karen.

"Well, I'm very impressed. Do you want to tell me how you did that?"

"Jonathan, do you want to explain?" said Karen.

"Shall we refresh the drinks first?" said Mac.

Mac refilled the glasses, relaxed back into his chair and said, "All right, Jonathan. Explain how you did it."

"I actually put your brain into a temporary seizure for a minute or two," said Jonathan. "Your brain was shut down just as if you were asleep. Karen took the plates away. Then I woke you up. Simple, when you know how!"

"I have no memory of being put out like that," said Mac.

"Have you ever had a sense of 'déjà vu', you are somewhere new and you have a sense of having been there before?"

"Yes, I have. It's a weird feeling."

"That is your brain going into a spontaneous seizure. It shuts down for about half a second. When it comes back, you have a sense that you were there before."

"Exactly."

"Well, you were there before, half a second ago."

"I understand, yes. What just happened felt a bit like déjà vu. How do you do it?"

Jonathan related the story to Mac as he had related it to Karen a couple of weeks before, about the coma following the car crash and about how he started to hear the thoughts of people around him. He told how his ability to communicate with people's minds had developed over a couple of years and he described his capability of being able to influence people's thoughts by concentrating on their eyes. Mac sat in silence as Jonathan related his story.

"My God!" said Mac as Jonathan finished. "How many people know about this?"

"You and Karen. The doctors who treated me in California knew a little bit about it in the early days but they put it down to mental illness. I have kept very quiet about it."

"Probably just as well," said Mac. "You know, if you had just told me about this I would have thought you were crazy but that practical demonstration you gave was pretty convincing. It was a clever move to do that as a surprise. Is there anything else that you can do with these mental tricks?"

"Well," said Jonathan, "I can do three things at the moment. I can cause temporary brain shutdowns, as I just did with you. I can also get into other people's minds and experience their memories and I can also plant thoughts and ideas in other people's minds."

"That's all you can do?" said Mac and then he burst out laughing. "I can make very good use of your skills, Jonathan."

"Do you want to see another demonstration?" said Jonathan.

"Yes, indeed!" said Mac.

"Go into the library and shut the door," said Jonathan. Take a book off the shelf, open it at a page somewhere in the middle, and read a couple of sentences out loud, but not so loud that we can hear. Then come back and bring the book back with you, please, but don't let me see it."

"All right, we'll give it a try," said Mac and he stood up and walked towards the double doors at the end of the Great Hall. A few minutes later the doors of the Great Hall creaked open again and Mac entered, walked over to his seat at the head of the dining table, and sat down, holding the book in his lap. Jonathan focused once more into Mac's eyes and soon he began to see Mac's memories of the last couple of minutes.

There was a misty image of a library full of books.

Then Jonathan heard the words "The Complete Sherlock Holmes."

After a pause, he heard "Page one hundred and sixteen."

Out of the mist in Jonathan's mind came an image of an open book.

The first words on the left hand page were "'We had all been summoned to appear before the magistrates...'"

Jonathan was writing it all down on a piece of paper as he kept focus on Mac's eyes. When he had finished writing, Jonathan broke his concentration and Mac, who had been in a temporary seizure while Jonathan had been reading his memories, shook his head.

"'The Complete Sherlock Holmes'," said Mac, holding up the book, "Page one hundred and sixteen."

He opened the book at that page and read aloud the first sentence. "We had all been summoned to appear before the magistrates..." He picked up the piece of paper that Jonathan had placed on the table and unfolded it. A broad smile appeared on his face.

"Unbelievable! Stunning! Amazing!"

Mac stood up and extended his right hand towards Jonathan. Jonathan stood and they shook hands.

"Well done! Well done!" said Mac. "I don't know how you do it but well done!"

Jonathan and Mac both sat down and Mac turned to Karen.

"Karen my dear, you were so right to bring Jonathan to see me. I think he and I can work together very well. Here is what I'd like to do, if it's all right with you folks. It's getting a bit late now and you're probably tired from your journey so why don't we all turn in for the night? Then tomorrow I would like to take Jonathan out for a walk and a chat."

Mac looked at Jonathan then Karen for approval.

"Karen," said Mac, "I've got at stack of papers to add to the memoirs. Perhaps if Jonathan and I went out for a couple of hours after breakfast you could review the papers and we could all meet up back here for lunch."

"That will work for me," said Karen.

"Sounds like a good plan," said Jonathan.

"Right then," said Mac, "I'll cook breakfast for eight-thirty."

Jonathan and Karen stood up.

"Thanks again for a wonderful evening," said Karen.

"See you at breakfast," said Jonathan as he and Karen walked together towards the double doors that led into the hallway. As they climbed the stairs towards their rooms, Jonathan said, "I would love to know what he's got planned. I've been trying to hook into his mind but I can't get any clear images."

"I expect you're tired," said Karen, "but I think you impressed him. Aren't you glad you came?"

"I'll let you know after tomorrow," said Jonathan as they parted company outside Karen's room.

"Good night," said Jonathan as he unlocked his door.

"Sleep well. See you at breakfast," said Karen as she stepped inside her room and closed the door.

Chapter 12

As Jonathan walked down the staircase next morning, he could detect the delicious smell of bacon coming from the Great Hall.

He walked into the hall and saw that Mac and Karen were already eating breakfast. A bright, low winter sun shone through the tall windows of the Great Hall, casting bright bands of light and sharp shadows across the floor and the dining table.

"There's fresh coffee on the sideboard," said Mac as Jonathan approached.

Jonathan poured himself a cup of coffee and took his place at the table.

"Good morning," said Jonathan.

"Good morning," said Mac. "Did you sleep well?"

"Yes, thank you. I was very comfortable."

"There's some bacon and eggs in the kitchen if you want to serve yourself," said Mac. "Karen and I were just catching up on some publishing business."

Jonathan went out to the kitchen and came back with a plate of bacon and eggs. As Jonathan tucked into his breakfast, Mac continued his conversation with Karen.

"I've got a package of material," said Mac. "I found some old photographs and letters which might be useful."

"I'll review those while you are out with Jonathan this morning. When you get back I would like to go through the printers proofs I brought with me, for you to check the copy editor's changes. But this package will keep me busy most of the morning."

"Good," said Mac. "Jonathan, are you ready to get out and about this fine morning?"

Jonathan nodded as he swallowed a mouthful of breakfast.

"Did you bring walking boots and foul weather gear with you?"

"Yes, I did," said Jonathan. "I'll go and get changed as soon as I have finished breakfast."

"Right," said Mac. "I'll meet you by the front door in half an hour."

Mac got up from the table and walked towards the kitchen.

Karen turned to Jonathan. "I'm really fascinated to find out what he has got planned."

"Me too!"

Jonathan finished his breakfast and stood up. "I'll see you later, then."

"Yes, I've got plenty to keep me busy this morning," said Karen

Jonathan left the Great Hall and went up to his room to change.

When he came back downstairs, Jonathan found Mac waiting in the hall, by the front door. Mac opened the front door and they stepped out. The cloud had thickened since breakfast and the highest hill tops were shrouded in cloud. Mac climbed into the driver's seat of the Range Rover and Jonathan climbed into the passenger seat beside him.

"It looks like the clouds are settling in over the hills this morning," said Mac, as he started the engine. "I think we ought to head for the coast."

"Fine with me," said Jonathan.

Mac pulled out of the driveway and turned right. Jonathan recalled that they had driven this way when they had come up to the castle from the town last night.

"So," said Mac, "You told me last night about your life in America but you really didn't say why you had moved back to the United Kingdom."

“To be honest, after Jill died, I was homesick. I never lost my deep love for the UK when I was overseas.”

At the bottom of the valley, Mac turned left. “This will take us over to the road alongside the loch.”

Jonathan nodded.

“California weather is better and the scenery is quite spectacular.”

“The usual clichés, Mac!”

Mac snorted a laugh. “I know, Jonathan. Don’t forget I spent several years in the United States. I think I know where you are coming from.”

“It’s a cultural thing. America can be a very exciting place but I constantly found myself at odds with the culture. The ‘American Way’”. Jonathan drew quotes in the air with his fingers.

“You don’t really have to explain,” said Mac. “I actually felt much the same way after I had been there for a few years, although the British Embassy did provide a certain amount of ‘cultural quarantine’”. Mac imitated Jonathan’s finger quotes then quickly grabbed the steering wheel again.

“Quite frankly, I do worry about the future of Britain though Mac,” said Jonathan. “I mean, I live a fairly sheltered life in Ravensgill Bridge and it seems far away from politics and war and all that stuff. But I do sometimes think that our way of life in Britain is changing for the worse. It’s almost as if we have no control of our own affairs any more, what with Europe and cultural pollution from America. Having lived in America I can see the way that that country has gone with unbridled greed and competition and...”

Jonathan looked over at Mac who was dividing his attention between the road ahead and what Jonathan was saying.

“...And?” said Mac.

"Oh, perhaps I'm just becoming an old curmudgeon in my retirement."

Jonathan saw that they had been driving along the edge of a sea loch, which was beyond a low wall along the right hand side of the road. Hills rose steeply on the left.

"No! At least you care about your country and you think about it. It's apathy about this country that is half the trouble. Your problem is that you feel helpless to do anything about it. Am I right?"

"Exactly! I get very disheartened about it."

Mac pulled the Range Rover over to the side of the road, switched off the engine and turned to Jonathan.

"Would you like to be part of an organization that is working to make a difference?" said Mac.

"What kind of organization?"

"Let's go for a walk alongside the loch and we can talk about it."

Jonathan could detect a tone of enthusiasm and excitement in Mac's voice. They climbed out of the car. There was a cold wind blowing off the loch and Jonathan could taste the salt on the air. The waters of the loch were grey and the wind was causing wavelets to break on the surface. Looking back to his right, Jonathan could see the town of Fort William at the landward end of the loch. They started walking side by side on towards the seaward end of the loch.

"Did you get a chance to read that draft of my memoirs that Karen had?" said Mac.

"Yes, I did."

"So you know all about the Army and the Diplomatic Service and the Intelligence Service?"

"Yes, indeed. A fascinating story. But I did detect a touch of tension in there around your retirement."

"Quite perceptive, young man!" said Mac with a broad smile. "For most of the time I was in MI5 I was proud to serve my country and I felt I was doing a good job. But towards the end, things started to change."

Mac paused for a moment and looked at Jonathan but Jonathan made no comment.

"There has been a steady shift in the mission of MI5 over the last few years and it has been largely as a result of political pressure. It's almost as if the government of the day wants to use MI5 as some kind of private army to avoid the legal niceties of life, prevent embarrassing situations for ministers and politicians and to generally support the establishment."

"What exactly do you mean by the establishment?" said Jonathan.

"The power structure. The people who wield power in this country. The people who make the important decisions."

"But this is a democratic country," said Jonathan. "Doesn't the ultimate power lie in the hands of the people?"

"I am not sure that we have ever been a truly democratic country, and certainly not in the last few years. Do you realize that less than one quarter of the people actually voted for the political party which now forms the government? Frankly, I think our so-called democracy is a sham and getting more so every year."

"Do you think people are apathetic?"

"That is certainly part of it. But that apathy is encouraged by the government who seem to have an agenda that is independent of our elected parliament. And that is not even considering the unelected folk who have a massive effect on our daily lives."

They reached a small brick and glass shelter overlooking the loch.

"Do you want to sit for a while?" said Mac

"Sure," said Jonathan, "this is an interesting discussion."

They sat side by side in the shelter, which provided some protection against the wind blowing across the loch.

"So who are these people that have such an effect on our daily lives?" said Jonathan.

"People with enough money to buy influence. Financial people. Bankers. Business owners. The media, or at least that part of it that is controlled by private money, much of it from overseas. Thank God we still have the BBC!"

"I am inclined to agree with you," said Jonathan, "but I have not been able to put it into words quite as clearly as you have. But you talked about an organization that was working to make a difference..."

"I'll get on to that, but first I need to tell you a bit more about what is going on in MI5. Stuff that I didn't put into the memoir."

"You mentioned how MI5 had changed," said Jonathan, "how it had become a tool of government."

"Yes. There is a dark side that is separate from the main part of MI5. It doesn't play by the same rules. Informally it's called 'MI5 Black Ops'.

"What kind of things does MI5 Black Ops do?"

"Well, they are geared towards keeping the status quo for the establishment, keeping power in the hands of the few, and above all else avoiding embarrassment for the government."

"How do they operate?"

"They often make 'awkward' people disappear. In a couple of cases Black Ops actually convinced foreign governments that these people were British spies and the foreign governments did the dirty work."

"Ugly business!" said Jonathan.

"Indeed! People often met with accidents.

"Were you involved in any of these operations?"

"No. It was when I began to see what was happening that I resigned from the service. I was going to blow the whistle on what was going on but I had seen what happened to whistle blowers in the past, so I decided to retire quietly and see what I might be able to do from the outside."

"Have you done anything yet?"

"Not yet. I've been keeping a close eye on what is going on. But there are some people in this country who share my concerns about these things and some of these people have resources."

"Are you still in contact with former colleagues in the service?"

"A few of them. We have to be discreet. It would be bad for their careers if they were too close to me. We arrange to bump into each other in pubs, on trains, that sort of thing."

"How does MI5 Black Ops recruit its operators?"

"A variety of sources, within MI5 and outside. Usually ex-military people, sometimes MI6. Then there are the freelancers."

"Freelancers?"

"Yes, mercenaries if you like. They are often people of very questionable backgrounds but with very special skills. Often of the criminal variety."

"It's interesting that you can get so many people to engage in questionable activities like that."

"The army have been doing it for years. The army can take a perfectly peaceful young man off the streets and turn him into a killing machine in a few months. It's all a question of training and psychological conditioning. MI5 Black Ops uses the same techniques."

"Does the official MI5 admit to what is happening in MI5 Black Ops?"

"MI5 keeps an arm's length relationship with MI5 Black Ops. They like to maintain what the call 'plausible deniability'. They provide some finance to MI5 Black Ops but they stay well away from day to day operations. Black Ops gets its assignments directly from cabinet level."

"I was wondering how they were financed."

"Apart from their official funding their budget is supplemented with...how should I put it? Additional activities."

"Presumably of a questionable variety?"

"Very presumably! Drugs, protection money, even donations."

"Donations?"

"Yes. There are people in this country who are very happy to support an organization that they see as maintaining the power of the establishment."

"Do you have any examples of MI5 Black Ops operations?"

"Yes, there is one I can tell you about. We had a case of a translator at GCHQ several years ago. You've heard of GCHQ, haven't you?"

"Government Communication Headquarters?"

"Yes. They are actually the third arm of the security services. Their job is to gather intelligence by intercepting communications. It used to be mostly radio intercepts but these days it is also internet and telephone. Anyway, this translator had previously worked as a translator at the British embassy in Moscow and he had been recruited by the KGB, but we never uncovered him. He finished his assignment in Moscow and he moved back to the UK and was assigned to GCHQ, where he continued his espionage activities. He was eventually caught, arrested and taken for interrogation."

"I don't remember that case in the newspapers."

"No, the security services like to keep a low profile, especially when they have been caught napping.

While he was being interrogated, this character starts to tell his interrogators what he knows about illegal monitoring activities he came across when he was working at GCHQ."

"Illegal monitoring activities?"

"There is a clandestine unit at GCHQ called the Commercial Unit. Their job is to monitor phone calls and emails between British companies and pass on commercial intelligence to the government. The government used that information to influence competition and to benefit companies that the government favours."

"Why would the government favour one particular company over another?"

"All sorts of reasons. At the nice end, political contributions. At the other end, bribery?"

"So this spy threatens to blow the whistle?"

"He starts to try to cut a deal with his interrogators. He tries to get the charges reduced in exchange for his silence. Surprise, surprise! One morning he is found dead in his cell, died of a heart attack during the night."

"Can you show any evidence of these illegal operations? Could you take it to the authorities?"

"Well, that's the problem. These operations are so clandestine, they cover their tracks very well. It would be their word against mine and if I started going public I don't think I would last very long."

"I think I see what you mean. Is there anything that you can do?"

"I want to fight what is happening. I want to defend the people against this stuff. This is rotting away the very foundation of British democracy. I do have a close circle of friends who are of similar mind, including one who outranks anyone who might be involved."

"Outranks the Prime Minister?"

"Technically, yes."

Mac was smiling. Jonathan was puzzled.

"Royalty?" said Jonathan

"Outranks the Prime Minister."

Jonathan made a soft whistling sound at this piece of information. He looked out to sea and saw that the low cloud of earlier had broken up. The low winter sun was illuminating the hills on the other side of the loch. A small fishing boat was making its way into the loch from the sea.

Jonathan turned to Mac. "So you're trying to fight this?"

"I think with your skills you could be a great help to us. We call ourselves 'Operation Checkmate'. We plan to thwart these people, frustrate their plans, stay one step ahead of them and outwit and outsmart them?"

"What would I have to do?" said Jonathan.

"Well, I hope we could adapt your skills to help us find out what MI5 Black Ops are up to and get ahead of them. So you could provide us with information and intelligence."

"I would be interested in helping. I certainly share your views about this stuff. I am nervous that I might not match up to your expectations."

"Well, think about it for a few hours. It's time to head back for lunch. Think about what I have told you this morning and we can talk about it over dinner tonight."

"I'll do that," said Jonathan. "It's certainly a big challenge."

They stood up from their seat in the shelter and started walking back down the coast road towards the Range Rover.

Chapter 13

Mac stopped the Land Rover in front of the castle and he and Jonathan jumped out and went inside. As they entered the Great Hall, they saw Karen sitting at the dining table where she had spread out papers, photographs and letters.

"Hello boys!" said Karen, looking up from her work. "Did you have a good trip?"

"Yes, thanks," said Jonathan. "Have you had any lunch yet?"

"Not yet," said Karen.

"There's some stuff in the kitchen to make lunch," said Mac.

"Why don't you two get changed while I make some sandwiches?" said Karen. "I'll also clear up this mess on the table."

"See you in a few minutes then," said Jonathan as he and Mac left the Great Hall.

Jonathan returned to the Great Hall twenty minutes later to find that Karen had cleared all the papers off the table and had replaced them with three place settings and two large plates of sandwiches. Karen was standing at one of the tall windows looking out over the gardens.

"How was your walk?" said Karen.

"We walked along the edge of the loch," said Jonathan as he moved over to stand beside Karen. Jonathan stood silently for a minute wondering how much to tell Karen about his conversation with Mac.

"It was an interesting conversation," said Jonathan, eventually.

"Do you think you might be able to work together?"

"I'm thinking about it."

Mac entered the room. "Thank you for making lunch, Karen," he said. He picked up a plate, loaded it with a selection of sandwiches and brought it over to where Karen and Jonathan were standing.

"It's a beautiful view, isn't it?" said Mac, nodding towards the window. He offered the plate of sandwiches to Karen and then to Jonathan and they each took one. "Does your place in the Pennines have a view, Jonathan?"

"Yes, on a clear day I can see as far as Morecambe Bay."

"I find the hills very inspirational," said Mac. "One of these days I'll have to get inspired to write a novel based on my life."

"There's enough excitement for a couple of novels," said Karen as she picked another sandwich from the plate.

"I'd like to come down and see your place sometime, Jonathan," said Mac.

"You'd be very welcome, Mac."

Mac placed the plate of sandwiches on the window seat in front of Karen and Jonathan. "You guys finish these off. I have some paperwork to attend to this afternoon. I need to go over those printers proofs that you brought me, Karen. Can you two entertain yourselves for an hour or two? Then we could all get together for dinner this evening. You will stay another night, won't you?"

"Is that all right with you, Karen?" said Jonathan.

"Sure," said Karen. "I don't need to be back in the office until after New Year."

"I'll see you at about six o'clock for cocktails. I've got my housekeeper coming in this evening to cook for us."

Mac walked out of the Great Hall.

Jonathan and Karen sat down together in the window seat, the plate of sandwiches between them.

"So, you were thinking about it?" said Karen. "Can you tell me more?"

"Well, I'd prefer Mac to tell you if he chooses to, but he wants me to help him fight corruption and bribery and the dark side of the government."

"Isn't that dangerous?"

"I don't think he wants me to be involved in the front line operations. He wants me to use my mental tricks to find information for him."

"What do you think?"

"It sounds interesting. At least it would give me some purpose in life. You never know where it might lead, and I'm sure if it didn't work out Mac and I could just part company."

"Jonathan, I don't want to think I have led you into something bad!"

"Karen, I'm a big boy! I need some excitement in my life. I'm going to give it a try."

"Well only if I can be involved too. You need someone looking out for you!"

Jonathan laughed. "All right then!"

"Did you show him any more tricks while you were out?"

"No. I did think about bringing a nuclear submarine into the loch while we were down there, but I think we ought to take things steadily with him. We don't want to show all our cards to him right away, just as I'm sure he is not showing us all his cards."

"Take it step by step? Good idea," said Karen. She stretched her arms above her head and yawned. "I've been working in here all morning. I'd like to go for a quick stroll around the castle gardens before it gets dark."

"I'll walk with you if you like," said Jonathan.

"You've already had some exercise today. Why don't you take a rest this afternoon? I won't go far from the house. I'll meet you down here just before six, all right?"

"Works for me if you're sure," said Jonathan. "I'll take an afternoon nap."

Chapter 14

When Jonathan came back down to the Great Hall, it was already dark outside and the Great Hall was beautifully lit. Once again, a bright log fire was burning in the huge fireplace. Karen was sitting in one of the enormous armchairs near the fire, a glass of white wine in her hand. Jonathan sat down opposite her.

"Did you have a good rest?" said Karen.

"Very good, thank you. I slept for a couple of hours. How was your walk in the garden?"

"The gardens are beautiful. I should think Mac has a professional gardener to look after them. They must be spectacular in the summer."

Jonathan noticed an elderly lady wearing an apron, standing in the shadows.

"Jonathan, this is Mrs. Johnson."

"Good evening, Mr. Long," said Mrs. Johnson, in a soft Scottish accent. "Can I get you something to drink?"

"Thank you. I would like a glass of beer, please."

Mrs. Johnson walked off towards the kitchen. She returned with Jonathan's drink just as Mac walked in.

"I see Mrs. Johnson is looking after you," said Mac. "My usual, please, Mrs. Johnson."

Mac sat down in the third armchair. "Well, Jonathan, have you thought any more about our conversation this morning?"

"Yes, sir, I have. I certainly share your sentiments about the way that British democracy is being eroded and for a long time I have felt powerless to do anything about it. I would like to see if I can contribute something."

"From what I have seen of your party tricks so far I am sure you will be a key player in our efforts."

"There is one thing I would like to ask," said Jonathan.

"What would that be?" said Mac.

"That I can keep Karen involved, just to have someone to bounce ideas off."

"Well," said Mac, "for obvious reasons our work must be kept very secret but Karen and I have been working together for quite a long time now so I'm happy for her to be involved."

"Very well," said Jonathan, "I'm in."

"Good! Good!" said Mac. "Let's shake hands on it." Karen, Mac and Jonathan did a three way handshake. Mac picked up the malt scotch that Mrs. Johnson had placed on the table beside his chair.

"Let's drink to that!" said Mac, raising his glass and Jonathan and Karen raised theirs in response.

Mac's attention was distracted as the doors of the Great Hall swung open and a Scottish piper in traditional dress appeared at the door and started to play.

Mac looked towards Jonathan and Jonathan smiled. The piper continued to play as he walked slowly up the length of the hall. He stopped a few feet short of Mac, who was looking thoroughly confused. The piper finished his tune then faded away to nothing.

Mac sat down and exhaled loudly. Jonathan and Karen also sat down.

"All right," said Mac. "What the hell was all that about?"

"It's known as an induced hallucination," said Jonathan.

"You did that?" said Mac.

"Actually, it was a joint effort," said Jonathan. "I imagined the piper then transferred the mental picture over to your mind. It then appeared to you as a waking dream."

"But he was there. I could see him. I could hear him."

"Have you ever had a very vivid dream?" said Jonathan.

"Of course! Everyone has dreams."

"Well, an hallucination is simply a dream you have when you are awake."

"Is this another one of your tricks?"

"Yes, it is. It's probably one of the most difficult ones to do. Sometimes I simply can't make the connection but having been in fairly close contact with you over the last twenty four hours I was able to make the connection with you."

"So let me get this straight. If you can make the connection you can freeze people's minds or see inside their heads or make them imagine things that don't exist?"

"That's about it, yes."

"Do you have to be right next to the person to make it work?"

"Yes, I'm afraid I do have to be within eye contact, so as long as I can see them I could do the connection across the room."

Mac leaned back in his chair and made a soft whistling sound. "This is quite amazing. Are you sure no-one else knows about this ability of yours?"

"No-one. I've been keeping it rather secret, to be honest. I was afraid people might think I was crazy."

"If we use these abilities wisely, it will totally change the playing field between us and MI5 Black Ops. For once, we will be able to stay a few steps ahead of them."

"It will give me a sense of purpose," said Jonathan.

Mrs. Johnson appeared alongside Mac. "Dinner is ready, sir."

Mac put his hand on Mrs. Johnson's shoulder and said, "Are you real?"

"I beg your pardon, sir?"

"Never mind," said Mac, "my little joke!" and he laughed. "Let's eat, guys."

They walked over to the dining table and sat down as Mrs. Johnson walked back to the kitchen.

"Fish tonight," said Mac, "so white wine I think?" and he poured three glasses. Mrs. Johnson arrived with three bowls of Lobster Bisque and placed one in front of each person.

"When we have finished dinner, Jonathan, I would like to show you the people we are dealing with. The top guy at MI5 Black Ops is called Grendan West and the main go-between in the government is a guy called Lord Mendellson. He communicates between West and the Prime Minister "

"Do you have any recordings of them?"

"Mendellson is on news sites all over the web and it's easy to get information about him but West stays in the shadows and avoids publicity. However, I do have a DVD of him at an MI5 conference that I attended just before I retired. I managed to liberate some materials when I left."

Mrs. Johnson cleared away the empty soup bowls and returned with three plates of Baked Sea Bass in a lemon sauce.

"Can you explain something to me?" said Mac, between mouthfuls of fish. "If you can connect with my mind, how do you disconnect? Or do you stay connected twenty four hours a day?"

"It takes a great deal of concentration to make and keep the connection. It is really quite easy to turn it off or even lose it accidentally and then I would have to deliberately focus on the person again to try to re-establish the connection."

"So you are not likely to see me in the shower, or in bed?"

Karen sniggered quietly.

"It's not very likely," said Jonathan with a smile, "and if I do I promise I'll look away."

All three laughed heartily.

"I suppose you will be heading home in the morning?" said Mac.

"Yes," said Karen, "we will need to be at the station by about seven-thirty so we need to get a fairly early start."

"Well, if you can make do with coffee and toast first thing I will buy you proper cooked breakfast at the café next to the station. We should be ready to leave here about six in the morning."

When they had finished eating, Mrs. Johnson cleared their plates and Mac said, "Would you like to come into the study and take a look at West and Mendellson? You too, Karen?"

They all stood up from the dining table and Jonathan and Karen followed Mac out of the Great Hall. They turned left, past the bottom of the staircase and Mac opened the door to his study. There was a large cherry wood desk with a matching dark red leather executive chair, a tall window and shelves filled with rows of books. There was also a workbench with various computers, printers, fax machines and DVD and VCR machines.

"Take a seat," said Mac, pointing towards the workbench where there were three office chairs. Meanwhile, Mac started looking on one of his bookcases. Eventually he pulled out a DVD case. "Here we are! I think this will do the job."

Mac sat down at the workbench next to Jonathan, turned on the television and the DVD player and put the disk into the player. The image that appeared on the screen showed a conference room with rows of chairs occupied by people. Someone in a suit was standing at the front of the room, a chart of some description on the screen behind him and he was talking to the people in the room.

"The guy standing up at the front of the room is Grendan West. He is now the Director of MI5 Black Ops," said Mac. "When this recording was made he was in charge of some MI5 section or other. Counter terrorism I think."

Mac turned up the volume on the television. Jonathan concentrated intently. The recording lasted for about fifteen minutes then the television screen went black.

"What do you think, Jonathan?" said Mac.

"Since Mendellson is the more public of the two, I think I can get to West through him."

"My thinking exactly."

"I'll do some research on the web when I get back to Ravensgill Bridge. Is it possible to get a copy of that DVD to take back home with me?"

"You can take that one. I have a copy. Just let me have it back when you have finished with it."

Mac took the DVD out of the player, placed it back in its plastic case and handed the case to Jonathan. "West and Mendellson could be cooking up some new project. We need to keep an eye on them and find out what they are up to."

"I'll do my best," said Jonathan.

Mac stood up. "An excellent evening's work! How about we go back into the Great Hall and have a nightcap before we turn in for the night?"

"Great idea!" said Jonathan and Karen in unison and they stood up and followed Mac out of the study.

Chapter 15

Mac, Jonathan and Karen were all up well before dawn next morning and by six o'clock they had loaded their bags into Mac's Land Rover and were on their way to Fort William along the dark roads through the hills.

"I've got a question, Mac," said Jonathan. "I really need to make a mental connection with that Lord Mendellson."

"I agree," said Mac. "He is the key link between the government and MI5 Black Ops. He will probably know more than anyone."

"How can I find out more information about him?" said Jonathan.

"Mendellson is pretty much in the public eye. He's a member of the cabinet and is always coming and going between Downing Street and the House of Lords. I reckon that if you look on the BBC website for him, particularly BBC News or BBC Parliament, you should find a bunch of archive footage. He's always being interviewed on those late night news magazine programmes."

By now, they were driving through the outskirts of Fort William and there were a few more lights.

"Keep me in touch with anything you find out. We must find out their next project as soon as we can. Don't use mobile phones, though. Use landline phones. Much more secure. But in any case be careful what you say."

"How about email?"

"No! Far too insecure! You can use fax, though, as long as it's over a landline. If we are talking about an operation, perhaps we can come up with some sort of code."

Mac pulled the Land Rover into a parking place in front of Fort William station and checked his watch.

"We've got nearly an hour before your train leaves," he said. "I'll buy you breakfast at the café next door."

It was barely light as the train pulled out of Fort William at the start of its journey to Glasgow. Jonathan and Karen were facing each other across a table.

"Well, what do you think?" said Karen as the train gathered speed.

"I think you solved my boredom problem. It actually looks quite interesting. We'll have to see what develops."

"I hope it's not dangerous."

"So do I, I'm a devout coward!"

Karen laughed. "I hope you don't end up hating me for dragging you into this."

"Don't worry, it will be interesting."

By late afternoon and after two changes of train, Karen and Jonathan were on the last stage of their journey home. Jonathan would be getting off the train at Ravensgill Bridge and Karen would be continuing on to Leeds.

"Do you have any plans for New Year 's Eve?" said Karen.

"Not really. I'll probably go down to the Ravensgill Arms with a few friends. I never do much at New Year. I'm usually in bed by one o'clock!"

"I'll probably get together with my sister. Why don't we plan to get together for lunch after New Year? I need to go down to the London office for a few days but I could come out at the weekend."

"I've got a spare room," said Jonathan. "Why don't you come out on a Saturday morning and stay overnight? You could meet some of my friends."

"That would be great! Let's get back to normal after New Year and then I'll give you a call."

The train slowed down as it prepared to stop at Ravensgill Bridge. There was just enough light in the sky for Jonathan and Karen to see the bridge as they passed over it. Jonathan stood up. "Have a Happy New Year!"

Karen stood up and gave Jonathan a hug. "It's going to be the best year ever."

Jonathan picked up his suitcase and made his way to the door at the end of the carriage. There, he turned round and waved at Karen. "Bye."

"Bye," said Karen, "I'll call you."

Jonathan stepped off the train onto the dimly lit platform of Ravensgill Bridge. He waited on the platform until the train started to pull out. He saw Karen in the brightly lit carriage and waved. When the train had gone, he crossed the footbridge and let himself into the station buildings that were his house.

It was good to be home.

Chapter 16

The next day, Monday, was New Year's Eve. Jonathan had breakfast, unpacked from his trip and then went up to his study in the signal box. The last couple of days had been rather intense for him and he needed to have some quiet time to reflect on what had happened and what he had to do over the next few days.

It was a cold but clear day and as he sat at his workbench, Jonathan could see the sun reflecting off the waters of Morecambe Bay, twenty miles to the west. What a wonderful place for quiet reflection, Jonathan thought, and a great place to come home to after a couple of days out in the world.

Jonathan was in the habit of keeping a daily journal. It was rather more than a diary and he tried to record not only what he was doing each day but also what was in his mind and what his plans were. Ever since the car crash he had had problems with focus and concentration and he had found that writing things down was a very good way of keeping himself organized and on track.

He wrote of the last two days and his visit with Sir Fergus and how he had developed more confidence about his mental powers. He realized that he had probably isolated himself from the world too much in the last couple of years and his chance meeting with Karen was going to lead him into some interesting adventures. He wasn't sure what these adventures would be yet, but that just made it more interesting.

He closed his journal and put it back on the shelf and started up his computer. He got onto the BBC Parliament web site and quickly found several references to Lord Mendellson. As Mac had said, Mendellson's main job was as a "fixer" for the Prime Minister and his cabinet. Jonathan found dozens of video clips showing Mendellson being interviewed in news bulletins and late night news magazine shows. He was often defending some unpopular government policy or arguing with a politician from an opposing party.

The more that Jonathan found out about Mendellson the less he liked him. Politicians were not Jonathan's favourite species in any case but Mendellson seemed to be a particularly sleazy example. He was a politician straight from central casting: overweight, grey hair, red faced and wearing a pin striped three piece suit. Jonathan felt very motivated to be working against this character.

Jonathan decided to brew a fresh pot of coffee. With a cup of coffee steaming on his workbench, he researched Mendellson on the web and found a biography of him. The more that Jonathan knew about a person the easier it was to make a connection.

Mendellson was a typical establishment stooge. Educated at Eton and Oxford, then into the City of London, a rising star in banks and other financial institutions, seats on boards all over British industry. Eventually he had come into politics, elected as a member for a constituency somewhere in Yorkshire. He had climbed the ladder of his party when it was still an opposition party. He had developed a reputation for a ruthless pursuit of power and had made many enemies on his way up. Eventually, when his party had gained a majority and formed a government, the Prime Minister had brought him into his cabinet as some kind of personal assistant. Mendellson had soon acquired a reputation as something of a 'fixer', sorting out problems for his boss, the Prime Minister and protecting the boss from political embarrassment.

What a piece of work, Jonathan thought.

There was not much that Jonathan could do until after the New Year's holiday. It would be Wednesday before everyone was back at work. He would call Mac then and discuss what they were going to do to get into Mendellson's mind. At the moment, Jonathan was quite baffled by the problem of getting close to Mendellson. He would need to rely on Mac's high level contacts to arrange it.

Jonathan was not really a New Year reveller. He decided that a few drinks with friends at the Ravensgill Arms and into bed by one o'clock in the morning would be adequate celebrations. Probably an afternoon nap would help prepare him for the evening.

Chapter 17

Mac had had rather more of a merry New Year celebration than Jonathan had. Mac was a Scot who was born in a land where Hogmanay was a traditional Scottish celebration of the turn of the year. For many in Scotland, it was a two day holiday, covering not only New Years Day but also the day afterwards. Mac needed to get back to work and the second day of the year saw him sitting in his library, going over the bills and other correspondence that had come in since the before Christmas, when his phone rang.

"Hello Mac, this is Jonathan."

"Jonathan! What can I do for you?"

"I need to connect with this Mendellson character. I did quite a bit of research on him."

"Good. Actually, I was just about to call you. I've got some good news for you. Do you ever watch the BBC programme Question Time on a Thursday night?"

"Yes, I watch it most weeks, if I don't fall asleep in front of the television."

"Mendellson is appearing on the show next Thursday evening, a week tomorrow. You know how the show comes from a different place each week? Next Thursday it is being recorded at Bletchley Park, about fifty miles north of London."

"That sounds great," said Jonathan. "Bletchley Park is a museum of codebreaking now, isn't it?"

"Indeed it is. It's a fascinating place to visit."

"How do you propose we get in to the recording?"

"All organized. I have a few contacts in the BBC and I just spoke to the producer of Question Time. She e-mailed me a couple of tickets so we can be in the audience Do you think you will be able to get into Mendellson's mind?"

“It’s worth a try. What travel plans have you got?”

“Today is Wednesday. I have some business in London next Tuesday. Can you meet me in London next Tuesday afternoon? We can travel up to Bletchley Park by train on the Thursday morning and browse around the museum until the recording starts in the evening."

"I would really enjoy that," said Jonathan. "I can get a train down to London next Tuesday morning. Where do you want to meet?"

"I'll send a cab to pick you up outside Kings Cross station. Send me a text when you are about an hour outside London and let me know your arrival time."

"What about accommodation?"

"I've got a flat we can use. The cab will take you there. Can you pack for about a week?"

"Will do," said Jonathan. "I'll see you a week from this afternoon, then."

Jonathan had a feeling that the early part of January was going to be a rather hectic time, given his new job working with Mac. He needed to take his time off as and when he could, so he was looking forward to a few quiet days at home before going down to London. There was some reading he wanted to catch up on and if the weather was reasonable he wanted to do some walking out on the hills.

Chapter 18

On the day before he travelled down to London, Jonathan called Karen. She was back in London now and working in her publisher's office, catching up on all the work that had landed on her desk during her Christmas and New Year holiday.

"Hello, this is Karen."

"Karen, this is Jonathan. I'm going to be down in London for a few days. I'll be coming down on the train tomorrow. I wondered if you might want to get together for lunch?"

"That would be great, Jonathan! How about the day after tomorrow, that's Wednesday? I'll give you a call that morning and we can decide where to meet."

"I'll speak to you the day after tomorrow, then."

After she finished the call, Karen thought for a few moments, then she called Mac and told him about Jonathan's call.

"Ha!" Mac laughed, "I thought he might call. Did he say why he was coming down?"

"No, he just said he would be getting here tomorrow afternoon and wanted to meet me for lunch the next day."

"So, he didn't tell you anything?" said Mac.

"No, nothing at all."

"Good man! He has a good sense of security. Well, I asked him to meet me in London. Can you be available? Usual terms?"

"Sure. How much does Jonathan know."

"I had him vetted after we met and he's clean. I'm just going to call Roger and check that the flat is available. I am planning a meeting of the team over dinner at the flat on Wednesday evening and I'll get Roger to join us. Can you be there?"

"I'd love to, Mac!"

"OK. See you there."

Mac hung up from Karen's call and called Roger Gregson's number. Roger confirmed that the flat was available and said that he would join the rest of the team for dinner the day after tomorrow.

Jonathan got off his train from Leeds when it arrived at its terminus, London Kings Cross. He walked out of the station and found the taxi rank with a dozen or more identical black London cabs waiting in line, one behind the other. The driver of the first cab on the rank pulled forward a few feet to draw alongside Jonathan.

"Where to?" the driver called but Jonathan told the driver he was waiting to be picked up.

"Up there, guvnor," said the driver, pointing forward to a separate pick-up area a few yards to Jonathan's left.

Jonathan thanked the driver and walked over to the pick-up area. Within a couple of minutes, another black London cab pulled up beside where Jonathan was standing. The driver wound down his window and in a broad Cockney accent called out "Jonathan Long?"

Jonathan nodded and the driver said, "Jump in, guv!"

He opened the rear passenger door. The passenger doors of London cabs are very heavily tinted, making it almost impossible to see any passengers inside, so Jonathan was very surprised to see Mac sitting on the far side of the long bench seat in the back of the cab and grinning broadly.

"Welcome to London, soldier!" said Mac as Jonathan lifted his case into the cab and climbed in.

"Mac! I didn't expect to see you!"

Jonathan closed the door and sat down.

"Well," said Mac, "I didn't have much going on this afternoon so I thought I would meet you and show you to the quarters that I've arranged for you."

The cab pulled away from the kerb and headed out into the London traffic. The afternoon London rush-hour was just getting underway and the traffic was very heavy but London taxi drivers have an encyclopaedic knowledge of the back streets of London and usually managed to bypass the busy main routes, which were choked with traffic.

Jonathan decided to let Mac drive the conversation. The cab was heading eastwards from Kings Cross Station, towards London's financial district with its array of impressive buildings both old and new. The old institutions of the City, such as the Stock Exchange and the Bank of England mingled with buildings that looked impossibly modern such as "The Gherkin Building", home to an insurance company.

"I suppose you'd like to know where we are going," said Mac, and Jonathan was suddenly snatched out of his study of the passing buildings. It was very different from the natural beauties that he was used to around his home in the Pennines.

"Yes, in fact I'd like to know what our plans are now that I'm here."

"Of course," said Mac. "We'll talk about that when we get settled into the flat."

"The flat?"

"Yes, you've never been there have you? It's down on the river near St. Katharine Dock."

"Is it your flat?"

"Oh no! I could never afford a place like that. I borrow it when I'm in town. It actually belongs to Sir William Harvey. He's currently the British Ambassador in Washington so he's abroad most of the time and the flat just stands here empty."

"That's very generous of him."

"I got to know him when I was Military Attaché at the Washington Embassy and he was First Secretary. He probably only uses the flat for a couple of weeks each year."

The cab pulled off a main road and passed through a security gate to reveal a marina full of pleasure boats. After driving over a bridge at one side of the marina, which allowed access from the marina to the river, the cab stopped next to a block of very exclusive apartments.

"Here we are," said Mac as he stepped out of the cab. Jonathan followed him out, carrying the suitcase. After paying the driver, Mac got a key out of his pocket and walked along a short path to the front door of the apartment block. Once inside the pair walked over to a lift and Mac put his door key into a key slot in the lift, which caused the lift to ascend to the fifth floor of the building. The lift doors opened to reveal Sir William Harvey's apartment.

What Jonathan saw when he walked out of the lift was impressive. In front of him was a large living room with varnished wood-panelled flooring and containing two sofas and four armchairs. There was a stone fireplace on one wall and there was a large screen television and audio equipment on another wall. An archway led to a well appointed kitchen. A couple of steps led up from the living room to what appeared to be a dining area with a large glass topped table and four dining chairs around it. There was a large floor-to-ceiling, wall-to-wall window beyond the dining area. Jonathan walked up the steps into the dining area and was greeted with a spectacular view.

The window faced south and the River Thames flowed past. Jonathan opened the sliding doors and walked out onto the balcony beyond. On the right of the apartment about half a mile away was the iconic outline of Tower Bridge and just visible beyond, the ramparts of the Tower of London. To the left the river curved away out of sight downstream. Alongside both sides of the river were grand buildings and small piers and jetties. On the river itself were small pleasure craft and working boats, pulling barges and still others were ferrying passengers to and fro up and down the river.

"Quite a view, eh?" said Mac and for the second time this afternoon Jonathan was tugged away from his reverie.

"Yes, quite amazing"

"Why don't you put your case in the bedroom and I'll get a couple of cold beers from the fridge. Then we can sit and enjoy the view. Come on! I'll show you where you are sleeping."

There were four bedrooms in the apartment, each with an en-suite bathroom. Mac showed Jonathan into the one of the bedrooms where Jonathan left his case and followed Mac back out to the living room. Mac stepped into the kitchen and collected two cans of beer from the fridge and he and Jonathan sat down at the glass-topped table near the window. The late afternoon sun was silhouetting Tower Bridge and reflecting off the river making it look like a silver ribbon winding its way through the city. Jonathan took a sip of his beer and felt very relaxed.

"Well, Jonathan, I think it is time to tell you a bit more about what we are up to."

Mac took another sip of his beer and stared out across the river. Jonathan just sat back, ready to absorb this latest batch of information. He seemed to have solved the problem of what to do in his "retirement".

"As I told you in Scotland," said Mac, "I am in the business of standing up for the British way of life and correcting some of the wrongs I see around me. Fortune, or perhaps chance has left me in a position where I am able to have a small influence on the way our government acts. I suppose some people might see battling against the government as treason but I think I have a strong sense of what is right and wrong. If the general public knew what I was doing, I'm sure they would support me".

"I'm quite sure they would," said Jonathan, "but I think the general public are at a serious disadvantage when it comes to dealing with the government."

"Exactly!" exclaimed Mac, slapping his hand on the table. "Exactly. There obviously has to be some secrecy in government but I think the government sometimes abuses that veil of secrecy. I think we are on the side of the people, trying to even things up a bit. Are we both agreed on that?"

"We certainly are, Mac."

"Jonathan, I have something I have to tell you. Since I saw you in Scotland before the New Year. I have had you vetted for security. Do you understand?"

"Of course! It's the least I expected you to do."

"Good, I'm glad we've got that out of the way. It means I can discuss our work with you more freely and in more detail. I think your skills can be very valuable to our organization."

Mac shook his empty beer can.

"Another beer, Jonathan?"

"Sure!"

Mac walked over to the kitchen and returned with two more cans of beer.

"Thanks, Mac. You referred to an organization. Are other people involved?"

"Well, I suppose I can tell you about one of them. He's a chap called Roger Gregson or rather Group Captain Sir Roger Gregson to give him his full title."

"Royal Air Force?"

"Retired from the RAF a couple of years ago. He's a very interesting chap. I've invited him to join us for dinner tomorrow night so you'll get to meet him. I think you two will get on very well. He was a pilot on the Diplomatic Flight, hauling ambassadors, politicians and civil servants around the world in VC10 aircraft."

"I remember, the RAF bought a whole bunch of those VC10 aircraft from British Airways a few years ago. I thought the RAF converted most of them to flight refuelling tankers."

"Yes, they did, but they kept a few of them for passenger service. Anyway, I'm sure that Roger will be only too pleased to tell you all about his flying exploits during dinner tomorrow evening. But, as I say, Roger is retired from the Royal Air Force now. He runs an office in London, which helps businesses to gain access to politicians and government departments. I understand that is quite a lucrative business. I think you would see that someone who has contacts in government departments would be very useful to us."

"Of course. I'm looking forward to meeting him."

Jonathan looked at his watch. Almost six-thirty. The sun had now set and Tower Bridge and the buildings across the river were illuminated. The lights reflected off the river below.

"Getting hungry yet?" said Mac. "I thought we could call out for delivery tonight. Will Indian food work for you?"

"Sure, I love it. Thank you."

Jonathan told Mac what food he would like and Mac pulled out his mobile phone and placed the order.

"It'll be about three-quarters of an hour," said Mac as he put away his mobile. "They're pretty busy at the moment. We can always put it in the oven if you want to talk some more. It's a bit chilly this evening. How about we light a fire?"

Without waiting for Jonathan to answer Mac stepped down into the living room, turned on some soft lighting and clicked a switch next to the fireplace. A gas firelighter burst into flame beneath the logs that had already been placed in the grate.

"There we go," said Mac, rubbing his hands together. "That will be roaring away in no time."

Jonathan stepped down into the living room and sank comfortably into one of the armchairs. Mac flopped down into another armchair."

"Can you tell me some more about Roger Gregson, Mac?"

"I don't think it will do any harm to tell you a little more," said Mac. "As I told you before, he was flying government VIP types around the world. In fact, that is how we got to use this flat. Roger knew Sir William because he used to fly him between London and Washington and of course, I knew Sir William because I was working in the Washington Embassy when he was there.

"How did you get to know Roger Gregson?"

"I first bumped into Roger when I was with MI5. Roger's aircraft had been converted to fly suspected terrorists. The whole aircraft was bugged so that they could listen to what the suspects were saying to each other and collect valuable intelligence."

"Did you fly on the aircraft?"

"Yes," said Mac, "I flew several times with Roger. There was a radio cabin installed behind the cockpit. I used to spend most of the flight in there, listening in to the bugs and recording them. Occasionally Roger would step out of the cockpit for a break and I would brew up some coffee and chat with him."

"I thought you said he was on the Diplomatic Flight."

"Well, yes he was, but the intelligence services "borrowed" this aircraft and converted it. Roger and his crew came along with the aircraft. It was only for a couple of years and then the aircraft was converted back to diplomatic service. It was converted back to its former luxury but the work was put out to a private contractor. Since the bugging was never in the original plans the contractor didn't know anything about it and so they never removed it."

"So, you've got a Diplomatic Flight aircraft flying around full of bugging equipment? I think I can see where this is going"

"I think you can visualize the possibilities," said Mac. "In the one place where these government people thought they could not be overheard we could listen to their every word. Roger would go back to the radio cabin and listen in."

"He could get hanged for doing that!"

"Well, not quite! But he was taking a hell of a risk. Of course, he didn't disclose what he heard, except to me. He told me what he was doing and asked my advice."

"What did you tell him?"

"I told him not to get caught, of course! Anyway, this went on for two or three years. It was during that time that Roger and I found out about MI5 Black Ops. I took early retirement from MI5 and Roger took early retirement from the air force. We knew that we couldn't do anything about it while we were working for the government so we would do it from the outside."

"So that is the origin of Operation Checkmate?"

"Indeed it is," said Mac.

"And now Roger works in London?"

"Yes. He made a great many contacts among senior civil servants and politicians during his time with the Diplomatic Flight and he started a business to take advantage of those contacts. He helps businessmen to get government contracts. He's got an office in one of the old government buildings in Horseferry Road."

The intercom buzzer in the apartment sounded and Mac went over to the panel next to the lift. It was the food delivery and Mac pressed the button to open the front door and to allow the delivery person to come up to the fifth floor in the lift.

A minute or two later the delivery man stepped out of the lift with tonight's supper. Mac paid him and he stepped back into the lift. Mac carried the food over to the kitchen counter and Jonathan joined him.

"Do you want to have supper on trays and watch the television news?

"Sounds like a plan to me."

Chapter 19

When Jonathan stirred from his bed the next morning, Mac was already up and cooking breakfast in the kitchen.

"Good morning, Jonathan!" said Mac. "The coffee is brewed. A Full English Breakfast for you?"

Jonathan sleepily poured a mug of coffee. "Yes, please." He took his coffee, walked across the living room and stepped up to the dining area. The day was overcast but dry which should make his trip out to see Karen more pleasant. He walked back to the kitchen and sat on a stool, watching Mac cooking breakfast. Sausages, bacon, fried bread, fried egg. A true Full English Breakfast.

Mac served up onto the plates and drew another stool up to the kitchen counter.

"Thanks, Mac. What are your plans for the day?"

"I've got a few appointments so I'll be out for most of the day. I'll give you a spare key so you can let yourself in and out." Mac took a bite of sausage.

"I'll be going out to see Karen for lunch. I should be back early afternoon."

"Good! We'll cook dinner ourselves this evening. Karen will pick up a few things on the way home. Give some thought as to what tricks you are going to use to impress Roger Gregson tonight."

Jonathan put down his coffee mug and tucked into his breakfast and both he and Mac ate in silence for a few minutes.

"I'll clear up while you get ready to go out, if you want, Mac"

"Thanks, I would appreciate that."

Mac headed off back to his bedroom and Jonathan washed the dishes and tidied up the kitchen, then he went to get showered and dressed.

He felt distinctly more awake as he returned to the living room and sat down in one of the luxurious armchairs. He was rather looking forward to a couple of hours of quiet time after the events of the last twenty-four hours. He needed to think through what he had learned from Mac yesterday.

Mac emerged from his bedroom smartly dressed in a suit and tie. "Here's a spare key," he said, placing a key on the kitchen counter. "Treat the place like home, Jonathan."

"Thanks Mac. I'll see you late afternoon."

Mac walked over to the lift and pressed the call button. "See you later then," he said as he stepped inside the lift and the doors closed.

Things had suddenly started moving rather quickly for Jonathan. Less than a month ago, he had been wishing that he had more challenge in his retirement and now he was surrounded by it. It was taking him a little time to adjust. He had no real wish to get into anything dangerous and he certainly was not keen on doing anything illegal but he couldn't help admiring people like Mac and this other chap, Roger Gregson and of course Karen who had introduced him to this world in the first place.

What was this Lord Mendellson up to? Mac had described him as "the government fixer". Perhaps Lord Meddlesome would be a more appropriate title. Jonathan wondered how he would deal with Meddlesome. Perhaps Mac and this other guy, the ex-pilot, Roger Gregson, would be able to advise. Given that he had spent a lifetime in the world of secrets, Mac seemed a fairly straight forward kind of chap.

Jonathan was almost dozing in his chair when his mobile phone rang. It was Karen.

"Jonathan, are you still on for lunch today?"

"Yes. When and where?"

"How about twelve-thirty? There's a pub just on the eastern side of Leicester Square that does good lunches. It's called The Moon Under Water."

"See you there at twelve-thirty." Jonathan ended the call and checked his watch. He had enough time to enjoy another cup of coffee and then take a gentle stroll to Tower Hill tube station about half a mile from the flat and travel over to his lunch date.

Jonathan sat back down with his fresh cup of coffee and began to think about his lunch with Karen. How much could he tell her about what Mac had told him. Best not to say anything about it. He would have to be careful not to give anything away. This was a tricky business he was getting into. He would just have to get used to it.

Eventually the grandfather clock in the living room chimed eleven-thirty so Jonathan put on an overcoat, picked up the key from the kitchen counter and left the flat.

The earlier clouds had begun to break up and a wintry sun was casting long shadows across the street. Jonathan enjoyed his walk to the tube station at Tower Hill. He walked alongside the river, though the archway beneath Tower Bridge and along Thames Path in front of the Tower of London. Then he turned right, away from the river, to reach the station.

He had one change of trains and about forty-five minutes after leaving the apartment he emerged into London's "West End". Dominating Leicester Square itself was the Odeon Cinema where British film premières were held. The square was relatively quiet on this midweek lunchtime but at night, it would be gaudily lit with neon signs announcing the latest play or film that was showing.

Jonathan found the pub, The Moon Under Water and walked in. It was a typical London pub with a lot of dark wood panelling and polished brass fittings everywhere. The bar staff were in crisp uniforms: white shirts, bow ties, dark trousers. It was not exactly Jonathan's idea of a country pub but he was in the Big City now. There was no sign of Karen so he bought a drink at the bar, picked up a menu and found himself a seat at a table near the door where he could keep an eye out for Karen.

He quickly scanned the menu and decided he would order a toasted sandwich for lunch but he would wait for Karen before ordering. He gazed idly round the pub and then his eyes fell on the back page of the menu. It was a photograph of a newspaper cutting and Jonathan started reading it. The newspaper article was entitled The Moon Under Water, the same name as the pub. The article had been written by the author George Orwell in 1946. Jonathan remembered that George Orwell had written at least two famous books, Animal Farm and Nineteen Eighty-Four, although he thought a book called The Road to Wigan Pier was also one of Orwell's works. As he read the article on the menu, he saw that Orwell had described his perfect city pub – the décor, the furniture, the lighting, the staff and the food and drink. The pub in which Jonathan was sitting was not quite up to Orwell's standard but it would probably pass muster as a lunch venue.

Jonathan was still reading the article when a cheery voice said "Hi there!" He looked up and standing before him was Karen.

"Hello Karen! Sorry, I didn't see you come in. I was reading about the background to the name of this place."

"You found out about George Orwell, then?"

"Yes. I would guess you've been here before?"

"Quite a few times."

"What can I get you to drink?"

"Just a lemonade please, Jonathan. I've got quite a lot of work to do after lunch."

While Jonathan went over to the bar to get Karen's drink, she looked over the menu. Jonathan returned to the table and placed Karen's drink before her.

"Made your choice?," he said.

"Yes," said Karen and she pointed out her selection on the menu.

"I'll go and order the food."

As with many English pubs there was limited table service in this pub so Jonathan went back over to the bar, menu in hand and placed the food order. When he got back to the table and sat down, Karen opened the conversation.

"How are you enjoying your stay in London, Jonathan?"

"Very much thank you." He had decided to avoid talking too much about his discussions with Mac the previous evening but Karen was obviously probing.

"How is Mac?" she said. "He is the reason you are down here, isn't he?"

"I saw him last night and he was doing just fine. He wanted me to come down to give him some advice on some computer problems he was having."

"Did you stay at the apartment in St. Katharines?"

Jonathan was absolutely floored. Karen clearly knew as much about Mac as he did. In fact, it looked like she probably knew a lot more.

"You know about that apartment?" he said.

Karen looked slightly sheepish. "I probably haven't been entirely straight with you, Jonathan. Perhaps it's time for a confession. I have actually been working with Mac for the last couple of years."

"You mean working with him on his memoirs?

"No. I mean working with him...operationally."

"So you recruited me right from the start?"

"Not exactly. When we first met, on the train, it was an accident, nothing planned at all. But after I came out to Ravensgill Bridge for lunch I could see that you had the potential to be a great operative for us."

"What about your work? For the publisher?"

"That's real. I work on contract for my firm, part time. That gives me the flexibility to work on Mac's operations when I'm needed."

"What kind of...operational work...do you do?"

"Mostly communications and research. I usually stay in London when Mac is on a case and work in the control centre."

"The control centre?"

"Yes, I'm sure you will learn more about the control centre at tonight's dinner."

"You know about tonight's dinner?"

"Of course I know about it. I'm doing the cooking!"

A waiter delivered their lunch to the table.

"Jonathan, the reason I could not tell you about any of this before is that we had to get you vetted for security."

"Well, that's a relief!"

"Are you mad at me?"

"Of course I'm not. After all I asked you how I could spice up my life, remember? You certainly delivered that!"

They both laughed, easing the tension considerably and they tucked in to their lunches.

"So what's on the menu for tonight?" said Jonathan, taking a break from his lunch.

Since there will be four of us I thought I would roast a large chicken with stuffing and roast potatoes and veggies."

"I'll help you prepare dinner."

They both finished their lunch then Karen said, "I've got some work to finish off this afternoon but I will pick up the things for dinner and bring them over to the apartment later. I expect we'll eat around eight o'clock."

"That lunch will keep me going until then! Where do you work in London, Karen?"

"Just off Russell Square."

"Opposite direction from me then. I'll walk with you to the tube station, though."

They got up from their table and left the pub. After walking the short distance to Leicester Square tube station they parted, because they were travelling on different lines.

"I'll see you later this afternoon," said Karen with a cheery wave as she stepped onto the escalator down to the Piccadilly Line. Jonathan waved back but Karen had disappeared from sight. He thought he could perhaps have time for an afternoon nap back at the apartment before everyone started arriving for dinner.

Chapter 20

It was nearly dark when Jonathan's afternoon nap was interrupted by the sound of a buzzer indicating that someone was opening the front door on the ground floor with the apartment key. Jonathan got up, looked at the small screen next to the lift and saw that it was Karen on her way up in the lift.

The lift doors opened and Karen stepped out, loaded with grocery bags. Jonathan grabbed a couple of bags and took them over to the kitchen counter. Karen followed with the rest of the bags. "Thank you," said Karen, rather breathlessly, as she lifted the last bag onto the counter.

"Is that all the groceries? There's enough to feed the five thousand here!"

"I've got to go down to get my suitcase, but that's all the groceries."

"You're staying over tonight?"

"I sure am!"

The buzzer sounded again and the face of Mac appeared on the screen alongside the lift as he came through the front door. Jonathan and Karen started unloading the grocery bags. Jonathan put the bottles of white wine in the refrigerator along with the cheesecake that Karen had bought for dessert.

"I'll finish putting things away and brew a pot of tea if you want to start preparing the meal," said Jonathan.

The lift doors opened and Mac stepped out. "Hello guys! Is there a cup of tea going?" He went to his bedroom and took off his overcoat then joined the others in the kitchen. Jonathan poured him a mug of tea. "Everything under control here?"

"Perfectly under control," said Karen as she finished washing the chicken and carried it to the roasting pan.

When Jonathan had finished putting away the groceries, he took his mug of tea across the living room and up to the dining table where Mac was sitting looking at the lights along the banks of the river.

"Did you have a good day?" said Mac.

"Very good. Karen told me that she was part of the team."

"Good. I was hoping she would. What do you think about it?"

"It's fine. I understand why she couldn't tell me until you had vetted me."

"You've got a good sense of security, Jonathan. That's important in our work."

"When I was working in the movie business we had to keep secrets about the films and the special effects that we were working on."

"I'd love to hear about your time in the movie business sometime but tonight I want to introduce you to Roger."

"I'm looking forward to that, he sounds like an interesting chap."

"He should be here pretty soon. Can you line up a couple of your tricks to show him? I haven't told him about what you can do."

"I'll give him an hallucination."

"That will be very impressive."

The lift doors opened and a man stepped out. He walked straight over to Karen, who was standing at the sink peeling potatoes and gave her a big, tight hug from behind.

"How are you doing my darling Karen?"

"Careful Roger, I have a sharp knife."

"Charming," said Roger and he poured himself a glass of wine and walked up to sit at the dining table with Mac and Jonathan.

"Introductions if you please, Sir Fergus!" said Roger.

Mac made the introductions and Roger and Jonathan shook hands.

"Very pleased to meet you, Jonathan," said Roger.

"The pleasure is mine, Roger. Mac has told me a lot about you."

Karen arrived at the dining table with a glass of wine in her hand and she sat down.

"Everything OK in the catering department?" said Roger.

"All OK, Roger," responded Karen.

Roger turned to Jonathan. "Karen does a terrific job for me in the control centre. You must come over to my office and take a look at it while you're in town."

"I'm sure he will," said Mac.

Suddenly Roger, jumped from his chair and ran over to the window. "Jesus Christ! What is that?"

Mac got up and stood beside Roger.

"There, coming up the river. It's the bloody QE2 for God's sake!"

"Well, blow me down," said Mac, who turned his head briefly towards Jonathan and winked. Karen simply sat quietly and took a sip of wine.

What Roger was seeing was a ship coming up the river towards Tower Bridge. It was of course an hallucination implanted in Roger's mind by Jonathan, but to Roger it looked as real as anything could be. Mac could not see the hallucination because Jonathan was concentrating on maintaining the it in Roger's mind, but Mac was playing along as best he could to help reinforce the hallucination.

"Look, Fergus! It's not slowing down! Hell, it's going to hit the bridge!"

The ship's bow, ploughing through the water, was getting closer and closer to the road level of the bridge, the part which normally opens up to let large vessels to pass through, but the bridge stayed firmly down and the ship showed no signs of stopping. It was about to hit Tower Bridge full on...and then the ship disappeared.

"All right Fergus," said Roger. "What the hell is going on here? Are you playing around with some hologram projection or something?"

Mac put his hand on Roger's shoulder and said, "It's all right Roger, let's sit down and I will explain."

Roger looked visibly shaken as he walked back to his chair at the dining table. Mac topped up Roger's wine glass and Roger took a long drink from it and pushed it forward for refill. For almost the first time since he had arrived, Roger was practically speechless.

"That," said Mac, "was why I have recruited Jonathan onto our team. What you saw there was an hallucination, a kind of waking dream, but it was created in your head by Jonathan. It's one of several very useful mental skills that Jonathan happens to possess."

Roger wiped his face with a napkin and took another sip of wine. "I don't know what to say. It was so real, like I could reach out and touch it."

"Just like your dreams seem to be real at the time," said Jonathan. "Full sound and glorious colour. You can even reach out and touch things in your dreams. This was just dreaming on a more conscious level. You were awake rather than asleep."

"But you triggered the dream or the hallucination or whatever in my head. How did you do that?"

Mac interrupted Roger's questioning and said, "By the delicious smell of things coming from the kitchen, I think that the lovely meal that Karen has cooked for us is probably just about ready. Why don't we serve up and then we can hear about Jonathan's rather unique and interesting mental skills as we eat."

They all walked over to the kitchen where Karen had prepared four plates. "Serve yourself to vegetables," she said.

Once they were all seated back at the dining table, Mac invited Jonathan to tell Roger about himself. Between mouthfuls of chicken and roast potatoes Jonathan related how he had been in the movie industry, how his wife Jill had been killed in a car crash and how he had discovered that the circuit placed in his head had caused him to have these curious mental powers. Roger listened intently to Jonathan's story. By the time Jonathan had finished they had all finished their meals and Karen got up to clear the table.

Roger turned to Mac and said, "We can certainly use Jonathan on the team. I need to absorb all this and work out how best we can use him."

Roger suddenly turned back to Jonathan. "I'm sorry Jonathan, I'm sitting here talking about you as if you were some new kind of spy equipment. I do apologize!"

"No problem, Roger. I'm just glad to join the team and do what I can to help."

"Let's just get this straight. You can trigger hallucinations and you can put people into temporary seizures. Right?"

"I can also sometimes hook into what they are thinking and seeing and hearing and I can dig into their memories."

Roger turned to Mac and said, "Fergus, now I know what the folks who cracked the Enigma code felt like. We must keep this thing ultra secret."

"Of course," said Mac, "but the great thing about it is that people have no idea that they have had a seizure. They just have a sense of déjà vu, and they usually don't recollect anything of their hallucinations."

"Right," said Roger. "I think I see what you mean. It's going to take me a while to get my head around this."

Karen had returned to the table to rejoin the group.

"What we need to do now", said Mac, "is to review where we are with the current project. Jonathan and I will be going up to Bletchley Park tomorrow morning. Mendellson is on the panel of Question Time which is being recorded in Bletchley Park tomorrow evening and Jonathan is going to see if he can get into Mendellson's head."

"Good idea," said Roger. "Why don't we get together on Friday morning at my office and review the situation then? Karen, can you bring Jonathan over to my office on Friday morning on your way to work and I will show him the control centre."

"I'll do that," said Karen. "My first meeting on Friday is not until eleven-thirty. I'll have plenty of time. I'll be going back to my flat in Finchley after work tomorrow so I will get down here at about nine-thirty on Friday morning to pick you up Jonathan. We should be at your office by ten, Roger. "

Jonathan looked at his watch then stood up from the table. "I think it's time for me to turn in," he said. "I'm very pleased to have met you, Roger. I'm looking forward to seeing you on Friday."

"Sleep well," said Roger.

"Let's plan to get going at about eight tomorrow morning," said Mac. "I'll knock on your bedroom door at seven."

Jonathan grunted his agreement and walked off towards his bedroom.

Chapter 21

Next morning Jonathan had a light breakfast of coffee and toast with marmalade and he was showered and dressed and ready by eight o'clock. He walked with Mac over to the Tower Hill station and they caught the Underground train to Euston where they would catch the train to Bletchley.

They each picked up a cup of coffee from a shop on the Euston station concourse. Jonathan yawned and said, "I might be awake by the time we get to Bletchley."

"Not a morning person, eh?" said Mac.

"Nah! I used to be but I think I used up all my early mornings some years ago."

The train from Euston to Bletchley was a suburban commuter train with basic accommodation and stopping at nearly every station along the line. It took almost an hour to reach Bletchley, just fifty miles north of London. Mac and Jonathan stepped off the train and began to walk along the platform to the station exit.

"It's only about five minutes walk," said Mac.

"Have you been here before?"

"Very early in my MI5 career, just before GCHQ moved to Cheltenham. I came here for a week's training course on cryptography. Last year I came back to visit the museum."

They left the station and turned right to walk along the road towards Bletchley Park. As they walked, they could just glimpse the main buildings through the trees. It was about a quarter of a mile to the front gates of the park. As they turned off the road and into the driveway, they could see the Victorian mansion that had been home to the Government Codes and Ciphers School during and after World War Two. It had been renamed Government Communications Headquarters (GCHQ) after the war and had eventually moved out of Bletchley Park to Cheltenham in the west of England. After lying empty for twenty years the mansion in the middle of the park had been restored by dedicated volunteers and had been opened as a Museum of Cryptography, celebrating the formerly secret labours of the brilliant cryptologists who had broken the German communication ciphers during the Second World War. General Eisenhower himself had said that, in his opinion, the efforts of Bletchley Park had shortened the war by at least two years.

Mac and Jonathan paused for a moment to take in the view. The driveway on which they were standing curved around a lake that lay in front of the mansion and then curved back to arrive at the front door. The mansion itself was an impressive structure built at the end of the nineteenth century in a rather quirky mixture of architectural styles. It was a two storey building of red brick construction but with grey and white stone columns and decorations surrounding the doors and bay windows. There was a two storey circular tower at one corner of the building capped with a copper dome, which had acquired an attractive green patina over the years.

"It looks just the kind of place where you would expect a bunch of boffins to work," said Jonathan.

"Actually, the mansion was mostly used for the administrative offices. The boffins worked in wooden huts around the park that were thrown together at the start of the war."

After admiring the view for a few minutes, Mac and Jonathan went into a building on their right where they bought tickets and a guide book and started their tour of the museum. They spent a couple of hours absorbed in their study of the museum's exhibits which told the story of how the code breakers of Bletchley Park had been recruited from the mathematics departments of Britain's top universities to find ways of breaking the codes used by the German military to keep their radio communications secret. They saw the Enigma cipher machines and the very earliest versions of computers, which had been developed and used in the darkest days of the war. Both Mac and Jonathan were so fascinated by what they had learned in the museum that they had entirely lost track of time.

Mac looked at his watch. "Good Lord! It's nearly three o'clock. I've just realised I'm hungry."

"Me too! Can we get lunch somewhere round here?"

"There's a cafe in Hut Four, or if you want something more substantial there's a pub called The Enigma Tavern just the other side of the railway tracks from here. Bear in mind that we have to be back at the mansion to go into the Question Time recording by six o'clock and it probably won't finish until about nine, so we are not likely to be able to get an evening meal."

"I think I would like to unwind for an hour or two before I start trying to get into Mendellson's mind," said Jonathan. "Why don't we walk over to The Enigma Tavern?"

"Good idea. These museum tickets can be re-used for a whole year so you can come back whenever you like."

With that, they left the museum and started walking back towards Bletchley railway station.

By the time that they had had a drink and a meal at the pub and walked back to Bletchley Park, it was almost six o'clock. The museum had closed but they showed their tickets for the Question Time recording at the gate and they were admitted by a uniformed guard who directed them to the mansion. Once inside, they were directed to a large room where other members of the television audience were gathering. Coffee and biscuits were available but both Mac and Jonathan declined and they took seats at one of the tables away from the crowd, to await the start of proceedings. There were cards on the table upon which they were invited to write questions to be asked during the programme but they did not want to attract unnecessary attention to themselves so they chose not to submit any questions.

After a few minutes, Mac spoke. "Jonathan, I've got a question for you. When you are getting into the mind of a subject you are concentrating one hundred percent on them, right?"

"Very much so."

"So how do you make sure that you are able to remember all the details that you see in their minds?"

"Good question. I have found that the memories in my head are very intense for a few minutes so if I can record my memories onto a notepad straight afterwards, or tell the details to somebody then I can make a pretty good record of it."

"Once the recording has started we won't be able to leave the studio until it's finished. Do you have a pen and paper to record your thoughts?"

"I always carry some kind of writing materials." Jonathan pulled a small spiral bound notebook and a ball point pen out of the pocket of his jeans and placed them on the table.

A man wearing a headset and microphone walked into the room and plugged his headset into an amplifier at the front of the room. "Ladies and gentlemen, could I have your attention please?" He paused briefly and the buzz of conversation that had been filling the room subsided. "My name is Greg Owen and I'm the studio manager. In a few minutes, we will all be moving into the studio to take our seats for the recording of

Question Time. Once we are seated, we will be doing a short rehearsal so that the camera and sound crews can check their equipment. Then David Dimbleby and his panel of guests will enter and we will start recording. We will record the programme straight through without a break so now would be a good time to make yourself comfortable if you need to. My assistant, Anne, will be here in a few moments to show you to your seats in the studio."

The studio manager unplugged his headset and left the room.

"Jonathan, quick, come with me," said Mac. They both stood up and Jonathan followed Mac as he walked quickly out of the room. Mac caught up with the studio manager in the corridor just outside the room.

"Excuse me, Greg," said Mac. "My name's Fergus McKinnon. Did your producer, Jean, mention me?"

"Yes, sir, she did. She asked me to make sure I looked after you. What can I do for you?"

Mac lowered his voice. "Is there any chance we can slip into the studio and get seats on the front row?"

The studio manager looked around rather furtively. "No problem. Come with me." He led Mac and Jonathan down a corridor and through double doors into the studio. The room was in fact the former ballroom of the mansion with high ceilings and tall windows along one side. The windows were covered with heavy curtains now in preparation for the programme. Rising on the left were rows of seats for the audience. To the right, at the front of the studio, was the familiar Question Time studio set that both Mac and Jonathan had seen on television many times before. There was a curved table where the panel and the chairman would sit. There were seven seats behind the table. Behind the seats was a series of tall background panels bearing the Question Time logo and on the floor in front of the table was the large black Q logo bearing the name Bletchley Park picked out in large white capital letters. Jonathan noticed that the centre chair behind the table, the one that would be occupied by the chairman David Dimbleby was a few inches higher than all the other chairs. He mused that this was probably a subtle way of giving the chairman a little extra authority over the guests.

"Take those two seats at the far side of the front row," said the studio manager, pointing across the room.

"Thanks Greg," said Mac and he and Jonathan walked across the room and took their seats. By the time they were seated the studio manager had left the studio again and they were alone. The room was very quiet.

"This is excellent," said Mac in a low voice. "You'll be just a few yards from Mendellson."

Jonathan looked around the room. The seats behind them rose up in about ten rows. Above his head was a lighting gantry that stretched across the width of the room and illuminated the studio set brightly, and in front of him were two television cameras, one each side of the studio, Cables snaked across the floor. Jonathan noticed a buzz of conversation at the double doors and the rest of the audience started to file into the room and take their seats. At the same time, technicians started to take up their places behind the television cameras. Other technicians were picking up sound booms.

Once the audience was seated the studio manager, Greg Owen, came in. "Right, ladies and gentlemen, we are going to do a short rehearsal so that our director and our sound and vision people can get all their equipment set up and adjusted. So I would like six volunteers from the audience to come out and play the part of our guest panellists."

About a dozen hands shot up and the studio manager selected six people from the audience, who stepped down to the studio floor and were directed to their seats behind the curved table. The studio manager settled himself into the centre chair. A couple of technicians fixed lapel microphones to the volunteers.

"I will ask a question and then I will invite each of the panel members in turn to comment on the question. I would also like contributions from the audience so if you would like to say something raise your hand and wait for me to call on you to speak. For the rest of the audience, applaud when you think fit."

Mac leaned over to Jonathan and said in a very low voice, "Do you want to try a practice run on the panellist nearest to you?"

"I don't think that will work, Mac. You see, I have to have some connection with the person, I have to know something about them in order to hook into their memories. For example, with Mendellson I can try various keywords like 'Prime Minister' or 'MI5' and get into his memory but with these panellists I don't know them from Adam."

Mac nodded and the pair watched as the studio manager called on each volunteer in turn to comment on the question he had asked. It took about ten minutes for all six panellists to say their piece, so Jonathan reckoned that at best he had about seven or eight minutes to get into Mendellson's mind and get out again before Mendellson was asked to comment on the next question. Mendellson would be in a temporary seizure while Jonathan scanned his memory stream so he would just be staring straight ahead and would not respond to anything said to him. It was a risky job but at worst, Jonathan could just drop his concentration, thus freeing Mendellson from the seizure.

After two rounds of questions to the volunteers, the studio technicians had their equipment set up and the studio manager instructed the volunteer panellists to return to their seats in the audience. Then the chairman of the Question Time programme walked onto the studio floor.

"Good evening, ladies and gentlemen. My name is David Dimbleby and I will be chairing this evening's discussion. I would just like to say that it is you, the audience, who are the key to an entertaining show so please do feel free to participate by asking supplementary questions and applauding when appropriate. And now please welcome tonight's guest panellists."

Dimbleby called the each of the guests by name and the audience applauded as each took their seat. The first guest was an opposition Member of Parliament who sat closest to Jonathan in the seat that Jonathan had hoped would be occupied by Lord Mendellson. The next guest called was a journalist working on one of the national daily newspapers. The audience applauded each guest as they were introduced. The roll call continued until Lord Mendellson was the last to be seated, farthest away from Jonathan.

"I was hoping he would be closer," whispered Mac.

"Me too, but because of the curve of the desk I am face on to him and that will definitely help me to make eye contact with him. Do you think he will recognize you?"

"Not likely. I've only met him briefly a couple of times and I am pretty much in the shadows sitting here."

The panellists settled into their seats and the audience became quiet as Dimbleby began to speak. "We will take one practice question as a warm up for the panel and a final technical check for sound and vision, then we will start the recording, so can we have our first question please?"

A member of the audience stood up and started reading a question from a card that she held. A technician with a boom microphone held it above the questioner's head and a cameraman with a chest mounted Steadicam closed in. Once the question was asked the chairman invited each of the guests in turn to comment on the question, starting with the guest closest to Jonathan and working through the panel so that Lord Mendellson was the last to be asked to comment.

"I'm trying to get into the rhythm of the show," said Jonathan.

"I understand," said Mac. "Take your time. The recording will last an hour. Just relax."

The pair watched as Dimbleby looked directly into one of the cameras that were moving about on the studio floor and the programme's introductory music played. Dimbleby began his introduction. "Good evening and welcome to Question Time. This evening we are in Bletchley Park in Buckinghamshire, fifty miles north west of London. During the Second World War, this park was home to the British code breakers who cracked the German Enigma military codes and by some reckonings helped to shorten the war by two years. For thirty years after the war, the heroic achievements of the code breakers were shrouded in secrecy but now Bletchley Park is a museum of code breaking, honouring those wartime achievements."

Dimbleby paused and there was applause from the audience. As the applause died away, he introduced the six members of the panel again for the benefit of the television viewers. Then he called on a member of the audience to read out the first question. He asked Mendellson to respond.

"Are you ready?," said Mac in a whisper.

"Just as soon as he has finished answering his question."

Mendellson spoke for just over two minutes in response to the question then the panellist to Mendellson's right pitched in with her answer. Jonathan caught Mendellson in eye contact and immediately put him into a light seizure and started thinking of keywords to start the memory trace.

"MI5 Black Ops."

An image started to form in Jonathan's mind.

I am in a car, sitting on the back seat. There is a driver wearing a peaked cap and uniform. I am travelling down Whitehall and I can see the tower of Big Ben ahead of me. The car is slowing down and making a right turn into Downing Street, where the Prime Minister works and lives when he is in London. The car is drawing up to a pair of ornate gates guarded by two policemen. I have been summoned by the Prime Minister to see him but I don't know what he wants to talk to me about.

One of the policemen is looking in through the windows of the car and now he is waving to his colleague who is opening the gates. The car is driving slowly through into the street beyond the gates. The car is stopping at the door of number 10. A policeman is opening the car door and I am stepping out. As I approach the door the policeman on duty is saluting me and the door is being opened from inside. I am stepping in through the doorway into the entrance hall and an aide is closing the door behind me. I have been here many times before.

Another aide stepping out of a side door, into the hallway.

She says "Good morning, Lord Mendellson."

I respond, "Good Morning."

"The PM is ready for you, sir."

With a broad sweep of her arm, the aide is inviting me into the Prime Minister's office. I am walking into the room and I see the Prime Minister sitting behind a large desk.

"Lord Mendellson to see you, sir," says the aide.

The Prime Minister says, "Good morning, George."

I respond "Good morning, Prime Minister."

"Take a seat."

I sit down at the opposite side of the desk from the Prime Minister. The aide is closing the door as she is leaving the room.

The Prime Minister is speaking again. "George, we are getting an increasing problem. We are losing support for our anti-terrorism efforts. Both in parliament and in the country. We are having trouble getting our anti-terrorist legislation through parliament and we have been getting a lot of demonstrations and protests around the country. We're also losing support for our military operations in the Middle East."

"I absolutely agree, Prime Minister. We are losing the battle for the hearts and minds of our own people."

The Prime Minister is continuing. "When we had the attacks in New York and later here in London we had a lot of public support but the longer we go without a terrorist attack the less support we get. It's almost as if people forget and when they feel safe they are less inclined to accept restrictions."

"Prime Minister, it's almost as if the more successful we are at fighting the terrorists the less support we get from the people. And don't forget our military operations. People are questioning why our troops are dying in the Middle East. It's as if people have lost track of why we are there."

"George, I want you to take on a task to rebuild popular support for our anti-terrorist policies. Do you think you can handle it?"

"Yes, sir. I am sure I can handle that. I think it might be a job for the Organization."

"George, as usual I do not want to know what you are doing. We must maintain plausible deniability."

"Very well, Prime Minister. Leave it with me."

The Prime Minister is pressing a button on his desk and I am standing up as an aide is opening the door.

"Good luck, George," the Prime Minister is saying as I turn to leave. As I reach the door, I turn to face the Prime Minister. "Thank you, Prime Minister."

I am being shown to the door by the aide. "Goodbye, Lord Mendellson," she says and I step outside. A policeman is stepping forward and opening my car door. The car has been turned around to face the other way, towards the gates that we came in through, because Downing Street is a dead end street. I am getting into the back of the car and the policeman is closing the door.

My driver is saying, "Where to, sir?"

"Back to my office, if you would."

"Very well, sir."

I need to call Grendan West over at MI5 Black Ops and set up a meeting with him to discuss what the Prime Minister has talked about. I am pushing the button to close the privacy window between the driver and myself. I am punching in Grendan's private mobile number on my mobile phone. It rings for a few moments then Grendan answers

"George, what can I do for you?"

"I need to set up a meeting with you."

"Well, today is Wednesday and I'm pretty much tied up for the rest of this week. Would Monday, the fourteenth do? Say, two-thirty in the afternoon? Usual place?"

"That will be fine. I'll see you then," I say and I disconnect the call.

Jonathan felt a nudging in his ribs and realized it was Mac indicating that Mendellson was about to be asked another question. Jonathan immediately broke concentration with Mendellson and started writing in his notebook to record what he had seen on Mendellson's memory trace. When he had finished his notes, without saying anything he showed the notebook page to Mac who nodded approvingly. Both Mac and Jonathan were relieved that no-one seemed to have noticed the seven or eight minutes during which Mendellson had been in a seizure.

Jonathan watched the remainder of the programme feeling much more relaxed that this first real use of his memory trace seemed to have gone well.

The audience applauded as the programme's closing music was played. When the recording was over the studio manager stepped onto the studio floor and asked everyone in the audience to remain seated. Dimbleby led the guest panellists out of the studio then the studio manager called on the audience to leave, one row at a time. Mac and Jonathan's row was among the first to leave. They did not speak until they were standing on the driveway, outside the front of the Bletchley Park mansion.

"I think that went rather well," said Jonathan.

"Yes, I think so too," said Mac. He looked at his watch. "Nine thirty-five. There's a train back to London at ten o'clock. I suggest that we walk back to the station and catch that train. We can talk about the information you gathered once we are on the train home."

They walked quickly in the cool night air and reached Bletchley station in plenty of time for the ten o'clock train. At this time of night, all the station facilities such as the coffee shop were locked up and dark so they sat on a bench on the platform to wait. After a few minutes, the train pulled into the station and came to a stop with a squeal of its brakes. Jonathan and Mac stood up from the bench and boarded the train. As the train began to move off, they found seats. They sat facing each other. There were very few passengers on the train and none in their carriage.

"Warmer in here than out on that platform," said Jonathan.

"Let's look at what we've got from Mendellson," said Mac.

Jonathan pulled out his notebook. "The Prime Minister has told him that the people and the parliament are becoming too complacent about terrorist threats because we haven't had any attacks for a couple of years and has ordered Mendellson to come up with a plan. What kind of plan do you think Mendellson will come up with?"

"I need to think about that. Before now MI5 have claimed that they have broken up a terrorist plot just to make the papers and the public feel more comfortable."

"This guy Grendan West has popped up again."

"He's the head of MI5 Black Ops. I used to work with him in the old days. I never really liked him though."

"Well, Mendellson is meeting him somewhere, sometime next Monday."

"I am guessing that they will decide the plan then so it would be good if you could do another memory trace on Mendellson after that meeting to find out what they are planning."

"How do you propose that I get within sight of Mendellson again?"

"I'm not sure yet but I'll put Roger onto that one."

The train rumbled on through the darkness, stopping at almost every station between Bletchley and London, and both Mac and Jonathan dozed lightly until the train arrived in London's Euston station. As they walked along the platform towards the exit gates, Mac said, "I think we should get a taxi back to the flat, rather than using the tube at this time of night."

The station clock showed that it was just after eleven o'clock. The pair walked out of the station towards where the taxis queued up waiting to be hired. There were several taxis there and nobody waiting so Mac and Jonathan got into the cab at the head of the queue. Mac told the driver to take them to the St. Katharines flat.

"You're going to see Roger's office tomorrow morning, aren't you?" said Mac.

"Yes, Karen is going to take me over there."

"I have to be out and about early tomorrow morning. I have a couple of meetings so I will meet up with you all at lunchtime. It will be all right to brief Roger and Karen about what we learned tonight. When I get there we can sort out what our approach to this should be."

The taxi pulled up outside the apartment building and Mac and Jonathan got out. Mac paid the driver and then the pair went into the entrance hall and up in the lift to the flat.

"I'm going to get straight off to bed, it's been a long day," said Jonathan.

"Me too, I've got an early start," said Mac and with that, they both went off to bed.

Chapter 22

Jonathan's alarm clock went off at seven-thirty next morning. He threw on a t-shirt and tracksuit trousers and went from his bedroom to the kitchen. A he brewed a pot of coffee and poured himself a mug full.

As he was drinking his coffee, Karen arrived.

"Good morning, Jonathan," she said. "How did it go last night?"

"It went really well," said Jonathan. "We got some good information out of Mendellson, but we'll probably need more."

"That's really good," said Karen. "Was the Bletchley Park museum interesting?"

"Yes, I enjoyed it, but I would love to go back there another time because there is just too much to see in one day."

"Well let's get down to business," said Karen. "Roger is expecting you at the office at ten o'clock. That gives you plenty of time to have breakfast and it gives me time to get to my eleven-thirty meeting after I drop you off."

"I'll cook breakfast," said Jonathan. "Do you want anything to eat?"

"I'll just have a piece of toast with marmalade."

"Mac said he would join us at lunchtime. Will you be there?"

"No, I'm going to be stuck in that meeting until mid afternoon at the earliest. We have several new books that we are developing and they are all my authors."

"Well, I'll tell you what we found out from Mendellson last night. Mac said it would be OK to tell you. Mendellson went to see the Prime Minister. The PM is worried that, because we haven't had a terrorist attack now for several years, people are getting resistant to anti-terrorist legislation. The PM asked Mendellson to fix the problem."

"Well, Mendellson is well known as the government fixer," said Karen.

"Mendellson is meeting with Grendan West on Monday."

"Grendan West. I have heard of him. Nasty piece of work, I understand."

"Mac has much the same opinion. We need to get inside Mendellson's head again after that meeting with West to find out what they are planning. Mac said he would get Roger to organize that. I need to make eye contact with Mendellson to get into his memory stream."

"Have you got any plans for the weekend, Jonathan?"

"Well, I thought on Saturday I might get a boat down the Thames to Greenwich and go to the Naval Museum and the Royal Observatory. I've never been to Greenwich before."

"Doing anything on Sunday?"

"Nothing planned."

"Do you want to come round to my flat for Sunday lunch? That will give me Saturday to clean up the flat and do my shopping."

"That's very kind of you. What's your nearest tube station?"

"That would be West Finchley, on the Northern Line. It's about ten minutes walk from my from my flat. I'll draw you a little map while you're cooking your breakfast."

Jonathan jumped up. "I'd better get on with that or we'll be late for Roger." He walked over to the kitchen and started getting pots and pans from the cupboards and the eggs and bacon from the fridge. Meanwhile Karen drew a map for Jonathan showing how to get to her flat from the West Finchley tube station.

After breakfast, Jonathan excused himself to Karen and he went back to his bedroom to get showered and dressed.

Half an hour later, they were both ready for the day.

"It looks like a nice day out there," said Jonathan. "What's the nearest tube station to Roger's office?"

"Westminster is about half a mile," said Karen. "That's the nearest. I'm ready to head out whenever you are."

"I'll get my coat," said Jonathan.

They went down in the lift and left the building to walk along Thames Path and up the hill, past the Tower of London to get to the Tower Hill tube station, from where they could get a direct train to Westminster.

They emerged into the wintry morning sunlight at Westminster tube station. The tower of Big Ben, the Houses of Parliament and Westminster Abbey dominated the view as they came up the steps from the station. They walked down Abingdon Street, past the Houses of Parliament. As they turned right into Horseferry Road, Karen pointed out Thames House, the headquarters of MI5.

Roger Gregson's office was in part of the Home Office building. Government budget cuts had resulted in some of the functions of the Home Office being moved out of London to cheaper accommodation in provincial cities like Newcastle and Liverpool. The theory was that modern technology such as video conferencing made it increasingly difficult to justify employing thousands of civil servants right in the heart of the capital city. The exodus had left empty office space which had been leased out to private companies. Roger Gregson had jumped at the chance to take a suite of offices. His company, UK Connections really needed to be in the heart of government to maintain the personal contacts that were so essential to Roger's business.

Karen and Jonathan entered the building and took the lift up to the third floor where Roger's office was situated. Karen used a key card to open the door and they were greeted by a receptionist in the outer office.

"Hello Mary" said Karen. "We have a visitor today. This is Jonathan Long."

Mary extended her hand.

"I'm Mary Robertson. I'm so pleased to meet you, Mr. Long."

As Jonathan shook Mary's hand, Roger appeared from the inner office. "Mr. Long is going to be doing a lot of work for us, Mary. I think you'd better get him a badge and a key card. Authorisation level three on the key card."

"I've got to get to a meeting," said Karen. "I'll leave Jonathan in your very capable hands. See you later."

Karen left the office, closing the door behind herself. Mary stood up and retrieved a camera from a filing cabinet.

"Just stand against that wall and smile, Jonathan."

She took the photograph and checked the image on the preview screen. "I think that will do. I'll have the key card and the badge ready for you in about half an hour or so. Here is a visitor's badge which you can use until your own badge is ready." Mary picked up a badge from her desk and clipped it on to Jonathan's shirt breast pocket.

"Come on through to the inner sanctum," said Roger as he waved Jonathan through to the inner office.

Roger had a large desk with a studded leather executive chair and had his back to the window. Through the window and across the roofs of buildings, Jonathan could just see the top half of Big Ben. The rest of the office had dark wood panelling from floor to ceiling. The wall opposite the door was filled with a bookcase, which held hundreds of books. There were two rather less luxurious chairs for visitors in front of Roger's desk.

"This is where it happens," said Roger as he sat down behind his desk. He then took a key from his pocket and turned it in a lock in one of the drawers of his desk.

"Actually, this is where it all happens!"

Jonathan heard a rumbling sound behind him. He turned and saw that the dark wood panelling was sliding back to reveal an array of television screens, computer monitors, keyboards and other control panels along a workbench that ran the width of the room. In front of the workbench were three executive chairs on wheels.

"Behold! The Control Centre!" said Roger as he got up from his chair and walked across the room. He turned on a red switch on the wall and all of the screens slowly came to life. The television screens were showing a variety of street scenes while the computer screens showed a logo. When Jonathan looked closer, he could see that the logo consisted of a chess board in a circle with a chess Knight in the centre. He then noticed that Roger's ID badge, clipped to his waistband, had the same logo.

"What do you think?" said Roger, spreading his arms out as if to embrace the whole array of technology.

"Amazing" was about the only word that Jonathan could come up with as he realized that his mouth had been hanging open as he tried to take in the scene before him.

Roger pulled out two of the wheeled executive chairs from the counter.

"Come on, sit down and I'll give you a guided tour."

Jonathan sat down next to Roger who was sitting in front of one of the computer screens. Roger pointed to the television monitors. "These are all showing traffic around here in central London. We collect signals from CCTV cameras on buildings and other places. We control which cameras we use with these computers."

Roger unclipped his ID badge from his waistband and scanned the barcode on it across the lens of a webcam. He then placed his left thumb on another device on the worktop.

"Fingerprint recognition," said Roger.

A map of the United Kingdom came up on Roger's monitor. He clicked on an area of the map near Birmingham and the screen zoomed in. Several thumbnail images of roads appeared. Roger clicked on one of the thumbnail images and the image it contained appeared full size on his television monitor.

"That's the M6 just north of Birmingham," said Roger.

The image showed three lanes of very slow moving traffic.

"Always a nightmare there," said Roger. "I use the M6 toll road myself."

"I use the train myself," said Jonathan.

Roger laughed. "Wise man. Very wise."

"Talking about trains," Roger spun his seat back round to his computer, he pressed a few keys, clicked on the screen a couple of times and on the screen appeared a railway train carriage with a dozen or so passengers sitting and a buffet trolley being pushed down the gangway between the seat. Roger looked closely at the bottom of the screen. "That's coach B on the ten o'clock train from Kings Cross to Leeds, just south of Peterborough now."

Roger looked very proud of himself. “Neat bit of kit, eh?”

“Neat indeed,” said Jonathan. “I’m not sure I want to know how you get all these pictures.”

“Most of it is surprisingly easy and surprisingly legal. You can get almost all these pictures quite freely on the web. All we did is write software to make some of the cameras easier to find and display. For some reason, this country went crazy with CCTV cameras a few years ago and they didn’t put too much thought into the security of the images. For the rest of it, we have friends in certain places. Let’s leave it at that, shall we?”

I could use a cup of coffee,” said Jonathan. “How about you?”

“Yes, I’ll get Mary to put on a fresh pot,” said Roger.

Jonathan put Roger into a seizure, got up from his chair and walked out to the front office.

“Mr. Gregson would like some coffee please, Mary.”

“I’ll brew a fresh pot and bring a couple of cups through.”

“Oh no, he’s working on something in the control centre. I’ll wait and take it through.”

“By the way, here’s your personal key card,” said Mary handing the laminated card to Jonathan,

“Thank you.” Jonathan pulled the visitor’s badge from his shirt breast pocket and placed it on Mary’s desk.

Mary opened a door in the corner of her office, which revealed a small cupboard containing a sink and a water tap. On shelves above the sink, there were coffee mugs and above them was coffee stuff like filters, coffee creamer and cans of Columbian coffee.

“Columbian is Roger’s favourite,” said Mary as prepared the brew.

"By the way, the men's room is to the right down the corridor."

"Thanks," said Jonathan. "I'll just pop out for a moment."

Jonathan stepped out of the office. When he returned, the coffee had finished brewing.

"How do you like yours, Jonathan?"

"Cream, no sugar."

Mary poured two cups of coffee and placed them on a tray, which she handed to Jonathan.

"There you go."

Jonathan carefully carried the tray back to the control centre and set it down on the workbench between himself and Roger. He looked at Roger, who was still in a seizure, his eyes closed as if he was asleep in his chair. He brought Roger out of the seizure.

Roger shook his head. "Wait a minute! Where did that coffee come from? I just said I wanted some and it's there. What's going on?"

Jonathan smiled broadly but suppressed the urge to laugh.

Seeing Jonathan smile, Roger said, "Is this another one of your mind games like the one that you did on me last night?"

"Yes, it is."

"You just made the coffee appear by magic? How did you do that?"

"I made it look to you as if the coffee appeared by magic. In fact, it took about ten minutes to brew the coffee and bring it in. I simply stopped most of your brain working for those ten minutes, so it appeared to you that the coffee appeared instantly as if by magic."

"You stopped my brain?"

"Most of it. It was as if you were asleep. It was actually a seizure."

Jonathan explained to Roger how momentary brain seizures were very common and they gave people a sense of déjà vu. Roger continued to shake his head in amazement as Jonathan gave the explanation.

"With that and the hallucination thing you did on me at the flat the other night we have the silver bullet. If we use your mental powers properly we can work miracles!"

"Don't let you coffee get cold," said Jonathan. Roger laughed and picked up his cup of coffee.

"Well, you've shown me a couple of miracles," said Roger. "Let me show you a couple."

Roger took a sip of his coffee as he turned back to his computer.

"Mac's Land Rover," said Roger as he typed in a registration number. A few seconds later, a picture appeared on a monitor above Roger's head showing Mac's Land Rover in the car park at Fort William railway station.

"Automatic Number Plate Recognition?" said Jonathan.

"Yes," said Roger, "but we've added a few bells and whistles so we can track a vehicle around the country and we can see a picture of the vehicle."

"Who put all this stuff together?"

"Well, I did most of the design work and I've got a tame programmer who did most of the technical stuff. There's one more thing I'd like to show you."

Roger pulled up a picture of Jonathan on his screen.

"That's the picture that Mary took this morning. She's already loaded you into the system. Now, let's take a look."

Roger punched a couple of keys and about ten seconds later, the monitor showed a picture of Karen and Jonathan walking past the Houses of Parliament.

"Automatic Face Recognition," said Roger proudly.

"No place to hide," said Jonathan.

"Pretty much, although this stuff is aimed at the bad boys, not innocent people like you and me. Don't forget, our work is aimed at tripping up the folk who misuse stuff like this. This is just about levelling the playing field a little bit."

"I get your point," said Jonathan.

"Let's get back to the project in hand," said Roger. "How did things go at Bletchley Park last night?"

Jonathan gave Roger the same short summary that he had given to Karen earlier that morning, including the planned meeting between Mendellson and Grendan West. Roger rubbed his chin, deep in thought.

"So you need another face to face encounter with Mendellson after his meeting with West?"

"I'm afraid so. Then we can hopefully get more information about what they are up to."

"I have an idea, though, since you came up with your seizure trick. What would you think about going into Mendellson's office?"

"Whoa! I'm not sure about that. I'm not a spy!"

"I think I can get you in without too much risk. You see, for security, many government departments insist on cleaning staff who cannot speak English. I have a cleaning company as one of my clients and they do the cleaning in Mendellson's building. All the cleaners are Spanish workers who do not speak any English at all. They are scheduled to clean Mendellson's building every Tuesday evening, so I reckon I can switch you with the regular cleaner and you can get in and snoop around."

"What if I can't get him into a seizure?"

"Well, then you'll just have to clean his office!" Roger laughed. "Let's step back into my office and talk about it a bit more."

They moved back to Roger's main office and Roger closed the sliding panels to hide the control centre. The desk intercom buzzed: "Sir Fergus McKinnon to see you sir," said Mary.

"Send him in," said Roger.

The office door opened and Mac stepped into the room.

"Hello guys!" said Mac. "What do you think of the control centre, Jonathan?"

"Quite interesting." Jonathan had rather more on his mind than the control centre. He was not at all sure that he wanted to follow Roger's plan. Mac sat down facing Roger.

"Anything on what Mendellson's up to, Roger?"

"I've just been talking with Jonathan here about a possible plan, haven't I Jonathan? I don't think that you're too comfortable about the plan yet, are you?"

"Right now, I'm bloody terrified!" said Jonathan.

"You'll be fine," said Mac. "What's your plan, Roger?"

"I was going to put him in as one of our Spanish cleaners then he could put Mendellson into a seizure and have a snoop around his office. He won't have to say anything and I can get Marcia, the cleaning supervisor, to introduce him."

"You're making the assumption that Mendellson will be in his office," said Mac.

"He always works late. There's every reason to believe that he will be there."

"What about uniform?"

"They all wear white overalls with the company logo. Marcia can arrange that. I'll take Jonathan down to their offices on Tuesday afternoon."

Mac turned to Jonathan. "This is your first operation. You're bound to have some first night nerves."

"You should only be in there for ten minutes or so," said Roger, "and I'll be right outside in the car. We'll wire you up for sound. Your job is to do a memory trace on Mendellson just like you did last night."

"Jonathan," said Mac, "why don't we go to lunch and have a chat then I can take you back to the apartment and you can take the rest of the weekend off. What time do you need him, Roger?"

"I need to be at the cleaning company office by five, so I'll pick up Jonathan at the apartment at four thirty on Tuesday afternoon. I'll call Marcia this afternoon and get it all set up."

"Good," said Mac. "So Jonathan, you are a free bird until four-thirty Tuesday afternoon. Let's go to lunch."

With that, Mac and Jonathan left Roger's office and went to lunch.

Chapter 23

On Sunday morning, Jonathan cooked himself a leisurely breakfast at the St. Katharines flat. He had enjoyed some time to himself since Friday afternoon but now he was looking forward to having lunch with Karen. After getting showered and dressed he left the flat and walked to Tower Hill tube station to travel to Karen's flat in Finchley, about ten miles north of central London. The journey took him just about forty five minutes and he used the map that Karen had sketched to navigate the ten minute walk to her flat. It was in a typical suburban London street with terraced houses down both sides, many of which had been converted to flats. Jonathan found Karen's address and walked up the short path to the front door. There was a box on the wall to the right of the front door with two bell pushes. Jonathan pushed the one labelled 'K. Wilson' and almost immediately, a voice came out of the scratchy speaker. "Hello, this is Karen!"

There was a click. "This is Jonathan." There was a loud buzz from the front door and Jonathan pushed it open and stepped inside. There was a hallway with a staircase rising on the right hand side of the hallway. Jonathan saw Karen coming along the corridor from the downstairs flat, drying her hands on a tea towel.

She threw the tea towel over her shoulder and hugged Jonathan tightly, kissing his cheek. Jonathan responded with a hug for Karen. "Jonathan, I'm so pleased you could come for lunch. Come on through to the kitchen." Karen grabbed Jonathan's hand and almost dragged him back along the corridor and into the kitchen, which was a bright and cheery place with a window overlooking a long but narrow back garden. "Let me take your coat," said Karen as she helped Jonathan to pull off his overcoat. She hung it on a coat hook in the corridor.

"Take a seat," she said, gesturing towards a table in the corner of the kitchen with two chairs. "Can I get you a drink? I've just opened a bottle of Chardonnay."

"I'll have the same, please."

Karen poured Jonathan a large glass of wine and placed on the table in front of him. "The lunch is pretty much under control. I hope you like lamb." There was an appetizing smell of roasting lamb and rosemary starting to fill the kitchen. "Roast potatoes all right for you?"

"All my favourites!"

"That's good."

Karen took a quick look in the oven to check everything was in order and then topped up her wine glass and came to sit at the table. "I have been so looking forward to this. Do you want to go and sit in the front room?"

"No, thanks, I'd like to sit here in the kitchen while the lunch is cooking."

"How was your trip to Greenwich yesterday?"

"I had a great time. The boat trip was a great way to see the river and The Royal Observatory was fascinating."

"I've never been there."

"Perhaps we could go together one day. There's a lot of interesting things to see there."

"That would be nice. I think we are going to be working together quite a bit in the future."

"It certainly seems that way."

They each took a sip of their wine. "You have a nice little garden here," said Jonathan, pointing through the kitchen window. "I would think that's a nice place to sit out in the good weather."

"I love it. It's a bit muddy and wintry at the moment. I really don't spend enough time out there."

"Do you spend most of your time in London?"

"Except when I have to go out to visit my authors or when I visit my parents and sister in Leeds. I would say I spend three weeks out of four here. I keep some stuff at my parent's house so I can travel pretty light when I go up there."

"Maybe you could store a suitcase here for me so I can travel light."

"What a good idea. I'm sure I could find a space for it in one of my cupboards."

Karen stood up. "I just need to put on the veggies." She walked across the kitchen and pulled a bag of mixed vegetables out of the freezer. "Perhaps you could lay the table." She poured the frozen vegetables into a saucepan of boiling water.

Jonathan hunted through the cupboards and drawers in the kitchen and eventually gathered together the plates and cutlery for two place settings. Meanwhile, Karen had prepared the gravy and was now carving the lamb. She brought over a plate of the sliced lamb and then returned to the stove to get the vegetables, the gravy and the roast potatoes. Jonathan refilled the wine glasses and they both sat down to eat.

"It's such fun to have someone visit for Sunday lunch," said Karen. "I usually eat on my own."

"No partner, Karen?"

"No, no-one. I have a few friends around Finchley who drop in occasionally or we meet up at the local pub or wine bar, but no-one I would call a partner. Yourself?"

"No, I don't have a partner either. It's taken me a long time to settle back into England and like you I have a few good friends but I just don't seem to have met anyone special yet."

They ate in silence for a few minutes then Jonathan said, "This is the most delightful Sunday roast. Just wonderful."

"Well thank you, Jonathan. It is nice to have my cooking appreciated."

They both finished their meals and sat leaned back in their chairs feeling very full and very satisfied.

"I've got some cheesecake for dessert if you've got room for it," said Karen.

"I'm absolutely full," said Jonathan, patting his tummy. "Perhaps a bit later I might be able to manage a small slice."

"Let's leave the dishes until later," said Karen. "Come on through to the front room."

She led Jonathan by the hand once more and took him into the front room. It was a modest but comfortable room with two armchairs and a two-seater settee. There was a television in the bay window and a stereo unit in the corner to the right of the window. There was a soft instrumental piece playing on the stereo. Karen led Jonathan to the settee and Jonathan sat down. "I'll go and get our wine," she said. She left the room and returned a few moments later with their wine glasses and the half empty bottle of wine. She set them down on the coffee table in front of the settee and sat down next to Jonathan.

"This is a very comfortable room," said Jonathan.

"Yes, I usually fall asleep in front of the television in here."

Jonathan laughed quietly. Karen grasped Jonathan's hand and rested her head on his shoulder. He moved a little closer. Karen sighed softly. They listened to the music together for a while, then Karen turned her face, pursed her lips and offered Jonathan a kiss to which he responded with a gentle kiss. Karen returned to resting her head on his shoulder. "That's the first real kiss I have had in several years," said Jonathan quietly.

"Me too," said Karen. They turned towards each other and hugged.

"I'm feeling sleepy after that lunch," said Jonathan.

"You can stretch out on the sofa or there's a bed you can lie down on if you want. Personally I would recommend the bed."

"Are you sure?" said Jonathan.

"Yes. Come on." Karen stood up and pulled Jonathan up from the sofa. She led him by the hand to the bedroom. "There you go." Jonathan kicked off his shoes and lay out on the bed on top of the duvet. Karen walked round to the other side of the bed and lay down next to him. They rolled towards each other and hugged and kissed, this time exploring each other's mouths, rather more passionately this time. After a while, they relaxed their hold on each other and they both fell asleep. Neither of them had been accustomed to sleeping next to a nice warm body for several years.

Jonathan awoke and looked at the clock radio on the bedside table. They had been asleep for about ninety minutes. He quietly got up from the bed and walked to the kitchen. He closed the kitchen door to avoid waking Karen, who was still sleeping, then he cleared the dirty dishes from the kitchen table and washed, rinsed and dried them. He put on a kettle of water to boil for making a pot of tea, and while the kettle was heating up, he explored the kitchen cupboards to find where to put the clean dishes away. While doing that he found the tea cups, sugar, teaspoons and a milk jug. He laid out a tray and made the tea in a teapot. He waited a few minutes for the tea to brew then he carefully carried the tray into the bedroom and cleared a space on the dressing table to place down the tray. Karen was still asleep. Jonathan quietly sat down on the edge of the bed, leaned over and kissed Karen on the cheek. She groaned, stretched out and opened her eyes to look up at Jonathan's face.

"How do you like your tea, sleepy head?"

"You angel, you've made a cup of tea. I like mine with milk but no sugar."

Jonathan stood up and walked over to the dressing table and poured two cups of tea then brought them over to Karen, who had by now pushed herself up to a sitting position. He handed a cup to Karen.

"Thank you so much. How long have I been asleep?"

"Close on two hours. I only just woke up myself."

"You are a perfect gentleman, Jonathan."

Karen and Jonathan both sipped their tea.

"I am so pleased that you came over today," said Karen. "Do you have any plans for this evening? I would love your company. We could put on a DVD to watch and I've got another bottle of wine and I've got some cheese and biscuits to munch on."

"I'm not sure when the last train leaves."

"Don't worry about that for now, I'll check it later on the computer. Now it's time for me to get up and wash the dishes."

Jonathan stood up and Karen handed him her cup and hauled herself off the bed. She walked to the kitchen and Jonathan followed. He put both cups down on the kitchen counter just as Karen swung round and threw her arms over his shoulders. "You absolute sweetie! You cleaned up the lunch things!"

Jonathan smiled and they kissed.

"Come on," said Karen, "let's go choose a DVD to watch."

Chapter 24

Jonathan chose a mystery while Karen chose a romantic comedy and they decided to watch the mystery movie first.

"I'll get the cheese and biscuits at the end of this movie, if that's all right," said Karen.

"Fine by me," said Jonathan as he sat in one of the armchairs. Karen turned on the television, started the DVD and stretched out on the sofa. They both became quite engrossed with the plot of the film and neither spoke for about ninety minutes. As the final credits started to roll, Karen said, "If you'll put in the next DVD I will go and get the cheese and biscuits and the wine."

Karen got up and walked to the kitchen. Jonathan got up and changed over the DVDs then joined Karen in the kitchen. "Need any help," he said.

"Perhaps you could open the wine and take it into the living room. You probably know where the wine glasses are by now."

Jonathan saw that the wine bottle had a screw cap so he grabbed a tea towel to help his grip as he unscrewed the cap. Then he collected a couple of wine glasses, took them and the bottle through to the living room and placed them on the coffee table that stood in front of the sofa. Karen followed shortly afterwards with plates and knives and a plate loaded with several different kinds of cheese and a selection of biscuits and crackers. They both sat on the sofa. Jonathan poured two glasses of wine and passed one to Karen. He raised his glass and said, "Here's to a wonderful Sunday afternoon."

"And evening," Karen said. They clinked their glasses together and each took a sip before placing their glasses carefully down on the coffee table. Jonathan got up to start the DVD and walked back to sit next to Karen.

"It's nice not having to worry about work," said Karen.

"A few weeks ago I would have disagreed with you but I think I am quickly getting myself into quite a bit of hard work since I started working with Mac."

"He is so glad to have you on the team now," said Karen, "and so am I!"

They both nibbled on the cheese and biscuits and sipped on the wine while the movie played on the television.

Karen leaned over and kissed Jonathan on the cheek. He returned the gesture with a kiss on her lips and put his arm round her shoulders. She snuggled in a bit closer. About half way through the movie, Karan laid he head on Jonathan's lap. He felt just the slightest arousal in himself. She was a really nice person to spend the day with and they were both footloose and fancy free, for the rest of today at least. He ran his hand gently through Karen's hair and stroked the back of her neck. He felt very peaceful and content at this moment.

As the movie finished, Karen sat up.

"It's probably time I made plans to head back home," said Jonathan.

"Please don't go, Jonathan," said Karen. "I would love you to stay over if you could."

Jonathan thought for a few moments. He did not want to take advantage of Karen but this was the first real female companionship that he had enjoyed for several years. "If you are sure that is all right."

"Of course it's all right. We are both grownups and just to get things perfectly clear I don't expect you to sleep on the couch. Come on, let's put the cheese and wine in the fridge."

Karen stood up, picked up the plates, and carried them into the kitchen. Jonathan followed with the wine and glasses. They put the cheese and wine in the fridge, put the glasses and plates in the sink. “They can wait until the morning,” said Karen with a rather defiant toss of her head then she took Jonathan by the hand and took him through to the bedroom. She pulled back the duvet to reveal crisp white sheets.

Jonathan pulled off his shoes and then said “Karen, it’s been quite a long time.”

From the far side of the bed Karen smiled very sweetly and said, “It has been for me too.”

They turned their backs to each other to undress. Jonathan decided to keep his underwear on just for the moment and Karen kept on her lacy white bra and panties. Each feeling rather shy they slipped between the sheets. They kissed and held each other tightly. Trying to be as tender as he could, Jonathan stroked Karen’s hair. She stroked his back and they each got used to being close to another person again. She gently massaged his chest and torso and they kissed passionately. He deftly unhooked her bra. He was starting to remember how to make love to a woman. He had always tried to be respectful to women when it came to love making. Karen pulled away slightly and cast her bra onto the floor beside the bed, then pressed her bare breasts against his chest. She kissed him again, passionately then she rolled over and pulled off her panties. Jonathan slipped his underpants off his legs at the same time and they rolled back together. She gave him another passionate kiss then said very quietly and sweetly “Ready?” to which Jonathan whispered “Yes.”

They made gentle love for a long time, in perfect rhythm until Jonathan said “Ready?” to which Karen responded “Yes!” and she pulled him closer and they both speeded up their movements. Karen’s first orgasm came accompanied with a powerful, repeated thrusting of her hips and just seconds later Jonathan came, causing Karen to have yet more powerful thrusts. Jonathan offered Karen a kiss and Karen responded with lips that were puffy from sexual arousal. Jonathan carefully rolled away to one side and lay holding Karen.

"Thank you for that," she said.

"Thank you too," said Jonathan, unsure what else to say at this particular moment.

Jonathan pulled the duvet cover up over them and they both were asleep within five minutes.

Chapter 25

The radio alarm on Karen's bedside table went off at six o'clock next morning. Jonathan saw that Karen was already up. He pulled on his jeans and shirt and walked out to the kitchen where Karen was cooking a breakfast of sausages and eggs. A pot of fresh brewed coffee stood on the kitchen counter.

"Good morning, Karen."

"Good morning. Why don't you jump into the shower while I finish cooking breakfast? There are some spare towels in the airing cupboard."

"I'll do that," said Jonathan and he found the towels and went into the bathroom. Freshened up but dressed in yesterday's clothes he went back to the kitchen, just as Karen was placing the breakfast plates on the kitchen table.

"Would you like any orange juice?" said Karen.

"No thanks," said Jonathan. "Coffee will be just fine for me." He poured himself a cup of coffee then sat down at the kitchen table. Karen sat down and they both started to eat their breakfast.

"Thank you for a great weekend, Karen,"

"It was a lovely day yesterday, wasn't it? I hope we can spend a few more weekends together when we have the time."

They finished breakfast and cleared away the dishes. "I'll wash the dishes while you get ready for work if you like," said Jonathan.

"What are your plans today," said Karen.

"I'm going back to the flat to get some fresh clothes then I'll probably go and see a movie. I don't have to be at Roger's office until tomorrow afternoon."

"I'll travel down with you on the tube as far as King's Cross, if you like. That's where I change trains to get to my office."

"I would enjoy your company on the journey."

Jonathan washed the dishes and put them away while Karen got ready.

They locked up the house and walked together to West Finchley tube station. They travelled together on the train until it reached King's Cross where Karen had to change trains.

"I may see you tomorrow evening at Roger's office," said Karen as she stood up to leave.

"See you then," said Jonathan and he waved goodbye. He continued on until Moorgate where he changed trains for Tower Hill, then took the pleasant walk back to the St. Katharines flat. He decided to shave and clean his teeth and take another quick shower after discarding his old clothes in his bedroom. After he got dressed again, he poured himself a glass of grapefruit juice and walked over to the table in the window to enjoy it and to plan out his day. He was actually rather at a loose end for the next twenty four hours or so. There were a couple of movies that had just been released which he hadn't seen so he decided to go and see those. He would not go to the centre of London where the cinema prices would be outrageous so he decided to take the tube to Richmond in south west London. It was just far enough out of London to be quieter and less crowded but easy to get to.

He thoroughly enjoyed his train ride out to Richmond and he found both of the films he saw very interesting as well as entertaining. By the time the second film finished it was late afternoon. Jonathan did not particularly fancy struggling through the London rush hour so he popped into a bookshop and bought a paperback book about spying, then he found a very pleasant pub where he spent a couple of hours enjoying a rather drinkable best bitter and reading his book. He left the pub and found an Indian restaurant a few doors along from the pub where he enjoyed a hot chicken curry. Finally, he went back to the tube station and headed home. Mac was at the flat when Jonathan got back. He was relaxing and watching television. He muted the sound.

"Hello Jonathan. How was your weekend?"

"Very enjoyable. I've had a pretty lazy day today."

"That's good. In this business you never know when you are going to get called out so you need to take your R and R when you can get it."

"What's the plan for tomorrow?"

"Roger has planned to get you into Mendellson's office as a cleaner. He will pick you up here at the flat at four thirty tomorrow afternoon. You are a free bird until then. We'll all have a meeting at Roger's office after you get back from Mendellson's office."

Jonathan slumped down in one of the armchairs and Mac turned the television sound back on. They sat there together watching the news then Jonathan hauled himself out of his chair and stood up.

"I'm off to bed, if you don't mind, Mac."

"Sleep well, Jonathan."

Chapter 26

Next morning Jonathan slept fairly late since he expected a late evening of work. He spent what was left of the morning reading the book he had bought in Richmond the day before. He made himself a lunch from some ham, cheese and a baguette that he found in the refrigerator and after lunch he watched an old black and white movie on television for a couple of hours. Before he knew it, it was nearly four thirty and Roger called to say he was waiting outside. Jonathan went down in the lift and out through the front door to Roger's car.

Jonathan and Roger didn't talk much as they headed across the river via Tower Bridge and drove into the southern suburbs of London.

"The cleaning company's office is just around the corner," said Roger as he pulled the car to a halt on the side of the main road. "I just want to go through what we are going to do and make sure that we have got a clear plan. Pass me that briefcase that's behind my seat, would you Jonathan?"

Jonathan reached behind the driver's seat, pulled out the briefcase and passed it to Roger. When Roger opened the briefcase, it was almost empty. Jonathan saw a small earpiece and an envelope. Roger picked up the earpiece and handed it to Jonathan. It looked like a typical hearing aid with a piece that fitted behind the ear, and had a smaller piece, on a thin wire, that fitted inside the ear.

"This actually is a hearing aid," said Roger, "but we've modified it to transmit and receive so I can talk to you and you can talk to me. Remember, Mendellson thinks you only speak Spanish, so unless it is a critical emergency I think you should just grunt quietly – one grunt for yes, two grunts for no. Got that?"

Jonathan grunted once. Roger burst out laughing and pulled an earpiece on a wire out of his jacket pocket.

"Can you hear me?" said Roger.

Jonathan grunted once.

"Everything all right?" said Roger.

"Sure. I'm starting to look forward to this mission."

"That's the way it usually goes," said Roger. "When you are waiting around for the action to start you are as nervous as hell, but once you are on the way the adrenalin kicks in and you are ready for anything."

Jonathan smiled.

"I'll take you round the corner to the cleaning company office in a moment. We'll be seeing Marcia who runs the company. She will get you a uniform and then we'll come back to the car and drive over to Mendellson's office just off Whitehall. Marcia will follow us and get you into the office, and I will wait outside. I'll pull you out as soon as I can.

Roger got out a small piece of paper with some writing in Spanish.

"He terminado limpieza de su oficina, señor."

Jonathan read the words aloud.

"Your Spanish accent is remarkably good," said Roger.

"Twenty years living in Southern California."

"Of course!"

Roger laughed as he started the car and pulled into a side road. He stopped again in front of a small row of shops, one of which had a sign on the front "City Contract Cleaning Services".

Jonathan and Roger got out of the car and Jonathan followed Roger up to the door of the shop. Roger opened the door and stepped inside and Jonathan followed. A counter ran across the width of the shop, and behind it was a door to the rest of the building. On the counter was a bell, which Roger hit smartly. The door opened and out stepped a lady.

"Roj!" she said and held her arms out wide.

"Marcia!" said Roger, hugging the lady. "Long time no see. How's business?"

"We could do better, as always, but it is so good to see you, Roger. And who is your friend?"

"This is Jonathan."

Marcia came out from behind the counter and gave Jonathan a hug. "A friend of Roger's is most certainly a friend of mine."

She returned behind the counter. "Now, Roger, we have a little business to discuss, no?"

"Marcia, as I told you on the phone, just for this evening I want you to put Jonathan in to clean Lord Mendellson's office. Could you do that?"

"Everything is arranged. I have given the regular guy, Pedro, the night off. There is no problem. But Jonathan, you come with me. I will get you a uniform. Come."

Jonathan went behind the counter and followed Marcia through the door and into the back of the building. He emerged five minutes later wearing a crisp white overall bearing the City Contract Cleaners logo and the name badge embroidered with the name Pedro.

Marcia emerged from behind Jonathan with a beaming smile. "He looks good Roger, no?"

"Perfect, just perfect."

"He can keep the overalls as a gift from me, Roger."

"What do you think of that, Pedro?" said Roger.

"Perdone, yo solo hablo español, señor," said Jonathan with a grin.

"Excellent!" said Roger, clapping his hands.

Roger then opened his briefcase and took out the envelope. “Here’s a little donation to the next office party, Marcia,” he said as he passed her the envelope.

“Roger! You really shouldn’t. I’m just so glad to help you. But thank you, you are so kind. Is there anything else I can do to help you Roger?”

“Actually there is, Marcia. Can you meet us outside Lord Mendellson’s building and take Pedro in?”

“Of course, Roger, I will see you there at seven o’clock this evening.

“Goodbye until then,” said Roger and he stepped outside, followed by Jonathan. They got into Roger’s car.

“I’m actually starting to feel more confident about this,” said Jonathan as Roger started the engine and pulled away from the kerb.

“That’s good,” said Roger, “you certainly look the part in that uniform. We really cannot go anywhere with you dressed like that. Why don’t we park up on the Albert Embankment for a while and then we can meet Marcia.

Roger drove through the streets of South London and eventually reached the river and the Albert Embankment, which ran along the opposite side of the river from Big Ben and the Houses of Parliament. He parked the car alongside the kerb.

“You can see both the MI5 and the MI6 buildings from here,” said Roger. Pointing, he said, “MI5 are right across the river from here, Thames House, and MI6 are on this side at Vauxhall Cross.”

“Hiding in plain sight?” said Jonathan.

“That’s the general idea,” said Roger. “The theory is that everyone is so occupied by their magnificent buildings that they don’t notice the detail! Have you seen the GCHQ building down in Cheltenham?”

“No.”

"Bloody enormous great doughnut shaped building. Probably half of the population of Cheltenham work there, but it's still a pretty secure place."

"I'd be interested to see GCHQ sometime."

"You will, Jonathan, I'm sure you will. Now we have you on our side, we can get involved in a lot more projects. We've had to let several projects go because we just did not have the resources to pursue them."

"You know, it was less than a month ago that I was telling Karen how bored I was."

"I don't think you'll be bored working with us."

They sat for a while in the gathering gloom of twilight, watching as the lights on buildings on both sides of the river turned on. The lights along the Albert Embankment illuminated the road on which they were parked.

Roger checked his watch. "Time to go."

Jonathan breathed very deeply and exhaled. "Let's do it."

Roger drove down the Albert Embankment and crossed the river using the Vauxhall Bridge. He then worked his way up through Westminster, round Parliament Square and up into Whitehall. He turned off Whitehall into a side street between rows of government buildings.

"This is where Mendellson's office is," said Roger as he pulled up next to the kerb. "Marcia should be here in a few minutes."

A white minibus with the City Contract Cleaning logo on the side pulled up in front of Roger's car and eight cleaners, all in matching white overalls, climbed out. Marcia climbed out of the driver's seat and led the group into the building. She emerged about ten minutes later and walked over to the passenger side of Roger's car. Jonathan opened the door and got out to meet her.

As they walked towards the entrance to the building, Jonathan heard Roger's voice in his earpiece.

"Everything OK?"

Jonathan gave one grunt.

"Good man!" came the response in the earpiece, "now go break a leg!"

Jonathan recognized the encouraging phrase given to actors just before they stepped onto the stage. By this time, they had reached the entrance to the building and Marcia was unlocking the door. They entered the building and Marcia walked over to the lift. The doors opened and she and Jonathan stepped inside. She pressed the button for the fourth floor. The doors closed and the lift started up.

"I don't want to know what you are up to, Jonny boy, but whatever it is, good luck. Your cleaners trolley is in the utility cupboard just there. I'll be waiting at the front door when you come out."

Jonathan smiled. The lift reached the fourth floor and the doors opened. "It's the third office on the left," said Marcia. His name is on the door. Just take out the trash and run your feather duster over all the woodwork, just like you would clean your own room, Jonny boy."

Jonathan suddenly felt very nervous, but there was no turning back now. He stepped out of the lift. Marcia remained in the lift as it returned to the ground floor and Jonathan felt very alone. He collected his cleaner's trolley from the utility cupboard just across from the lift and he pushed it along the corridor, stopping outside the third door on the left. He knocked on the door. "Limpiador, señor".

"Come in," said a gruff voice from inside the office.

Jonathan picked up his feather duster and opened the door. Lord Mendellson was not at his desk, he was sitting in a leather chair near the window, reading a sheaf of papers and making notes on them occasionally. He appeared to be totally uninterested in Jonathan.

Jonathan picked up the waste paper basket and took it out into the corridor. He emptied it into the larger trash bin on his cleaner's trolley and returned the empty basket to the side of Mendellson's desk. He started to clean the furniture with his feather duster, trying not to look at Mendellson. He dusted over the books and the bookcase.

Then he faced Mendellson and put him into a seizure. Mendellson's eyes closed and he looked as if he was asleep. Jonathan breathed a sigh of relief.

Jonathan jumped as a voice came through his earpiece. It was Roger.

"Are you into his office yet?"

Jonathan grunted once.

"Have you got him into a seizure?"

Jonathan grunted once again.

"Good man, take care in there."

Jonathan started thinking about key words to start retrieving the memory stream.

"Grendan West. Black Ops. Meeting. Terrorism."

The memory stream started to flow.

I am in my car, driving myself this time. I don't want my government driver involved in this because I must keep it ultra secret. It is the middle of a gloomy January afternoon. I am driving down a country lane in the Thames Valley near Marlow. This is near where Grendan lives and we always have our meetings in remote places. I can see a pub ahead on the left. It is called The Queens Head. That is where I am meeting Grendan West. We need to talk about the assignment that the PM has given me. I am turning left into the pub car park. There is only one other car in the car park and I recognize it as Grendan's Mercedes. I hope that we will not be disturbed in our conversation. I am pulling up next to Grendan's car. I am getting out and walking across the car park and I am having to bend low to walk in the door because it is a very old building. I am looking round the bar and I see Grendan sitting at a table in the corner, with his back to me. I am buying an orange juice from the lady behind the bar and now I am walking over to Grendan's table.

"Good afternoon, George," says Grendan in his gravelly voice, without looking round.

I am sitting down across the table from Grendan.

"Good afternoon."

"So what do you need on this particular occasion?"

I tell Grendan about the assignment that the PM has given me, to raise people's acceptance of anti-terrorism legislation.

"Well, we need another terrorist attack. That would wake the buggers up." Grendan sounds almost disinterested as he talks about something that could kill or maim many people.

I tell Grendan that we need to avoid injuries to our citizens.

"How about a mock terrorist attack?" says Grendan.

I say, "Good idea if you can pull it off."

"Damage the infrastructure but avoid injuries. That way it will cause the most inconvenience but at the least risk," says Grendan.

I say, "Will you handle it?"

He says, "When do you want it done?"

I say, "Couple of weeks. Does that give you long enough to organize it?"

He says, "Leave it with me, old chap. You'll know when it happens. I'll get our tame terrorist Sean Donnelly to do it. He needs a purpose in life, something to keep him out of the pub."

I don't know who Sean Donnelly is and I don't need to know.

I stand up and say, "Remember, no civilian casualties."

Grendan waves me away and I leave the pub.

Jonathan picked up his feather duster and dusted the top of the filing cabinet, then he moved over towards the door. He brought Mendellson out of his seizure. Mendellson opened his eyes, shook his head and went back to reading his papers.

"He terminado limpieza de su oficina, señor."

Mendellson made a dismissive sort of wave and Jonathan opened the door, slipped out into the corridor and quietly closed the door behind him. He felt thoroughly drained. He returned the cleaner's trolley to the cupboard at the end of the corridor, then walked over to the lifts and pressed the call button.

It seemed to take an age for the lift to arrive. Jonathan got in and pressed the button for the ground floor. The lift door closed and the lift started down. He realized his brow was damp with sweat, and wiped it with his sleeve. The lift finally arrived at the ground floor, the doors opened, and Jonathan stepped out into the entrance hall. There were the other cleaners sitting on benches in the hall and Marcia was standing talking to the night watchman who was sitting at his desk. Marcia took no notice of Jonathan.

He walked over and sat on the bench with the other cleaners. Presumably, they had finished their work and were waiting for the rest of the cleaners to finish. He prayed that the cleaners would not engage him in conversation. He had pretty much exhausted his knowledge of Spanish. He folded his arms and closed his eyes, pretending to be asleep.

He thought he might have dozed off for a few minutes because the next thing he felt was a hand on his shoulder, gently shaking him. He opened his eyes and was relieved to see it was Marcia. He stood up and followed her to the front door where the other cleaners were waiting.

Jonathan stepped outside, careful to be the last cleaner to leave. As they reached the pavement, the group of cleaners turned left to follow Marcia to the minibus, and Jonathan turned right. He hoped that none of the cleaners would notice he was not travelling with them. Roger drew up in his car and Jonathan quickly got in. He rubbed his face and exclaimed "Jeez! I'm glad that's over!"

Roger pulled away from the kerb, passed the cleaners' minibus, and drove down the street. "We'll go back to the Horseferry Road office. Fergus and Karen are already there. Can you pull off those overalls as we drive?"

Jonathan slipped off his shoes and unzipped the overalls, then he squirmed around in the passenger seat to pull his arms out of the overalls, then pulled his legs out. He bundled up the overalls and threw the bundle into the back seat. He slipped his shoes on again.

"By the way," said Roger, "you did a cracking job there."

"I've never been so nervous in all my life!"

"You did well for a first mission."

It was only a short drive back to the Horseferry Road office and Roger pulled the car into an underground car park below the building. They got out and rode up in the lift to the corridor where Roger's office was situated. As they entered the office, there was a loud pop of a champagne cork and Mac was pouring glasses of champagne.

"No longer a virgin, Jonathan?" said Mac. He put down the bottle of champagne and shook Jonathan very firmly by the hand. "Well done, well done." He handed Jonathan a glass of champagne. Roger had already served himself, as had Karen who was sitting in the chair usually occupied by Mary during the day.

Mac raised his glass. "Here is a toast to the latest member of Operation Checkmate. He has certainly earned his stripes tonight!. To Jonathan!"

Roger and Karen raised their glasses and echoed, "To Jonathan!" and everyone took a sip of their champagne. Mac refilled all the glasses and perched on the corner of the desk.

"First things first," said Mac. "Jonathan, did you get a successful memory trace?"

"Yes I did. I need to dictate it to you while the image is still strong."

"Let's go inside," said Mac.

They all transferred to Roger's inner office and Roger opened the sliding doors to the control centre. Karen flipped on the main switch and all the monitors and computer screens came to life. Roger sat at his desk and everyone else sat facing him.

Karen picked up a pencil and notepad and Jonathan related the meeting between Mendellson and West, the planned mock terrorist attack and the name Sean Donnelly."

When Jonathan had finished, Mac said, "Excellent work, Jonathan, really excellent. Well I think we can safely say that Mendellson is now out of the loop. He is too close to the PM to be involved in the actual operation."

"Who is Sean Donnelly?" said Jonathan.

"Bomb maker," said Mac. "He used to be in the Provisional IRA. I bumped into him when I was doing a stint in Belfast when I was with MI5. When the Provos disarmed during the peace process in 1998, some of the Provos refused to disarm and they formed a new group called the Real IRA to carry on the fight. Sean had been a bomb maker for the Provos and then he joined the Real IRA as a bomb maker. He was arrested in 1998, trying to drive a car load of explosives across the border. Sentenced to thirty years."

"So how can he be involved with Grendan West?" said Karen.

"MI5 got him let out of jail after he had served thirteen years," said Mac. "They wanted to pick his brain about the Real IRA bombs so they could defuse them. His specialty was using mobile phones to detonate his bombs."

"So now he's working for Black Ops?" said Jonathan.

"It certainly looks that way," said Mac.

"Have you got a picture of him?" said Roger.

"I'm sure we could find one fairly quickly," said Mac, "When he was arrested his face was in every newspaper in the country. Karen, can you try to pull up a picture and then start AFRS and see if we can track him down?"

Karen rolled her chair over to the control centre desk and started on her task.

Meanwhile Mac continued to analyse Karen's notes. He was thinking aloud. "An attack on infrastructure like a railway line or a bridge would have the desired effect, and it could be done when no people were around."

"We are not going to be able to get close to Grendan West," said Roger, "so it looks like we will need to find Sean Donnelly."

"Last time I heard of him he was living in a house that MI5 had bought for him in North West London."

"Found him!" Karen called from the control centre. "Twenty five AFRS hits in Willesden."

"Of course," said Mac. "Willesden has a large Irish population. He would fit in there without being noticed."

"Can we do anything more with this tonight?" said Roger.

Mac yawned, "I think we have all had a long day. Why don't we go and get something to eat and get an early night and we can take a fresh look at all this tomorrow."

The rest of the group murmured their approval, and they all walked out of the office with Roger bringing up the rear and locking up the office behind them.

Chapter 27

By the time Jonathan woke up in his bedroom at the St. Katharines apartment next morning, the apartment was quiet. Jonathan looked at the clock on the bedside table: 09:45. He threw on a pair of jeans and a sweatshirt and walked out to the kitchen. On the counter was a note from Mac:

Good morning, Jonathan! We thought you would benefit from a lie-in this morning after your adventures last night. We are all over at Roger's office this morning, working out what our next steps will be. Come over anytime you are ready.

Jonathan prepared a fresh pot of coffee and while it was brewing, he quickly got shaved and showered and dressed in fresh jeans and a clean shirt. He prepared himself a couple of slices of buttered toast for breakfast and within half an hour he was putting on his overcoat and on his way out of the apartment.

He followed the same route that he and Karen had taken yesterday and he caught the tube to Westminster then he walked to the Horseferry Road building where Roger's office was located. He took the lift to the third floor and walked down the corridor to Roger's office. He used his new key card to open the door and went in.

Mary was sitting in the outer office. The door to the inner office was closed.

"Good morning, Jonathan," said Mary. "Go on through, they're all in there waiting for you."

Jonathan opened the door to the inner office. Roger, Karen and Mac were sitting at the conference table.

"Hello, Jonathan," said Mac. "Grab yourself a cup of coffee from Mary and come and join us."

Jonathan turned to go back to the outer office to get his coffee but before he could take a step, he was greeted by Mary, who was carrying a steaming mug of coffee on a tray. "I'll bring it over to the table," she said.

Jonathan sat down at the spare seat between Karen and Mac. Mary placed the coffee in front of him and she withdrew to the outer office.

"Using our face recognition technology, we've finally tracked down Sean Donnelly to a house in Willesden," said Mac. "It took a lot of processing time. We did a search of CCTV pictures for the last month and we found a cluster of hits around Willesden. Then we narrowed down to his street and we have a pretty good idea what house number he is in. We don't have a camera actually looking at the house but there's one at the end of the street. There's a car parked in the street outside the house, which we think, is his and we have got the registration for that.

"Is the car registered to him?" Jonathan asked.

"No, it's registered in another name but at the same address," said Mac. "He probably registered it in a false name. It's very easy to do that."

"So what is our next move?" said Karen.

"It's my suspicion," said Mac, "that Sean is going to build a bomb and explode it somewhere near a railway line or bridge. I think the intention is to cause infrastructure damage but not to kill people. That means he will probably hit track or signalling or possibly tunnels. I think, of all the targets, tunnels provide the best return on investment for him. A damaged tunnel would take months to repair."

"Do we have any idea when he might move on this?" said Jonathan.

"West told Mendellson that it would probably be within two weeks," said Mac, "so I would say we have at least a week before we have to start worrying. But we still have no time to waste. We should keep a round-the-clock watch on Sean and his car and track him if he moves."

"Agreed," said Roger. "Karen and I can take turns keeping watch. Mac, when he moves you can use my car to follow him. I don't think we should involve the police until we have more definite information on what he's up to. Jonathan, you'll probably want to go with Mac. Are we all agreed on that?"

The other three around the table nodded in agreement. Karen got up from the conference table, walked over to the control centre and sat down in the swivelling chair. "Still no activity," she said. She swivelled round to face the others. "Why don't you guys organize some coffee and sandwiches for lunch? I'll keep watch here."

Roger, Mac and Jonathan trooped out of the office while Karen remained at the control centre desk. She was thinking about the problem of how to get close enough to Sean Donnelly to allow Jonathan to get a memory stream. She slowly scrolled through each of the forty eight CCTV cameras in the Willesden area and then a thought struck her. One of the cameras showed the entrance to a pub just round the corner from the street where Donnelly lived. The pub was called The Skipton Arms. Could this be Donnelly's local pub? It was certainly the nearest, probably no more than five minutes walk from his house. She did an AFRS scan for Donnelly's face on this CCTV camera and sure enough, she got twelve hits over the last two weeks. Donnelly was a man of habit. Almost every night he went into the pub at eight o'clock and left again to go home at ten o'clock. If Jonathan could be in the pub at the same time as Donnelly, perhaps he could get close enough to Donnelly to do a memory trace.

Karen was lost in her thoughts as the boys returned with sandwiches and coffee. She excitedly told them what she had discovered while they were out as Roger handed her a package of sandwiches. They all sat around the conference table.

"Good work, Karen," said Mac. "I think the plan should be for you and Jonathan to go in as a couple having a drink and spy out the land for the first night. Why don't you go out there tonight? Don't attempt a memory trace, Jonathan, just look around and find out what goes on in that pub."

"Do you think West will have had enough time to meet up with Donnelly yet?" said Roger.

"Probably not," said Mac, "but tonight's a dummy run. He may have had a meeting by tomorrow night. I'll organize a car to run you around this evening, Jonathan. Are you going back to your flat, Karen?"

"No, I've got to go into the office for a while and then I'll probably go back to the St. Katharines apartment if that's all right. The car can pick up Jonathan and me from there. Probably about seven thirty?"

"Consider it done, Karen," said Mac. "All right with you, Jonathan?"

"Fine with me."

"I think we've done enough for this afternoon," said Mac. "We'll leave you in peace to do some real work, Roger. I have a meeting this afternoon so I have to get away. It looks like you've got a quiet afternoon in store, Jonathan."

Chapter 28

Precisely at seven thirty that evening, Karen received a call on her mobile. The driver for her and Jonathan had arrived outside the St. Katharines apartment block and was ready whenever she was. She and Jonathan pulled on their overcoats and went down in the lift to the ground floor. Outside they found a black BMW with a uniformed driver sitting in the driving seat. They climbed into the back seats of the vehicle.

"I have been instructed to take you to The Skipton Arms in Willesden," said the driver. "Is that still correct?"

"Yes, that's right," said Karen. The vehicle moved off.

After a while, Jonathan said, "I'm starting to enjoy this work."

"It's a lot more fun than an office job," said Karen.

"I've never had a real office job," said Jonathan. "I mean a clerical pen pushing kind of job."

"Lucky you!"

It took about twenty minutes for the car to reach Willesden. The car pulled up to the kerb of a very nondescript street full of warehouses and industrial premises.

"I'm going to drop you here rather than in front of the pub," said the driver. "Mr. McKinnon asked me to do that just in case someone might be watching. The main road is just ahead. Turn left and you will see The Skipton Arms. Miss Karen, give me a call when you are ready to be collected and I will pick you up on the corner up there."

"Thank you very much, driver," said Karen as she and Jonathan stepped out of the vehicle.

They walked up to the main road and turned left as the driver had instructed and saw the pub just ahead on their left. Before he had left Roger's office, Jonathan had printed off a small head and shoulders picture of Sean Donnelly and now he pulled that picture from his inside overcoat pocket and took another look at it to remind himself of Sean's facial features. He showed the picture to Karen who studied it for a few moments then nodded and returned the picture to Jonathan.

They walked up to the pub and went inside. Jonathan checked his watch. It was five minutes before eight o'clock. The pub was fairly quiet, the after work trade had gone and the steady evening after dinner crowd had not yet arrived. It was a typical London suburban pub, dark panelled walls and dark mahogany furniture. There were bar stools around the semicircular bar. It was obvious to Jonathan that the separate public bar and lounge bar of the original pub had been knocked into one large bar. There were upholstered bench seats along the walls of the pub with tables and chairs in front of them.

"What would you like to drink, Karen?" said Jonathan as they stood just inside the front doors.

"My usual glass of white wine, please," said Karen.

Jonathan stepped over to the bar and ordered the wine and a pint of best bitter for himself. He carried the drinks over to a table and sat on one of the bench seats with his back to the wall so that he had a good view of the whole room. Karen sat beside him. He looked at his watch. It was exactly eight o'clock.

"Surveillance can be the most boring part of this job," said Karen quietly.

"Perhaps we won't have to wait too long," said Jonathan. "At least we can have a drink while we are waiting."

The pub started to fill up with a few more customers. A young couple came in and they were followed by an old man with grey hair and a walking stick. Jonathan took out the picture of Donnelly and placed it on the seat between him and Karen. One of the characteristics that Karen had noted about Donnelly when she was reading his description on the computer was that he was relatively short at five foot five, so she was looking for a short man. A man roughly fitting that description came in but he was wearing glasses and as far as they knew, Donnelly didn't wear spectacles.

The recent arrivals bought their drinks and dispersed themselves around the pub, some sitting at tables while some sat on stools at the bar.

The front doors opened again and a short, middle-aged man walked in. Jonathan looked at the man, looked down at the picture and looked at the man again. He nudged Karen with his elbow. She looked down at the picture and said very quietly, "He's a possible."

The short man walked up to the bar. "Your usual, Sean?" said the lady behind the bar and she started pouring a pint of Guinness. This time Karen nudged Jonathan.

"I think that's our man," said Jonathan.

Donnelly carried his drink over to a corner table on the far side of the room from where Jonathan and Karen were sitting. "I can make eye contact from here," said Jonathan.

"We are supposed to be just surveying the place," said Karen. "At least give him time to get settled with his drink."

Jonathan kept watch on Donnelly, whose head was down in a newspaper. Jonathan could not get a memory trace unless he could make eye contact. After a long time Donnelly put down his newspaper, picked up his Guinness, and looked around the pub. Jonathan thought that Donnelly had looked at him suspiciously but decided that it was just his own nerves. As Donnelly put down his glass, Jonathan started concentrating on his eyes. Within a few seconds, Donnelly's eyes glazed over and he was in a seizure, looking straight ahead. No one else in the pub seemed to be taking any notice of the short man in the corner, staring into space.

Jonathan started to think of keywords. "Grendan West." "Terrorist attack."

Soon the memory stream started to flow:

I am sitting in a pub in Kilburn in the middle of the afternoon with a pint of Guinness. Grendan West has asked me to meet him here because he has an assignment for me. Apart from the barman, I am the only person in the pub. This pub is usually deserted in the middle of the afternoon so it is a good place for a private meeting.

The front doors of the pub are opening and Grendan West is walking in. I have worked with Grendan West before. He was the one who hired me into MI5 Black Ops to help him to defuse bombs. West is dressed in jeans and a leather jacket over a T-shirt. He is buying a pint of lager at the bar and now he is walking over to my table and sitting down.

He says, "Good afternoon, Sean."

I say, "Good afternoon, Mr. West."

He says, "I have an assignment for you if you want it."

I say, "How much?"

He says, "Thirty thousand pounds. Half up front, the rest on completion."

I say, "What's the job?"

He says, "I want a terrorist attack on one of the tunnels north of Kings Cross station. I don't want any people hurt, just damage and mayhem."

I think for a moment. It sounds like fairly simple job. It will probably take a week, maybe less.

"Thirty thousand pounds, you say."

"Half up front."

"When do you want it done?"

"How long will it take you?"

"A few days. Where are we? Today is the Wednesday the sixteenth. I could do it next Sunday, the twentieth."

"Good." West is pulling an envelope out of his pocket. "Here's the first fifteen thousand."

"I'll need to take a short break out of the country until the chase dies down."

"I'll organize that. I'll call you."

West has left half of his drink and has stood up.

"Remember, damage only. No people killed or injured."

Now West is leaving the pub.

Jonathan released Donnelly from his seizure and watched while Donnelly picked up his pint of Guinness and took a long drink from it. He was behaving as if nothing had happened.

Jonathan took a notebook and pen from his jacket and made notes about the memory trace that he had just received. When he had finished his notes, he pushed the notebook across to Karen so that she could read.

"That gives us plenty to work with," said Karen after reading the notes.

"What do you think that Mac and Roger will do with the information?" said Jonathan.

"I am sure Mac will want to avoid the tunnels being blown up, so I think he will want to somehow get the bomb disarmed. His main objective is to be a pain in the butt to Black Ops and to thwart their operations."

"I think we should wrap things up for tonight," said Jonathan. "I don't want to risk Donnelly noticing what we are doing. Perhaps we can come back tomorrow after we've had a meeting with Mac and Roger. Let's finish our drinks and then you can call up the car."

Ten minutes later, they were climbing into the BMW. When they were safely inside the vehicle, Jonathan said, "Are you coming back to the St. Katharines flat, Karen?"

"No, I think I'll go back to my own place this evening, if that's all right with you."

Karen leaned forward and gave the driver the address of her flat. She would be dropped off first because her flat was much nearer to their present location.

"I suppose we will need a meeting with Mac and Roger tomorrow morning," said Jonathan.

"I'll call Mac when I get back to the flat and arrange it for ten thirty," said Karen.

As the car pulled up outside Karen's flat, she gave Jonathan a peck on the cheek and said, "A good evening's work. Well done Jonathan!"

"I'll see you at ten thirty," said Jonathan.

It was ten o' clock in the evening by the time Jonathan was dropped at the St. Katharines flat. When Jonathan stepped out of the lift and into the living room, Mac was watching the television news.

"Successful evening?" said Mac.

"Yes," said Jonathan as he walked over to the kitchen and collected a bottle of wine from the fridge and a wine glass from the cupboard. He sat down in the armchair next to Mac, opened the wine and poured himself a drink.

"Did Karen call you?" said Jonathan.

"Yes," said Mac. "Meeting at ten thirty, right?"

"That's right," said Jonathan.

Jonathan told Mac about the memory trace and the plan to blow up the railway tunnel just outside King Cross.

"What do you think our next move should be?" said Jonathan.

"I think we should have that conference with Karen and Roger before we make any more plans," said Mac. "We can share a taxi over to Roger's office. Can you be ready to leave by ten o'clock tomorrow morning?"

"I'll be ready," said Jonathan as he poured himself a second glass of wine. He woke up at two o'clock in the morning with a half full glass of wine on the table next to him. The memory traces made him more tired than he realised. There was no sign of Mac, who had presumably gone to bed. Jonathan hauled himself out of the armchair and walked towards his bedroom. Without getting undressed, he lay on the bed and fell straight back to sleep.

Next morning, Mac and Jonathan shared the taxi to Roger's office. Karen was already there and by ten thirty, all four were seated around the conference table. Mary, the office assistant had provided coffee and biscuits for the group. Roger had set up a large electronic whiteboard and had collated together on the board the information that Jonathan had reported from the memory traces together with some background information that Mac had provided.

"Let's review everything we've got and see if we can spot any gaps in our information," said Mac.

"We know who, what, where and when," said Karen. "What else is there?"

"I want to keep a close eye on Sean," said Mac. "For that matter I want to keep a close eye on Black Ops. The main thing here is to discredit Black Ops in the eyes of the public. If we can prevent the bomb going off but publicise the plot, that will be the best of all possible worlds. I had a meeting with one of our supporters yesterday who has pledged a tidy sum of money to boost our coffers if we succeed with this project. I suggest that Jonathan and Karen go back out to The Skipton Arms tonight for one more memory trace on Donnelly. Are you up for that? Jonathan? Karen?"

Both said they were.

"We'll meet here again at ten thirty tomorrow morning," said Mac. "Everyone agreed on that?"

There was a general nodding of heads in agreement. Mac continued, "I'll send the car round to the St. Katharines flat, same as last night. Roger, keep an eye on Donnelly from the control centre, just in case he makes a move."

"I've got to go into my office for a while," said Karen. "So, if that's all I will head out now."

The meeting broke up and Jonathan caught the tube back to Tower Hill. He bought a sandwich on the way and after he had eaten his lunch, he lay on the bed and took an afternoon nap.

Just before eight that evening Jonathan and Karen were back at The Skipton Arms. They sat at a different table than the night before, hoping to minimize the chance that Donnelly might recognize them. They watched as the pub gradually filled with people but there was no sign of Donnelly. They nursed their drinks for nearly an hour and then Jonathan got up and bought more drinks.

"I suppose we might as well enjoy our drinks if he's not going to turn up," said Jonathan as he placed the drinks on the table.

"I'm going to give Roger a call and let him know," said Karen. "Perhaps he knows where Donnelly is."

She made the call. "We have not tracked him anywhere," said Roger. "His car is still parked outside his house so we think he is probably still at home."

"Are you still at the office?" said Karen.

"Yes, I'll be staying all night to keep an eye on Donnelly. I've got a camp bed here that I can doss down on. I want to make sure Donnelly doesn't get away during the night."

"We'll see you at ten thirty in the morning unless something happens during the night," said Karen.

Karen ended the call then said, "You might as well relax and enjoy your drink." She told Jonathan about the rest of the call.

"It's a damn pity that we couldn't do a memory trace on Donnelly tonight," said Jonathan. "It leaves us with a bloody great gap between now and when he blows the tunnel sky high next Monday, and we don't know where he is going to go to ground either. Somehow we need to get close enough to him to get another memory trace."

"Roger is keeping an eye on Donnelly tonight and we can discuss our strategy with Mac tomorrow morning," said Karen. "Enjoy your drink and mull over the problem."

"Cheers!" said Jonathan and he took a long drink, finishing his pint of beer. "I could do with another one of those. Same again for you?"

"I'm not driving. Make it a large one!"

When they had finished their drink, Karen called for the car and they were taken back to the St. Katharines flat.

They were woken up at seven thirty next morning by a sharp knock on each of their bedroom doors from Mac. He cooked fried eggs and sausages and brewed a pot of coffee while Karen and Jonathan got washed and dressed.

"Roger tells me that Donnelly was a no show yesterday evening," said Mac as they sat around the dining table enjoying their breakfast.

"It seems to me that we have a big hole in our information between now and when he detonates the bomb," said Jonathan. "It would also be nice to know where he is going to go after the attack."

"I really want to avoid the bomb actually exploding, so I need to find out how he plans to detonate the bomb and stop him. Anyway, we can talk about this in Roger's office. I'll call a taxi while you two finish your breakfasts. At least the good news is that Donnelly has not moved his car overnight."

They shared the taxi to Roger's office. Mary was brewing a fresh pot of coffee as they arrived. "Go on through," she said. "I think he's awake. I'll bring the coffee through in a minute."

Roger was awake and in fact, he was just finishing shaving with an electric razor that he kept in a desk drawer for just such occasions.

"Good morning, crew," said Roger with a broad smile. "Let's get settled." He gestured towards the conference table. They were all seated when Mary brought the coffee through. "Mac, can you bring us up to date with where we are and what we know?"

"We know his plan is to detonate a bomb in the tunnel north of Kings Cross station sometime next Monday. We don't know what time of day but we can safely assume that it will be during the small hours between Monday and Tuesday, because he has been told to avoid killing people. There are fewer trains overnight."

"What information are we still missing?" said Karen.

"Pretty much everything before and after the detonation," said Mac. "We don't know how he is going to get the explosives and we don't know where he is going to build the bomb. We don't know where he is going to hide out after the attack, except it will probably be overseas."

"Today is Friday, so if he is going to blow up the tunnel on Monday, he needs to start getting his act together soon," said Jonathan. "I really need to get another memory trace out of him."

"I can make some reasonable assumptions based on his methods in Ireland," said Mac. "I am pretty sure he is not keeping explosives in the house. That's not his style."

"What is his style?" said Roger. "What do you expect him to do?"

"I expect the bomb will be detonated by mobile phone," said Mac. "He will be miles away when the bomb goes off. I also expect he will get his explosives from his mates in the Republic of Ireland. Of course he might steal them from somewhere here in the UK."

"Where from?" said Jonathan.

"Quarries are a good bet," said Mac. "They usually have a lot of explosives and they are not always too careful with their security,"

"Everything I have heard here tells me that we need to stick to Donnelly like glue," said Roger.

"Jonathan and I should get out on the road," said Mac "and at least get out around the Willesden area to be ready to follow him when he moves."

"You can use my car," said Roger, "but I think you should wait until he actually makes a move."

Chapter 29

"You're right, Roger. We'll wait," said Mac.

"I don't think you'll have to wait long," said Karen who had left the conference table and walked over to the control centre. "He's just walked out of his house and put a suitcase in the car." Karen was watching the image from the CCTV camera at the end of Sean's street. Everyone came over and stood behind her, looking at the screen above her head, which carried the same image as on her computer screen. After a few moments, they saw Sean Donnelly step out of his house, open the driver's door of his car and get in.

"Lights! Camera! Action!" said Roger. On one of the other large screens, Karen brought up a map of the Willesden area. The ANPR system showed Sean's car as a bright, white, flashing dot on the screen. Every few seconds the dot jumped to a new location as Sean's car moved into the range of a different CCTV camera.

"It doesn't show the exact position of his car," said Karen as she turned towards Jonathan, "just the last time a camera saw him."

As they all watched, the tracking dot moved away from its original position and started moving eastward through Willesden. The group continued watching intently as the white dot continued its halting progress.

"Do you think he knows that we are watching him?" said Jonathan.

"Probably not," said Roger. "If he did he would use back roads and we would lose him. Back roads don't have as many cameras."

"He's turning north on the Edgware Road," said Mac. "He's going to go up the M1." The M1 was a motorway that ran north from London to the north of England.

"Right, Jonathan. Let's hit the road," said Mac. "We'll head out on the M1 and catch up with him. Roger, stay in touch on the mobile. I'll also have Jonathan track Sean on the laptop while we are in the car. Don't lose him!"

"You can use my car," said Roger. "You don't have time to rent a car."

"Keep us on your tracking screen, Karen," said Mac as he and Jonathan pulled on their overcoats. Roger threw his car keys to Mac.

"Take care," said Roger, "and don't bend the Beemer".

Mac and Jonathan stepped out of the office and closed the door. They took the lift to the underground car park and Mac led Jonathan to Roger's silver BMW. They got in, Mac driving, and he reversed out of the parking space. They emerged onto Horseferry Road and Mac turned right. He drove up Park Lane to Marble Arch and then he was on the Edgware Road, which would lead him directly to the start of the M1.

"Give Karen a call," said Mac. "Tell her we will be on the M1 north bound in ten minutes. Find out what's going on."

Jonathan put the phone on speaker so that Mac could hear the conversation, then he dialled Karen's number. When Karen answered, he passed on their position information then said, "How's the tracking?"

"Sean turned onto the M1 north bound about five minutes ago," said Karen.

"How fast is he going?" said Jonathan.

"I'd estimate around sixty, maybe sixty five."

"OK, thanks, Karen. We'll stay in touch."

Jonathan ended the call then turned to Mac. "What do you think he's up to?"

"I'm not sure yet," said Mac. "If his target was in the middle of London, why would he be heading out into the country?"

"To collect something?" said Jonathan.

They were both quiet for a few minutes while they pondered the question as Mac threaded his way through the busy traffic. They had just reached the motorway and Mac was accelerating up to the speed limit when Jonathan was struck by a thought.

"Could he be collecting explosives?"

"Good thinking," said Mac. "When I worked in Northern Ireland, the bombers did not keep a stockpile of explosives in their homes in case they were searched. The collected explosives that were hidden south of the border each time they built a bomb."

Jonathan's mobile phone rang. He answered it and put it on speaker. It was Karen. "We are tracking you guys now," she said, "and you're about twenty miles behind Sean. He is still heading north"

"Thanks, Karen." Jonathan ended the call.

"I think we'll push up the speed a bit," said Mac. "If he turns off onto a country road he could be out of CCTV cover and we might lose him."

Mac increased his speed to eighty miles an hour. Even at that speed, the BMW was being overtaken by many vehicles. At that speed, they would probably catch up with Sean in about an hour. Mac dare not push his speed beyond eighty. The last thing he needed was to waste time getting pulled over by the police for speeding

For a long time the only sounds in the car were the roaring of the engine and the rumble of the tyres as the BMW ate up four miles every three minutes, closing the twenty mile gap between Sean and his pursuers by a mile every four minutes.

Jonathan spoke up: "I was just calculating that we are about sixteen miles behind Sean. What are we going to do when we catch up with him? Arrest him? Call the police?"

"He hasn't actually broken any laws yet," said Mac. "I want to follow him from a safe distance and see what he does. He may lead us to other people."

"If both Sean and us stay on the road and stay at this speed," said Jonathan, "we should be caught up with him in about an hour. Of course he could speed up or turn off this road at any time."

"Let's keep our fingers crossed that luck is on our side," said Mac.

They drove on through a grey winter's afternoon, closing in on Sean.

"I expect he will need to stop for fuel at some point," said Mac, "or at least to stretch his legs. I'd like to catch up with him before he does that. I've got a sneaking suspicion where he might be going, or at least the general area, and I don't want to lose him."

"Where do you think he's going?"

"Let's leave that open for now," said Mac. "Why don't you check in with Karen and see how things are going back at base?"

Jonathan dialled Karen's number.

"Hello Jonathan! How goes it?"

"Gaining on him steadily, we hope," said Jonathan.

"We are tracking him on the M1," said Karen. "He's maintaining about sixty miles an hour. You're about twelve miles behind him."

Mac shouted over towards the phone. "Call us straight away if you see him turn off the road or if you lose him."

"Will do," said Karen.

Jonathan ended the call.

They drove on in silence. Jonathan was calculating their progress in his head as they slowly closed the gap. Ten miles. Nine miles. Eight miles. Every four minutes another mile ticked off. Eventually there were just two miles separating them from Sean's vehicle.

"Two miles, by my reckoning," said Jonathan. "I'm going to check with Karen." He called Karen's number.

"Yes, I think he's about two miles ahead of you," said Karen.

"We'll close up another mile and then stay behind him," said Jonathan.

"If he stays on the motorways we will be able to track him but if he turns off onto local roads it will be a lot more difficult," said Karen. "You'll have to try to get close enough to follow him visually."

"Stay in touch. We'll close up on him," said Jonathan. He looked over at Mac for approval and Mac nodded. Jonathan ended the call.

Within a couple of minutes Jonathan saw a car up ahead that looked like the car he had seen in Willesden on CCTV, the gold coloured Renault 307. Soon they were just a hundred yards behind the Renault and Mac dropped his speed to maintain that distance.

"There are some binoculars in my bag," said Mac. "Pull them out, would you?"

Jonathan reached over to Mac's bag on the back seat and after rummaging around for a while, he found the binoculars.

"Can you see the registration number from this distance?" said Mac.

Jonathan put the binoculars to his eyes and adjusted the focus. He checked the registration against the note that Karen had written for him. "That's him."

"Good! We'll keep him in sight. Give Karen another call and give her an update."

Jonathan called Karen again. "We've got him visual now, Karen. We are staying a hundred yards back."

"Good work!" said Karen. "We'll continue tracking him for as long as we can. Our tracking is showing you right on top of him. Be careful!"

Mac was letting other vehicles pull in between him and Sean's car from time to time, to try to avoid Sean suspecting that he was being followed.

The winter sun had now set and the motorway was dark although a full moon rising in the east provided hope that Mac and Jonathan might have a bright moonlit night.

As they motored on, Sean maintained his route along the M1, but there was a maze of possible routes around Birmingham, the city at the centre of England, and Sean could head off in almost any direction. Mac and Jonathan just had to keep him in sight and see where the pursuit took them.

Still following a hundred yards behind, Mac and Jonathan approached another major junction, which might clarify Sean's intended route. Sean took the M6 west towards Birmingham rather than the alternative northerly direction, which would have taken Sean further towards northern England or even Scotland.

"I think I know where he's going," said Mac, "I'd bet he is heading for Wales"

"Why Wales, Mac?"

"Let's see if you can work it out. What is the name of the body of water to the west of Wales?"

"The Irish Sea?"

"Right, and beyond that?"

"Ireland?"

"Exactly! I'll bet you he is going to meet up with someone who has come over from Ireland with his explosives. He's on a trip to pick them up."

"Now I see it", said Jonathan.

"I've been in the intelligence business a long time. You develop a sixth sense about these things."

The pursuit continued. Sean continued west on the M6 passing around the north of Birmingham, then Mac and Jonathan followed him as he turned towards Wales on the M54.

"Look!" said Mac. "He's turning off!"

Sean's car had its left turn indicator flashing and he pulled off the motorway into Corley service area. Still keeping a safe distance, Mac followed Sean's car into the service area. As with all motorway service areas in England, there were two distinct areas. As vehicles entered the service area there was a road which ran directly to the fuel filling station so that people who just needed to stop for fuel could proceed straight back to the motorway and continue their journey. A second area was for travellers who wanted to take a longer break. This area had a large car park, restaurants, and shops. There was a direct road to this area, bypassing the fuel filling station and there was a loop road back to the car park for those who needed fuel and a break from driving.

Mac stopped a couple of dozen yards back from the fuelling area as Sean's car pulled up on the right side of a fuelling island.

"I'm betting he will pay cash," said Mac. "That means he will have to go into the shop and pay the cashier rather than paying at the pump with a credit card."

"Why would he pay cash?" said Jonathan.

"Cards leave a trail."

Mac pulled forward and drew his car up to a fuelling island two over from where Sean was parked so that he could watch Sean's movements without being seen.

"Jonathan, here's my debit card. Get out and fill her up with premium, would you? But before you start would you hand me my bag, please?"

Jonathan got out, then retrieved Mac's bag from the back seat and put it on the front passenger seat from where Mac could reach it. Then Jonathan went to attend to the refuelling of the BMW. Mac reached into his bag and pulled out three items. The first was a laptop computer and the second was the computer's power supply. He placed both of these items on the seat beside the bag. He then returned to the bag and drew out the third item. It was a plastic box, coloured brown and about the same size and shape as a box of cigarettes. On top of the box was a shiny metal disk.

Mac got out of the car and stood behind it where he could see Sean clearly. He watched as Sean walked over to the shop to pay for his fuel. As soon as Sean's back was turned, he ran over the Sean's car and crouched behind it. Using the magnetized disk, he attached the plastic box to the underside of Sean's car where it could not be seen unless Sean crawled under the vehicle. Mac stood up, dusted off his knees and walked nonchalantly back to the BMW. When he got there, Jonathan had just finished refuelling and he handed to debit card over to Mac.

Mac kept his back to Sean's car and said, "Jonathan, keep an eye on that car and let me know when he moves off and which way he goes. He could loop back to the shops but I suspect he will get back on the road. Tell me if he is carrying anything when he comes out of the shop."

Mac opened the driver's door and lifted his bag over into the back seat. He placed the laptop computer and power supply into the passenger foot well and then closed the driver's door and stood up.

"He's coming out now and he's carrying a brown paper bag," said Jonathan. "Now he's getting into his car and he's heading back onto the motorway."

"Good!" said Mac. "Let's go and take a bio break and pick up some sandwiches. I can't do a pursuit on an empty stomach and I missed lunch."

"Are you going to let him get away?"

"He won't get far!"

Leaving the car at the fuel pump, they walked over to the shop and after a bathroom break, they selected a couple of sandwiches and a couple of soft drinks each and went to pay for them.

On the way back to the car, Jonathan said, "You seem very relaxed about this pursuit, Mac."

"I put one of my little toys into operation. He has a GPS tracker stuck on the bottom of his car. It sends a signal by satellite to the control centre in Horseferry Road."

"So they can keep us informed about where he is?"

"Better yet. I've got a link from the control centre to my laptop and we can see where he is in real time."

By now, they had reached the car. "Be careful getting in," said Mac. "I put the laptop on the floor in front of your seat."

Jonathan climbed carefully into the passenger seat and picked up the laptop. He plugged one end of the power cable into the car's cigarette lighter outlet and the other into the laptop. Mac handed him the bag of sandwiches and drinks and Jonathan placed the bag on the floor in front of him. Mac started the car and moved off, away from the fuel pump and the bright lights of the filling station and out into the darkness of the road.

"Get that computer fired up," said Mac as he accelerated the BMW to join the motorway traffic, "then call Karen and tell her we have put a tracker on Sean's car."

Jonathan did as Mac had asked. When Karen answered, he said, "We just got on the road again and we put a tracker on Sean's car."

"I know," said Karen. "It just appeared on our display. Can you ask Mac to turn on the BMW tracker for me so I can keep an eye on you?"

Mac heard the request on the speaker and pressed a button on the dashboard. A red light appeared showing that the car in which Jonathan and Mac were travelling was now sending a GPS tracking signal to Karen in the control centre.

"We've got you," said Karen. "Have you got any idea what Sean is up to?"

Jonathan looked over at Mac who shook his head. "Nothing yet, but we're working on it" said Jonathan.

"Keep safe out there," said Karen.

Jonathan ended the call. By now, the laptop had started up and its screen glowed brightly in the darkness of the car.

"Now click on the GPS tracker icon," said Mac.

Jonathan clicked and after a few seconds, a screen opened showing a map of the whole of the United Kingdom from the Shetland Islands in the far north to the Scilly Isles in the far southwest. After a few more seconds, two white dots appeared, very close together and roughly in the middle of England.

Intuitively, Jonathan clicked on one of the dots and the map image zoomed in to a more detailed map, with Bristol in the southwest corner and Newcastle upon Tyne in the northeast. Jonathan clicked again twice and the map now showed the tangle of motorways and highways around Birmingham.

"Right, which way did he go?" said Mac.

Jonathan studied the map. The dot representing Sean's car was still progressing west on the M54 towards Wales. Jonathan reported the position to Mac.

"I'm glad we had a chance to get that tracker on Sean's car," said Mac. "This modern technology makes pursuits so much easier."

Jonathan laughed. "Takes some of the fun out of it though?"

"I'd like to say it balances the odds a bit better," said Mac. "Could you hand me a drink and a sandwich?"

Jonathan closed the laptop lid and picked up the bag. He passed a sandwich and a drink to Mac, and got the same for himself.

Jonathan opened the laptop again. When they had left the service area, Sean had gained about ten miles ahead of them but now they had halved that distance as Mac maintained a steady eighty miles an hour, ten miles an hour above the legal speed limit. Jonathan's phone rang. It was Roger.

"I've taken over the watch from Karen," said Roger. "I reckon he is going to head out west on the A5 and head into mid Wales.

"Wales was our thinking too," said Jonathan. "Do you need to speak with Mac?"

"No, let him concentrate on the driving. I gave Karen a few hours rest. I have a feeling we're going to be working late tonight. Keep on Sean's tail, Jonathan."

"Keep an eye on that screen," said Mac. "I think he's going to make a straight shot for the coast. We'll only average about forty miles an hour on that part of the route."

As Jonathan watched the screen, it slowly scrolled to keep the two dots towards the right of the screen and the road across Wales to the coast spread out towards the left. Sean's car remained about four miles ahead, slowed by the narrow, winding roads.

"It's a pity it is dark," said Mac, "This is a really pretty part of the world."

The next significant navigational point was Shrewsbury, a typical market town, serving the farming community surrounding it. From there, there were no more significant towns until Aberystwyth, on the coast of Wales, just a few small villages as the road wound its way across Wales.

Jonathan kept watch on the dots, moving westward in unison, five miles apart. There was very little traffic in either direction on the road. Jonathan felt he was in the middle of nowhere. "Do you want me to give you a rest from driving, Mac?"

"I'm all right for now," said Mac. "Perhaps you can drive us home. This road is hard work after the motorway!"

"Yes, tracking these white blobs is mesmerizing too! Let's have another drink. I need the caffeine to keep me awake!"

"Me too!" said Mac and he laughed. Jonathan pulled two more cans out of the paper bag and passed one to Mac.

Eventually, after two and half long hours of rather uneventful driving, the computer map showed Sean's car approaching the coastal town of Aberystwyth. Here he had a choice of turning either north or south. The computer map showed Jonathan and Mac still five miles behind.

"You might want to zoom in a bit more so you can track him through the streets of the town," said Mac.

Jonathan clicked on one of the white blobs a couple of times and the map revealed the detail of the streets of Aberystwyth. Sean skirted around the southern edge of the town and turned south on the coastal road. Jonathan gave another situation report to Mac.

"He's probably going to pull off this road somewhere," said Mac. "Keep a close eye on him."

As Mac turned the car south onto the coast road, the full moon illuminated the sea to their right. After their long drive across Wales, it was refreshing to be on the coast road as it followed the edge of the Cardigan Bay and the Irish Sea.

They had travelled about sixteen miles south along the coast when Jonathan saw that Sean's car had stopped and the BMW was now only two miles north of Sean's position.

"We need to close up in stealth mode," said Mac. "No lights. Then we'll get out and walk the last half mile. We can hide the car in the sand dunes. With this moonlight, we'll have to be really careful not to be seen. Bring the binoculars."

Mac turned off the lights on the BMW but the bright moonlight made it possible to continue slowly along the coast road until they were about half a mile north of Sean's position. Mac turned right off the road and toward the ocean and pulled the car to a halt between two sand dunes.

Sean's car was about fifty feet closer to the ocean than the BMW, and it was parked near what appeared to Mac and Jonathan to be a boathouse. Sean got out of his car and walked towards the boathouse as he was watched from the BMW. Sean reached into his pocket. Jonathan focussed the binoculars again and saw that Sean was holding a set of keys. Sean walked to the back of the boathouse, farthest away from the ocean, and unlocked it and stepped inside, closing the door behind him.

"Let's get out of the car and move forward a bit," said Mac. "Bring the binoculars."

"He might see us in this bright moonlight," said Jonathan.

"He's only likely to spot us if we are moving or if we break the skyline. Anyway, there's some clouds blowing in from the west and that will give us a better cover."

They got out of the car and very quietly closed the door then they crawled behind the dunes and moved forward very carefully, hiding behind each dune until they were at the top of the beach. They were now at the level of the beach hut, which was about fifty yards away to the south. They crawled up a dune and were careful to keep hidden by the tufts of grass that sprouted from the top. Mac silently signalled for Jonathan to pass over the binoculars and he looked over towards the boat house. There was no sign of movement. The wind was strengthening from the west and at the water's edge, the surf was becoming noisier.

"How come he had the keys to the boathouse? For that matter, how did he know the boathouse just happened to be here?" said Jonathan in a whisper.

"Sean's a very meticulous operator," whispered Mac. "He will have rehearsed this exercise a couple of times and he would have taken a Plasticine impression of the lock and made a duplicate key."

Suddenly the large double doors at the front of the boathouse swung open and a few moments later Sean emerged drawing a two-wheeled trailer on which was mounted what looked like an open boat, about twelve feet long. There was an outboard motor mounted on the stern of the boat. Sean pulled the boat and trailer clear of the boathouse and closed the front doors, then he emerged from the back door, which he locked. He then walked over to his car and lifted a black package out of the boot. He carried the package over to the boat and threw it into the craft.

Sean looked around, looking along the beach in either direction, looking at the sand dunes to the north and south of the boathouse. Mac and Jonathan pushed themselves close to the sand, to avoid being spotted.

Apparently satisfied that he was not being watched, Sean picked up the trailer again and wheeled it around so that the stern was now facing the sea. He then pushed the trailer down the short beach and into the water.

Mac was observing this procedure through the binoculars while Jonathan was looking out to sea. Suddenly, Jonathan tapped Mac's shoulder.

"I think there are lights out there at sea," said Jonathan quietly.

Mac turned his binoculars in the direction that Jonathan had pointed. "You're right. He's got a rendezvous with that trawler."

"Picking up explosives?" said Jonathan.

"I'd put money on it," said Mac.

"Do you want to try and stop him?"

"Not at this stage. I want to get as much information from Sean as I can."

There was the sound of an outboard motor and they both looked up to see Sean jumping into the stern of the boat and steering it straight out to sea through the surf that was breaking in the shallow water near the beach.

"I think we've probably got an hour or two to relax now," said Mac. "Are there any sandwiches left in the car?"

"Yes, there are. Do you want me to fetch them?"

"No, let's get in the car and warm up a bit."

Mac and Jonathan stood up and stretched, then they walked back through the dunes to the car. Just before getting in, Mac took another look out to sea through his binoculars, then got into the car. Jonathan was already in the car and was pulling sandwiches and drinks from the brown paper bag.

"So what's the plan now?" said Jonathan.

"We'll wait for him to come back from the trawler. Then I think he will head back towards London, probably on a different route. Now we've got the GPS tracker on him we should have no trouble following him."

"If you want to take a nap for a while, I'll keep watch," said Jonathan. "I'll get out of the car for a while and give Roger an update if you like"

"Thanks, Jonathan. An hour's shuteye will do me good. Then I'll keep watch and you can get some sleep."

Jonathan got out of the car and called Roger to update him on the last hour's events, then he walked down to the waterline and looked out to sea through the binoculars. The trawler was still in the same position. He estimated that it was about four miles offshore. No doubt the trawler would be appearing on a radar scope somewhere, but the vessel was perfectly legal. Sean's boat was probably too small to be picked up by radar.

The clouds had thickened considerably since they had first arrived and now the full moon was only visible through the occasional break in the clouds. The sea and the beach, which had previously been bathed in a bright silver light, were almost hidden in the gloom and the sand dunes appeared as dark smudges at the top of the beach. The wind had picked up considerably too, and the sound of the surf crashing on the beach was much louder.

Jonathan pulled up the collar of his overcoat and walked back up the beach to where the car was parked. As he approached the car, he saw that Mac had reclined his driver's seat and appeared to be sleeping. Jonathan set the alarm on his mobile to one hour and as quietly as he could he climbed into the car and sat in the front passenger seat alongside Mac.

Jonathan started to feel sleepy after just a quarter of an hour sitting in the car. He decided he would have to spend most of his shift outside if he were to stay awake. No doubt, he would be able to sleep when they got back on the road. He climbed out of the car and quietly closed the door. He thought the best way to pass the time and to stay alert would be to walk back and forth along the beach, about two hundred yards each way. Periodically he scanned the sea with his binoculars. The lights of the trawler remained stationary offshore, but he could see no other signs of activity.

He jumped when the alarm on his mobile went off, but he gathered his thoughts quickly and shut off the alarm. He walked back to the car and had almost reached it when he heard the sound of an outboard motor. He scuttled behind a sand dune and looked out towards the surf. He saw the boat just as it grounded itself at the water line. The outboard motor soon cut out, but there was no one aboard. Jonathan scanned left and right along the water line, but there was no sign of Sean.

Jonathan ran back to the car and tapped on the driver's window. Mac stirred from his sleep and Jonathan pulled the door open.

"What's up?" said Mac, rather sleepily.

"The boat is back, but no sign of Sean."

Mac climbed out of the car, and took the binoculars offered by Jonathan. He scanned the beach and looked out to sea. The trawler's lights were no longer visible.

"Sean is not in the boat," said Mac. "He might have fallen out, which I rather doubt. He might have stayed on the trawler, but then why send the boat back to shore? He could have easily sunk it or even dragged it aboard the trawler."

Mac made another scan of the beach with the binoculars. "He's not on the beach. Let's go down to the boat and see what we can find."

Mac and Jonathan walked down the beach to the boat. It was completely empty except for some water, swilling around in the bottom of the boat as it gently rocked in the surf.

A car engine roared into life and headlights illuminated the beach. Mac pulled Jonathan down onto the sand in the shadow of the boat. The car swung towards the coast road and the beach was once again plunged into darkness. Mac stood up and helped Jonathan to his feet. Their clothes were wet and peppered with sand.

"Damn! He must have swum ashore," said Mac.

They walked up the beach to where the car had been. There was a heap of black clothing, which Jonathan picked up.

"A wet suit," said Jonathan. "You're right, he swam ashore. But why?"

"Probably to make sure he wasn't being followed," said Mac.

"If he had swum ashore in a black wetsuit, no one would see him and he would have been able to make a run for it if he had seen us. As I told you, Sean is a pretty cool operator. Let's get back to our car and get after him."

They walked through the dunes and past the boathouse and reached their car. They both made an effort to brush the sand off their clothes but with the clothes still damp, it was not a very successful exercise.

"I'll get Roger's car cleaned when we get back," said Mac as he got in.

"Get that laptop started up again, and let's see what direction he went."

Mac started the car, turned it around to face the road, and waited with the engine running while Jonathan got the computer started and brought up the tracking software. It seemed to take an age while everything started up, but eventually two white dots appeared on the screen.

"He's headed south on the coast road," said Jonathan, "about five miles down the road from where we are."

Mac spun the wheels in the sand as he put the BMW into gear and pulled out onto the coast road, turning right to follow Sean.

It was not long before the road turned inland, away from the coast and was now passing through the low coastal hills.

"Give Roger an update, would you?" said Mac.

Jonathan called and the phone was answered by Karen.

"I couldn't sleep so I came back in," she said. "What's the latest?"

Jonathan related the evening's events so far including Sean's trip to the trawler and his spectacular departure.

"I think Sean's pretty obviously on his way back to London by a southern route, probably the M4," said Karen. "If you guys want to pull off and get some breakfast, we'll make sure we keep an eye on him."

"We'll let you know," said Jonathan, and he ended the call.

"What do you think, Mac?"

"I'm pretty sure he picked up explosives from that trawler," said Mac. "There could be no other reason for him going out there. He wouldn't want to assemble the bomb and then transport it a long distance, so he's probably going to assemble it somewhere in London just before he places it."

By now, Sean had turned onto a road that wound through the hills of south Wales. He was on the road to a town called Carmarthen from where he could head east towards London, just over two hundred miles away. He continued to drive in an exemplary manner, even more important now that he had a hundred pounds of explosives in the boot of his car. He was feeling tired now, as were his pursuers. It would be getting light soon and that time of half-light was always a bad time for falling asleep at the wheel.

"He will have to take a break soon," said Mac. "It would make a hell of a mess if he crashed with what he's got on board! As long as we stay within half an hour or so of him, I think we will be OK. He's got to get some sleep before he starts assembling that bomb."

"Don't forget I would like to get close to Sean to try to pick up another memory trace," said Jonathan.

"There's a service area right at the start of the M4, a place called Port Abraham," said Mac. "Let's see if he stops there. If he does, he will almost certainly go into the restaurant to grab some breakfast and you might be able to catch him in there. There's another service area at Bridgend, about thirty minutes farther on."

Jonathan called Karen to tell her what the plan was. After he ended that call, he looked at the tracking screen on the laptop and saw that Sean was indeed stopping at the Port Abraham service area. When the BMW reached the start of the motorway about five minutes later, Mac increased the speed to eighty miles an hour until he reached the service area, where he pulled off into the car park.

"I am just going to use the toilets and the shop and then I'll come back to the car," said Mac. "I don't want to risk Sean recognizing my face."

Jonathan walked into the restaurant. It was a self-service arrangement and at this time of day, it was serving hot and cold breakfast items. He spotted Sean serving himself a full cooked breakfast and he waited until Sean had paid for his food and taken his tray to a table. With luck, Jonathan thought, Sean will be here for a good thirty minutes, which should be enough time to get a memory trace.

Jonathan went over to the counter and served himself a full breakfast of sausages, fried eggs, toast and baked beans. When he had paid for his meal, he selected a table giving him a clear view of Sean. He caught eye contact with Sean and put Sean's brain into seizure, confirmed by Sean's glazed eyes staring straight ahead.

Jonathan thought of some keywords. "Explosives." and "Kings Cross". The memory stream started to flow.

I phone my friend Michael O'Leary in Dublin.

"Michael," I say. "I need a package for a job over here."

"Sure," says he, "When do you want it?"

"Tomorrow night would be good," I say. "I'm sorry for the rush but it's a special job and the client doesn't want to wait. I don't want to upset this client, they could make a lot of trouble for us."

"There's a boat going out of Waterford tomorrow morning and I can get the package on that one for you," says he. "Usual pick up point?"

Usual pick up point is three miles off the coast of Aberaeron, just south of Aberystwyth.

"I'll be there at midnight tomorrow," I say.

"What size package do you want?" says he.

"Two kilos, usual terms" I say.

"Payment before shipment," he says.

"I will send the cash by express mail today," I say. "You should get it tomorrow morning before you ship the package."

"You've got a deal," says he.

I will drive over to Aberaeron to meet the trawler. I will leave after lunch tomorrow. When I get the package back to London I will get some sleep and then I will take it out to one of the deserted places to put the units together.

The memory stream faded out.

Jonathan made some hurried notes then took a couple of bites of his breakfast and a sip of tea. He looked over to where Sean was sitting quietly eating his own breakfast. Jonathan had some good information but he needed another memory trace from Sean and he did not know if there was going to be another chance to be this close to him.

He started again, putting Sean into another seizure and thinking of keywords. "Escape." "Detonation."

I am at home in Willesden. The telephone rings and it is Grendan West.

"The first half of your payment is in your bank account," says he. "I transferred it this morning."

"Thank you," I say.

"Now listen carefully," says he. "You are to deliver the package to its final location at midnight on Saturday. After you have delivered the package, you are to drive overnight to York. You are to leave the company car in the York railway station car park and we will deal with it. Then you are to catch the eight o'clock train to Newcastle on Sunday morning. You will catch the afternoon ferry from Newcastle to Bergen. You are to detonate the package at midnight on Sunday when you are halfway across the North Sea. When you arrive in Bergen, you should lose yourself in Norway for exactly two months. You are to return to Newcastle on the boat that leaves Bergen on March 21st and your car will be waiting for you at the Newcastle Ferry Terminal car park."

I am making notes so I will remember everything exactly. Grendan West ends the call.

Once again, the memory trace faded out but Jonathan had all the information he needed. He quickly wrote down notes of the memory trace and then finished off the remainder of his breakfast Sean was finishing his coffee as Jonathan left the restaurant. He walked back to the car where he found Mac taking a nap. Mac jumped as Jonathan tapped gently on the window. Rubbing his eyes, Mac opened the window.

"How did it go in there?" said Mac.

Jonathan said nothing and just opened the notebook at the pages he had written and handed the notebook to Mac. While Mac read the notes, Jonathan walked round the car to the passenger door and got in.

"Excellent work, Jonathan," said Mac. "We don't need to track Sean back to London. We can pick up the trail when he goes out to assemble the bombs this evening. Let's head home and grab some sleep before the real action starts." He started the engine and drove out of the car park to join the motorway and continue his journey eastwards through South Wales.

The day had dawned cloudy but dry and cold, exactly the kind of weather that Mac enjoyed when he was driving. He crossed from Wales into England over the magnificent Severn Bridge. About fifty minutes after passing Swindon, Mac was reaching the outer suburbs of London and he nudged Jonathan awake.

"Call Karen and let her know what we are doing."

Jonathan called Karen again and told her what they planned to do.

"I'm going to head back to the flat and get showered and changed."

Mac made a signal to Jonathan that he wanted to use the phone, and Jonathan handed it over.

"I don't think we need the control centre anymore," said Mac. "You and Roger can get some rest. We'll see you back at the flat."

Mac made his way back to the St. Katharines Way flat through the relatively light traffic of London on a Saturday morning. Jonathan kept an eye on the image of Sean's street on the laptop, but apart from a couple of delivery trucks and an elderly lady pulling a heavily-loaded shopping trolley, there was no activity of any note.

Mac pulled the BMW into the assigned parking space for the flat.

"Bring the laptop in with you," said Mac as he pulled his bag from the back seat. They walked together across to the front door and pressed the button for the flat, both being far too tired to look for their own key. The door buzzed and they entered the hallway. The lift doors opened and they stepped inside and soon they arrived at the flat. Karen greeted them with a laugh and a hug as they stepped into the flat.

"I've put clean clothes on your beds," said Karen. "Go jump in the shower and get changed, and I'll make some coffee and some sandwiches for lunch."

Neither Mac nor Jonathan needed any encouragement to do exactly what Karen suggested. Both emerged about twenty minutes later looking and feeling much better.

"Quite a night," said Karen as Mac and Jonathan sat on the stools at the kitchen counter and tucked into the variety of sandwiches that Karen had prepared. As they ate, Mac told Karen about what they had seen and what they had found out about Sean.

"So you think he will go out to wherever he is building the bomb tonight and then he will plant the bomb and make an escape," said Karen. I've been keeping an eye on the CCTV while you've been getting changed. No activity yet."

"I don't think he's going to move before dark," said Mac, "but if you can keep an eye on him this afternoon I think Jonathan and I ought to get some sleep."

"Sure, I'll keep an eye on him and I'll wake you up in about four hours," said Karen.

With that, Jonathan and Mac retired to their bedrooms and they both fell asleep immediately.

Chapter 30

Karen had been keeping an eye on the image of Sean's street all afternoon, but had not seen anything worth noting, certainly not anything worth disturbing Mac or Jonathan from their much needed rest. It was now early evening and she had just put the kettle on to make them cups of tea when she saw Sean walking down the driveway to his car, carrying what looked like a sports bag. He loaded it into the car and walked back into the house. Karen switched the computer over to tracking mode and went down the hall to the bedroom area of the flat, knocking loudly on the doors of Jonathan's bedroom and Mac's bedroom before going back to the kitchen counter to keep an eye on the tracking screen and finish making the tea. Mac and Jonathan emerged a few minutes later, still drowsy from their afternoon's sleep.

Karen looked at the tracking screen, and saw that Sean's car was still parked in his driveway. Jonathan and Mac sat at the kitchen counter and sipped their tea.

"He came out a few minutes ago with a sports bag and put it in the car, but the car hasn't moved," said Karen.

"I think we ought to head off in the general direction of Willesden, so we can follow him when he makes a move," said Mac.

"I've packed you some sandwiches and a thermos flask of coffee so you could get off right away," said Karen.

"Are we expecting another all-nighter?" said Jonathan.

"I really don't know what to expect," said Mac.

"We will need to refuel the BMW, so perhaps we better get started," said Jonathan as he picked up the carrier bag in which Karen had packed the refreshments.

"I'm ready," said Mac, and he walked over to the lift and pressed the button. "Thanks for all you are doing, Karen. Are you going over to the control centre tonight?"

"Yes, I'll be heading out in a few minutes. Roger has been there all day, and he could probably use a break. I'll call him in a minute and let him know you are back on the road."

The lift doors opened, and Mac and Jonathan stepped in.

"Good luck!" shouted Karen as the doors closed.

"You know," said Mac as they settled into the car, "I'm not going to struggle through that central London traffic. Its evening rush hour now. I'm going to head east and go out to the North Circular Road. Then if he gets moving we can quickly get out to the M25."

"I'll rely on your judgment for that," said Jonathan, who had started the laptop computer again. The tracking software was still showing Sean's car in his driveway in Willesden.

Mac drove the car out of the St. Katharines Way complex and he drove east, past the great News International building and paralleling the north bank of the River Thames. He drove on through the old docklands of London, now gentrified with luxury flats or covered with huge office blocks. He stopped to refuel the car in the east London community of Poplar.

"Has he moved yet?" said Mac, after he had pulled up alongside the petrol pumps.

"No, still there," said Jonathan.

Mac filled up the BMW's petrol tank and paid at the pump with his debit card. He climbed back into the driver's seat and drove out of the forecourt and onto the road. A couple of minutes later he turned left and started to head north, away from the river on a dual carriageway.

"OK, he's on the move," said Jonathan.

"Which way's he going?"

"It looks like he's heading north."

"Keep an eye on him."

Jonathan kept watch on the white dot that represented Sean's car.

"He's heading out north on the Edgware Road now."

Mac accelerated the BMW and in a couple of minutes, they reached the start of the M11, which would carry them out to the M25 London Orbital Road in less than ten minutes.

"Now he's turning east on the M25."

"Yes," said Mac, punching the air. "Now we can get him. In a few minutes, we'll be heading straight at him. Keep an eye on him in case he turns off."

Jonathan zoomed out the tracking map until he could see both Sean's car and the BMW on the same screen, on the right and left edges of the map. Mac steered the car onto the M25 west. Jonathan did a rough estimate of the distance between the cars.

"You are about forty miles from him at the moment, closing at about two miles per minute."

"What I am going to do is pull off at the next exit and stop and watch what he does. There's any number of places he could turn off. Let's just keep watching for now."

Mac slowed for the exit and pulled off the motorway. He drove a few yards along a country road, then he turned the car in the road to face back towards the motorway.

Jonathan was concentrating on the white dot as it slowly moved around the north of London in a clockwise direction. Junction after junction, Sean kept going on the M25, getting closer and closer to where Mac and Jonathan were waiting.

"Are we going to follow him once he passes this exit?"

"Yes," said Mac, "keep up your position reports."

"He's about fifteen miles away, still on the M25. Estimate he'll be here in fifteen minutes."

Mac and Jonathan sat in silence in the dark car, illumination coming from the laptop screen. After about ten minutes, Jonathan gave another report.

"He's at the last exit before this one, four miles, estimate four minutes."

Mac started the car and pulled it up to just near the ramp leading back onto the motorway.

"Let me know when he crosses this exit," said Mac, leaving the BMW engine idling.

After a couple of minutes, Jonathan said, "There he goes!"

Mac accelerated up the on ramp to the eastbound side of the motorway.

"What's his speed?" said Mac.

"About sixty. He's about a mile in front of us."

Mac dropped his speed back to sixty miles an hour to stay behind Sean's car. "I think he's going into Epping Forest to do his bomb making".

In the short time that he had been working with Mac, Jonathan had learned that Mac had almost a sixth sense for predicting peoples' movements. Jonathan did not know this area very well and he had certainly never been to Epping Forest.

"He's turned north on the M11," said Jonathan.

"If I'm not mistaken, he'll turn off at the next exit," said Mac. "I'm going to close up on him a bit because we might have trouble following him when he turns into the forest." With that, Mac accelerated up to eighty miles an hour.

Jonathan took the tracking map to maximum zoom, which showed him the tracks in Epping Forest. "He's leaving the motorway now at junction seven."

"I think we might have a problem," said Mac. "If we follow him too closely into the forest with our headlights on he will know he's being followed."

"Why not wait outside the forest and see where he goes," said Jonathan, "and then we could go in on side lights."

"I've got some night vision goggles in that bag back there," said Mac. "Pull them out, will you?"

Jonathan reached over to the back seat and rummaged around in Mac's bag until he found some heavy goggles. He pulled them out of the bag. "You've got all the toys, haven't you Mac?"

"Toys that I know how to get hold of. I also liberated a few useful items when I left MI5."

Jonathan looked down at the tracking screen. "He's pulled off the road and he's entering the forest now."

Mac turned off the motorway and into the road that ran alongside the north edge of the forest. It was an unlit country road. Thick cloud was obscuring the moon and darkness enveloped them as Mac pulled up at the side of the road and turned off the car's headlights.

"OK, navigator. Where's he going?" said Mac.

On maximum zoom, Jonathan could see the white dot representing Sean's car moving slowly along the forest roads and into the heart of the forest. Eventually the white dot stopped.

"Let's give him five minutes," said Mac, "he might just be checking his map."

After five long minutes, the dot had not moved. Mac put on his night vision goggles and started the car engine.

"Here goes," said Mac. "Give me directions left and right to get me close to where he stopped."

"Turn right here."

Mac turned right, off the road and onto a dirt road into the forest. He did not need his car lights with his night vision goggles but Jonathan could not see anything through the gloom. He hoped that Mac's night vision goggles were doing their job.

"In a hundred yards take the right fork."

Mac continued on at walking pace, the dirt road crunching beneath his tyres. As Mac took the right fork, Jonathan said, "In two hundred yards, turn right." Mac grunted an acknowledgement but his attention was focussed on the road ahead.

Mac turned right, as instructed, and Jonathan said, "He's about two hundred yards ahead, off to the left of this track." Mac crawled forward until Jonathan said, "OK, he's in the woods about a hundred yards to the left of us."

Mac stopped the car and shut off the engine.

"We'll have to go on foot from here," said Mac. "I think we ought to get the car off this track and hide it because he will probably come out this way when he leaves."

Mac pulled the car forward a few feet then reversed off the road and he stopped the car behind some bushes. He pulled off his night vision goggles and put them on the back seat.

"Are you ready," said Mac.

"I'm ready," said Jonathan.

They got out of the car, pulled their overcoats off the back seat, and put them on. They walked out of the bushes and across the dirt road and stood facing into the trees on the other side. As their eyes got used to the dark, they saw a gated entrance to what appeared to be a driveway to a house. Sean's Peugeot was parked outside, facing away from the house and there were lights on in the house.

Mac signalled Jonathan to stop. As they watched, they saw signs of movement inside the house.

"My guess is he's in there assembling his bomb," whispered Mac.

"What's our plan?" whispered Jonathan.

"We'll wait for the moment. It's not likely us two could stop him. I want to keep an eye on him and see what he leads us to.

"Do you think he's killed the owners of this place?"

"I doubt it. Sean is not much into close quarters murder. He's a bomb man. It's much more likely he's been keeping an eye on this place for a few weeks and knew that it would be empty tonight. Sean is meticulous with his research."

The few moments that Mac had planned to wait turned into two hours. There was no sign of Sean. After the first twenty minutes, Mac and Jonathan had found a fallen tree on which to sit and watch the house. Now they were both feeling cold and stiff. Jonathan checked his watch. "It's eleven o'clock. What the hell is he doing in there?"

"Trying to avoid blowing himself up, probably," said Mac.

As Mac spoke, the front door of the house opened, throwing a beam of light into the darkness of the front garden. Sean stepped out carrying a cardboard box, which he placed in his car. He then returned to the house and closed the front door.

Mac signalled Jonathan to follow him and they moved closer in, using the cover of the forest to make sure they couldn't be seen from the house or the driveway. Sean came out of the house again, this time empty handed, and got into his car. He started it up and drove away from the house and down the driveway. He turned left onto the road and disappeared from view. The lights were still on in the house and the front door was still wide open.

"Let's go in and see what he's left behind," said Mac. "Don't touch anything – we don't want to leave any fingerprints."

They walked up to the open front door and went inside. To their right was a sitting room with a brick fireplace and a luxurious patterned carpet. Ahead was the kitchen and Mac led the way there. The oven door was open and inside was a package consisting of four cardboard tubes, bound together with tape and on top of the tubes was bound a mobile phone.

"That's Sean's style," said Mac.

"I can smell gas!" said Jonathan.

"Run for it! He's probably going to blow that thing any moment."

They ran out through the front door and were about fifty yards from the house when they were both thrown to the ground by a huge explosion behind them.

Mac picked himself up after a few moments. He was stunned but otherwise unhurt. Jonathan slowly sat up.

"Are you OK?" said Mac.

" I suppose this is what they mean by a 'baptism of fire!'"

"I'll take that as a yes."

What was left of the cottage was engulfed in flames. There was enough of a clearing around the house that the flames were not reaching the trees.

"We need to get out of here," said Mac as he helped Jonathan to his feet. "We need to catch up with Sean and get away from this place before we have to start answering some awkward questions."

They both trotted down the driveway across, the road and into the bushes to where the BMW was parked. They quickly pulled off their overcoats and threw them in the back seat and jumped into the front of the car. Mac got the engine started, put on the headlights and drove off the way that they had come.

As they reached the road at the edge of the forest, Mac stopped the car and said, "All right, which way did he go?"

"He's back on the M11, southbound, heading in towards London."

"Call Karen and tell her what's happening. Keep me up to date on Sean's position."

Jonathan called Karen and told her about the explosion.

"Are you both all right?" said Karen.

"Yes, we're fine, shaken but not broken," said Mac.

"You boys take care," said Karen.

"We will. We'll call you later," said Jonathan and he ended the call and turned his attention back to the laptop and the tracking screen. He zoomed out from street level until he could see all of north London on the screen.

Mac started the car again and turned left. "He's still on the M11, headed south, inside the M25," said Jonathan. Mac rounded a curve in the road and his heart missed a beat. There was a police car half blocking the road, its blue lights flashing, almost blinding Mac as he slowed down.

"Don't say anything, Jonathan. I'll do the talking."

Mac lowered his window.

"Good evening, officer."

"Good evening sir. May I ask why you are on this road tonight?"

"We've just been called out."

"Called out, sir?"

"Yes, didn't you hear about the bomb that's been found at Kings Cross?"

"No sir, we're checking cars because there was an explosion in the forest a while back."

Mac pulled out his expired MI5 identification card, carefully placed a finger over the date and showed it to the police officer.

"Very well, sir, I understand. Do you need a police escort, sir?"

"I don't think so, officer. We really don't want to attract too much attention to ourselves."

"I completely understand, sir." The police officer stood to attention and saluted. "Have a good evening sir and good luck."

He indicated to another officer who pulled a traffic cone out of the way and Mac waved and drove on.

"I gotta get me one of those cards," said Jonathan.

Mac laughed. "That can probably be arranged. It won't get you into MI5 headquarters, but it is useful when you're dealing with a country bobby!"

"Let's get back to the business at hand," said Mac. "Where is he now?"

Jonathan turned his attention back to the screen. "He is still on the M11, but getting very close to the southern end."

Mac steered the BMW onto the M11.

"So he's about ten or fifteen minutes ahead of us," said Mac. "I would like to close up a bit."

"He's on the North Circular, heading west."

The North Circular was the old ring road around north London, before the M25 was built. The old road was mostly dual carriageway but it had traffic lights and roundabouts. With luck, Mac and Jonathan could close the gap between Sean and themselves.

"I know he's going for Kings Cross," said Mac, "but I'm not quite sure about where he's going to place the bomb. I'm not so familiar with Kings Cross. When I come down to London on the train, I usually come into Euston. He's going to hit the tunnel just north of the Kings Cross station, isn't he?"

"If that tunnel was damaged, it would cause mayhem with the trains on the East Coast Main Line for weeks."

"What's above those tunnels?"

"Houses and roads, I think."

"Where is he now?"

Jonathan studied the screen. "He's turning off at Edmonton, now going south towards Tottenham."

Mac steered the car through the complex flyover at the southern end of the M11 and turned onto the North Circular Road heading west. It was getting late in the evening and there was fairly light traffic.

"I know a short cut to Tottenham," said Mac. We can save some time." He turned off the North Circular and wound his way through the back streets of Walthamstow until he reached Tottenham.

"Where is he now, Jonathan?"

"About a mile ahead of us."

"Keep the reports coming,"

Jonathan zoomed in the map to show the city streets.

"Still going south, passing Stamford Hill."

A couple of minutes later, "Still going south, a mile ahead, passing Stoke Newington."

Mac increased his speed slightly and closed the gap a little more. They were now about half a mile behind Sean's car.

"He's turning off!" said Jonathan, and he increased the zoom level. "Now heading west, no, southwest. He's heading straight for the tunnels, going southwest on Seven Sisters Road, still heading southwest."

"Now he's on Camden Road, still going southwest. Still on Camden Road."

"Now turning left on York Way."

Less than a minute later, Mac made the same left turn onto York Way, which ran parallel to the tracks into Kings Cross.

"Keep a close eye on him, Jonathan, let me know as soon as he stops."

"Heading south on York Way, now turning right on Goods Way and turning right again into a dead end road. And he stopped."

Mac pulled up on Goods Way opposite the road that Sean had entered. It was an unnamed road that ran for about a quarter of a mile beside some industrial and warehouse units. It ended at some derelict land.

"We are now parked right above the Kings Cross tunnels," said Jonathan.

"Let's get out and walk up a bit closer to see what he's up to," said Mac. He grabbed his overcoat and night vision goggles. Jonathan got his overcoat and Mac locked the car.

They walked a few yards up the road and saw Sean's Peugeot parked ahead. Mac drew Jonathan into the shadows of an industrial unit. There was a large cylindrical structure on waste land a few yards further up the road, right next to where Sean's car was.

"What is that structure?" said Mac.

"It's a ventilation shaft from the tunnels, originally built to clear steam and smoke from the steam locomotives, but they left it there to clear diesel fumes."

Mac looked out again, up the road. Sean was climbing a set of iron rungs that were attached to the outside of the structure. He was wearing a rucksack on his back. He reached the top, climbed over the rim, and disappeared inside the structure.

Mac and Jonathan waited in the shadows.

"Can he get right down to the tracks?" said Mac.

"I don't think so," said Jonathan. "He'll have to drop the package from the bottom of the ladder inside the ventilation shaft."

While they had been talking, Sean had climbed out of the ventilation shaft and returned to his car. They watched as Sean turned his car around in the road and headed back down the road to Goods Way. He turned left and disappeared from sight.

"We'd better get back to our car and keep an eye on him," said Mac.

"I'll give Karen a call and update her," said Jonathan as they walked back down the road. He pulled out his mobile phone and called Karen's number.

"Hi Karen. Sean has planted his bomb."

"Well, I'm tracking him here, and it looks like he's heading back north."

"Mac and I will walk back to the car and see if we can put a plan together. Is Roger around?"

"He's just stepped out for a break. I expect he'll be back within half an hour. Do you want me to try and contact him?"

"No need, we'll call you again shortly."

Jonathan ended the call.

"Wouldn't a simple timer be easier and more reliable than a mobile phone for detonating the bomb?" said Jonathan. "After all, mobile phones can be traced."

"No, timers are very outdated with bomb makers these days. They are into mobile phone detonators now. Usually they text a code to the phone on the bomb, and the phone software reads the code. If it's the right one, the software closes a relay and sets off the detonator which then sets off the bomb. The phone on the bomb is blown to smithereens and the bomber destroys the mobile that he used to set off the bomb. They always use pay-as-you-go phones so it is impossible to trace them."

"Surely bomb disposal could just pull the phone off the bomb, or just switch the phone off?"

"You'd think so, but they sometimes have a booby trap so that if the phone power goes off it will close the relay and detonate the bomb."

They reached the car and got in.

Chapter 31

Once they were back in the car, Jonathan started up the laptop again and brought up the tracking screen.

"He's heading north on the Edgware Road," said Jonathan.

"Going out on the M1," said Mac. "He is going to dump the car at York and go the rest of the way on the train. He's following his instructions from Grendan West to the letter. He's been instructed to be on the eight o'clock train from York to Newcastle tomorrow morning. That train leaves London at six o'clock, that's in five hours time. Why don't we go back to the St. Katharine's flat and get showered and changed and maybe grab something to eat. Then we can be back here for the six o'clock train."

"Are we just going to let him get away?"

"We know exactly what his plans are. It will take him at least three and a half hours to get to York by train and then I expect he will sleep on a station bench for a couple of hours. Call Karen and ask her and Roger to meet us at the flat."

Jonathan made the call as Mac drove back to St. Katharines.

"I'm already back at the flat," said Karen. "Roger is on watch. I'll call him and tell him to shut up shop and come back here."

The traffic on the streets of London was very light at this time of night and it took Mac only twenty minutes to drive back to the flat.

When Mac and Jonathan stepped out of the lift into the living room of the flat, Karen and Roger were watching a film on late night television.

Karen stood up. "Do you guys want a drink?"

"I'd murder a cup of tea," said Jonathan.

"Me too," said Mac.

Karen went to brew the tea while Mac and Jonathan sank into the armchairs. Once Karen had served tea and biscuits to everyone, Mac spoke. "We decided to have a few hours rest before we head north to follow Sean. Thanks to Jonathan, we know exactly what Sean's plans are."

"I'm rather worried that the bomb that Sean has planted might go off before we catch up with him," said Karen.

"Very little chance of that," said Mac. "He is following Grendan West's instructions to the letter and West told him to explode the bombs remotely on Sunday night, so that's almost certainly what he is going to do."

"Do you want to try and catch a couple of hours sleep?" said Roger.

"We should probably lie down for an hour or two," said Mac.

"I'll give you a knock on your doors at five o'clock," said Karen. "Will you want any breakfast when you get up?"

"Toast and coffee works for me," said Mac. "We can get a proper breakfast on the train."

"Same here," said Jonathan.

Mac stood up. "I'll see you all at five o'clock" With that, he and Jonathan went to their bedrooms.

By five twenty next morning Mac and Jonathan were showered, dressed in fresh clothes and ready to leave the flat. "I checked the location of Sean's car before we left," said Karen as she drove them out to Kings Cross station "As we expected his car is parked at York railway station."

"It sounds like he is still behaving exactly to plan," said Mac. "Let's hope our luck holds out."

Mac and Jonathan both stepped out of the car and Karen drove off. They were just in time to buy their tickets and catch the six o'clock train to York.

"Two first class singles to Newcastle," said Mac, offering his debit card to the ticket clerk.

He picked up the tickets and turned to Jonathan. "I think we've earned a bit of luxury this morning."

"Thank you very much," said Jonathan.

They walked over from the ticket office to the departure board to check on their train's assigned platform then walked onto the platform to board their train. The first class section was at the rear of the train and they were soon seated comfortably in the armchairs that comprised the seating in first class on this service.

The train started moving, slowly picking up speed as it cleared the station, crossed over the maze of tracks and points and entered the tunnel north of the station.

Jonathan looked at Mac and said, "I hope he doesn't choose to detonate that bomb right now!"

"I think that his project is designed to avoid any injuries. Remember, its main purpose is to swing public opinion in favour of anti-terrorist legislation. If the plot ever came to light and they had actually killed people, there would be more than hell to pay."

An attendant came to their seats and they ordered a large cooked breakfast each with a pot of coffee to accompany the breakfasts.

The train had now accelerated to its normal cruising speed of two miles a minute yet the ride was smooth and quiet, especially in the first class section with its improved suspension and superior sound insulation.

"I think we've done enough driving to last us several days," said Mac as he stretched out his legs and leaned back in his seat.

They were just finishing their breakfasts as the train slowed down and stopped in Peterborough station. It had covered the first eighty-four miles of its journey in just forty-five minutes. After a stop of about two minutes, the train got underway again, accelerating smoothly to its cruising speed.

Mac's mobile phone rang and it was Roger.

"We've been looking at CCTV from your train," said Roger. "There are two men in coach number four, seats twenty-two and twenty-three, that look like they could be a couple of MI5 spooks. We thought you might want to check them out."

"We'll do that and get back to you," said Mac, and he ended the call. He relayed the information to Jonathan.

"Do you think they are after us?"

"I don't think so. Of course, they might be on a completely different case, but I'd like to check them out just the same. Let's take a look at them on the screen first."

Mac selected the train and the coach and brought up the CCTV images of the passengers in coach four. He zoomed into seats twenty-two and twenty-three and studied the faces of the two men sitting there. He clicked on each face in turn and viewed a pop up giving details of the person: name, age, occupation. In both cases, occupation was blank, but one of the names rang a bell somewhere. He looked again at the face. It was a long time ago. The face was much older.

"Yes!" said Mac. "James Whiteley. I worked with him on a mission in Scotland years ago. I thought he'd retired."

"Perhaps MI5 is using retired officers these days," said Jonathan.

"It might make some sense," said Mac. "Easy to deny if anything went wrong, good experience, pay by results rather than keeping them on the salary. It could make a lot of sense."

"Who's the other guy?" said Jonathan.

"I don't recognize him."

"What should we do about them?"

Mac pondered the situation for a moment, then said, "I don't dare go up there in case Whiteley recognizes me. Can you take a stroll up there and perhaps do a memory trace without them noticing?"

"I'll see what I can do," said Jonathan as he stood up. He walked forward in the train until he reached coach number four. There were very few passengers in the coach on this early morning service, and Jonathan quickly spotted the two MI5 guys that he was looking for. They were seated either side of a table and there were newspapers and coffee cups spread out on the table between them. They both appeared to Jonathan to have nodded off to sleep. Thank would make the memory trace easier.

The four seats on the other side of the aisle were empty and Jonathan sat so that he could see the man that Mac had identified as James Whiteley. He concentrated on Whitley's face and closed his eyes.

At first, there was a fog, but that cleared and Jonathan was into Whiteley's mind. There was a jumbled picture of Whiteley and his companion getting onto the train. Jonathan concentrated on going backward through Whiteley's memories. A taxi to Kings Cross station. A pub in London. A phone call. Donnelly. Newcastle. York. It was getting jumbled again. Jonathan concentrated hard, what about Donnelly? Bergen. Overboard. York. York. What about York?

Suddenly the image in Jonathan's mind faded and he opened his eyes to see Whiteley looking across at him.

Jonathan got up from his seat and walked back down to the first class section of the train. When he got back to where Mac was sitting, he told Mac of the images and memories that he had seen in Whiteley's mind.

"Good work!" said Mac. "I suspected as much. These guys have been sent by MI5 or Black Ops to get rid of Sean before he can tell the world what has happened. They are going to do exactly the same as us and watch for Sean to join the train."

"What about Bergen? And overboard?" said Jonathan.

"I think that's how they plan to get rid of him," said Mac. "There is a daily ferry from Newcastle to Bergen, in Norway. They plan to kill him on board, and then dispose of his body in the middle of the North Sea."

"I suppose that solves a problem for us, unless Sean detonates the bomb before they do him in."

"No, I don't want them to get away with that," said Mac. "If they think they can just bring some guy out of jail to do their dirty work and then get rid of him, they will think they can get away with even more dirty tricks. On the other hand, if they know that we are around, they might just think twice."

"What do you plan to do with Sean?"

"I've been giving that quite a lot of thought. I want to try to bring him over to our side," said Mac. "If I can control him, I think he could be a good operator."

"Would you trust him?"

"Of course not!"

As the pair had been talking, the dawn had started to come up and the first rays of morning sunshine were streaming into the coach. Mac called for two more cups of coffee and the attendant brought them.

As they finished their cups of coffee, they felt the train starting to slow down as it approached York. The train stopped and Mac told Jonathan to step out onto the platform and look for Sean.

He looked up and down the platform and he saw a distant figure getting onto the train, and was pretty sure that it was Sean. He also saw the two MI5 men step off the train. They looked up and down the platform then got back onto the train. Then he stepped back onto the train and returned to his first class seat.

As the train started to move, Mac called Roger. "We are just leaving York for Newcastle. Jonathan is pretty sure he spotted Sean getting on the train. Can you confirm that?"

"We've been tracking him and he just boarded your train. He's sitting in coach number three. Your spooks are back in coach number four."

"Keep an eye on the spooks and on Sean," said Mac. "Let me know if there is anything suspicious."

"Right you are," said Roger and he ended the call.

"Time for a relaxing hour to Newcastle," said Mac as the train gathered speed. "Things might be a bit busier once we get to there. I suggest we get an hour's nap." He then noticed that Jonathan had fallen asleep. After all, they had both had little sleep for the past forty eight hours. Mac closed his eyes.

Chapter 32

As the train began to slow for Newcastle, Mac called Roger to inform him and to check on any activity by Sean or the MI5 men on the train. There had been nothing suspicious.

Jonathan and Mac left the train and walked toward the station exit. There were so many people milling around on the station concourse that it was unlikely they would be spotted either by the MI5 men or by Sean. In fact, the MI5 men were so busy watching Sean that there was little chance they would follow Mac even if they saw him.

"Let's concentrate on watching Sean," said Mac, "and let's not worry too much about the spooks."

They followed Sean out of the station to the area where buses and taxis stopped. Sean studied the notice board for a while, then moved to wait at a bus stop labelled "Shuttle Bus to Ferry Port". Meanwhile, the MI5 men were hanging around near the taxi stand but they did not appear ready to hail a taxi. Mac and Jonathan stood well back, behind the luggage trolley parking area and in the shadows where they would be less noticeable.

A shuttle bus arrived and they saw Sean step onto it. The driver got out and loaded Sean's suitcase while Sean took his seat on the bus. Meanwhile, the MI5 men had hailed a taxi. The shuttle bus drove away, followed closely by the taxi.

"We know where they are going, and the ferry doesn't leave for about four hours," said Mac. "We might as well stroll over and get a taxi. We don't need to follow them."

"The spooks also know where he is going," said Jonathan. "Why were they following so closely?"

"Because they are MI5 and we're not," said Mac. "Remember, they might be MI5, but they are still civil servants."

Mac hailed a taxi and they got in. "International Ferry Terminal," Mac told the driver. The taxi drew away from the kerb. Mac turned to Jonathan. "It's about ten miles to the port," he said. "Takes about fifteen minutes."

"This is the first time I've been to Newcastle, I think," said Jonathan.

"I expect that Sean is using this port because it is a long way from where the bomb will be detonated," said Mac.

They arrived at the ferry port and the taxi stopped outside the passenger entrance hall. Mac paid the driver, and he and Jonathan walked into the hall. They walked over to a desk labelled "Tickets and Reservations".

"Two open returns to Bergen," said Mac, "with a cabin in each direction, please."

The clerk printed the tickets and Mac paid with his debit card, then the clerk pointed towards the departure area. "We are boarding now, sir, and thank you for travelling with us today."

Mac looked around the departure area but could see no sign of either Sean or the spooks.

"Best if we get to our cabin straight away," said Mac, "Then you can have a stroll around the ship and see what's up. I would really like you to do a mind link to Sean and get an update on his plans. We need to stop him detonating the bomb."

They passed their bags through security, then boarded the ferry. It was a fairly large ship, designed for the rough waters of the North Sea. Mac led the way to the cabin, which had two single bunks, a bathroom with a shower, two armchairs and a table between them.

There was a large window, which right now showed the roof of the passenger hall. They stored their baggage in the cupboards provided.

"I'm going to give Roger a call," said Mac. "Why don't you have a quick look around?"

Jonathan went out of the cabin and found his way to the upper deck, which contained restaurants, bars and shops. He slowly worked his way through the various rooms until he reached a bar where he saw Sean sitting in a reclining seat with a glass of beer in front of him. Jonathan walked on past and looped round to the other side of the bar and saw the MI5 men sitting in similar reclining seats with coffees in front of them. He walked back to the cabin and reported his find to Mac.

"I think the most important thing is to get into a mind link with Sean before the spooks make their move," said Mac.

"I agree," said Jonathan. "I'll head back to the bar and start a mind conversation with Sean, and then with the spooks."

"Good," said Mac. "I'd better stay here in case I get recognized. I'll call for cabin service."

Jonathan left the cabin, returned to the bar, and took a seat a few feet behind Sean.

Hello, Sean. You are dreaming. What are you doing on this boat Sean?

Getting away from England for a while.

Why don't you go and see your family in Londonderry?

They could probably track me down there.

Who could track you down, Sean?

MI5 of course.

Why would MI5 want to track you down, Sean?

Because I did a job for them.

Don't you trust MI5, Sean?

No, I don't. They've killed us Republicans before to stop us talking.

What job did you do for them, Sean?

My usual job, put a bomb in a tunnel.

Is that the one at Kings Cross, Sean?

How did you know about that? Are you MI5?

Don't worry, Sean. I am on your side. I'm here to help you out. You can trust me.

I can trust you?

Yes, you can trust me. Have you detonated the bomb yet, Sean?

No, I was going to do it late tonight, when there are not so many trains around.

Why is that, Sean?

They told me not to hurt anyone.

Just to cause damage, but not to hurt anyone, right?

That's right. I put a special device on the detonator. It won't allow it to go off if there's any noise in the tunnel.

That's very clever, Sean.

I am a professional in the bomb game.

When are you going to set off the bomb, Sean?

Tonight, when we are in the middle of the North Sea.

How are you going to detonate it from the middle of the North Sea?

My usual way, with a mobile phone.

What if they track down the phone?

It won't matter if they do, I'll throw it overboard.

I don't suppose you can give me the phone number for the bomb, can you?

I'm not sure that I can remember it. It's in my phone.

I'm sure we can find it if we dig deep enough. It starts with 07 doesn't it?

I've got it, I think. 077...0090...0831.

Let me just read that back to you so I can remember it 077 0090 0831, is that it?

Yes, that's it.

What about the code to detonate the bomb?

What use is that without you having my phone?

Why do I need your phone, Sean?

Because the bomb will ignore you if you don't call from my phone,. It has to recognize that I am calling.

What's your phone number Sean?

Jesus, you are asking a lot of questions.

That's what I do, Sean. You're dreaming and dreams sort out all the stuff that's jumbled up in your mind.

Oh, I see! Now what were you just wanting to know?

Your phone number, Sean. The one you are going to use to blow up the bomb.

Yes, to blow up the bomb. Well I bought them at the same time, so it's nearly the same number. It just ends in 0832.

There's one more thing, Sean.

What's that?

The codes to detonate the bomb and to make it safe?

That's easy. Just text BLOW or SAFE to the bomb. But remember, once it's SAFE you can't blow it up.

That's very good Sean. In think you should wake up now.

Sean tossed his head back and blinked his eyes. He had just had the strangest dream. He took a drink of his glass of beer and looked very dazed.

Jonathan walked quickly back to the cabin and reported all he had discovered to Mac, and quickly wrote down the phone numbers before they could fade from his memory.

"We'll need to steal his phone, won't we?" said Jonathan.

"No need, now you've got the number," said Mac. "I've got a gadget here that will re-program a SIM card with any number."

"Another of your clever little gadgets from your MI5 days?"

"Well, not exactly. They didn't have mobile phones back then, but I do have a few contacts."

"Does it actually change the number?"

"No, I can't receive calls on that number, but it fakes out the number that shows up on the phone you are calling to."

"So, what we need to do is send the SAFE text to the bomb?"

"Yes, as soon as I've got this SIM card re-programmed."

"I'm going to go back to the bar and see what I can get from the MI5 guys."

"Good idea. I'll get on with re-programming this SIM." Mac was sitting on the bunk with the back off a phone and extracting the SIM card.

Jonathan made his way back to the bar and chose a seat just behind the MI5 spooks who were sitting reading newspapers.

He started his mind conversation.

You are dreaming. Can we have a little chat?
I suppose so. What do you want to talk about?
Are you MI5?
Of course. Proud to serve.
Black Ops Division?
Yes, I am. And we are on a black op right now.
What is that op?

We call it a clean-up operation.

What are you cleaning up?

A bomb maker who's on the run.

Would that be Sean Donnelly?

How did you know that?

Lucky guess.

What are you going to do with him?

Kill the bastard and throw his body overboard.

Do me a favour, will you?

What's that?

Wait until tonight, around midnight. All the other passengers will be asleep. We'll be right in the middle of the North Sea, his body will never be found.

Midnight. That's when we were planning to do it, anyway.

It's time to wake up now.

Whiteley shook his head and rubbed his eyes. He had had a really weird dream, but he really could not remember it.

Jonathan hurried back to see Mac in the cabin. He gave Mac the information he had got from Whiteley.

"I've got good news," said Mac. "I have re-programmed the SIM in my phone to make it look like calls are coming from Sean's phone. I need to test it by calling your mobile." Mac called Jonathan's number, then as soon as it rang, Mac ended the call. Jonathan compared the caller's number showing on his phone with the number of Sean's phone that he had written down earlier. The numbers matched.

"It works," said Jonathan.

"Good," said Mac. "Let's shut down that bomb of his." Mac typed in the text of SAFE and sent it to the bomb number. "Well, we are either in the clear or we just blew up the tunnel at Kings Cross."

"Perhaps we ought to keep an eye on the news," said Jonathan. "SKY News is available in the bar."

Chapter 33

When Mac and Jonathan got to the bar, there was no sign of Donnelly or the two spooks.

"Jesus!" exclaimed Mac, "They've already got him. Quick! Let's go out on the deck."

The deck was being swept by an icy North Sea wind, and was almost deserted.

"If they are going to throw him overboard, it will probably be over the stern," said Mac. "Less chance of anyone seeing and less chance of his surviving in the prop wash."

Mac headed towards the stern of the boat, closely followed by Jonathan. Just before the deck rail turned in towards the stern, Mac stopped and put his arm out to hold Jonathan back.

"Look! There they are!" said Mac.

The stern of the ship was poorly lit, and in the shadows of the deck machinery Jonathan could just see three figures. One of them seemed to be pointing a gun at one of the others, who looked like he was handcuffed to the deck rail.

"Can you do anything from here?" said Mac.

"I'll try a seizure," said Jonathan. "Gunman first?"

"Yes, do it! Now!"

Jonathan concentrated on the man who was holding the gun. No reaction.

"I need to get closer," said Jonathan. Without waiting for a response from Mac, Jonathan darted forward towards the deck machinery and crouched down behind a winch about ten feet from the group of three. He concentrated on the gunman and, in slow motion, the gunman crumpled onto the deck and dropped the gun. Jonathan concentrated on the second spook, who crumpled to the deck near his colleague.

Mac ran forward to Jonathan and they both ran to the deck rail at the stern. Sean Donnelly was still standing, handcuffed to the deck rail.

"Mr. Fergus, sir, what in the hell are you doing here?" said Sean.

"Watching out for you, Sean. Now, are you going to behave or do I need to leave you out here in the cold?"

"To be sure, Mr. Fergus, I owe you a big favour. But I'd love to know how you brought down those two guys. You didn't use a shooter, did you?"

"You've got a lot to learn about us, Sean," said Mac.

Mac pulled a key ring out of his pocket, picked one of the smaller keys and unlocked the handcuffs that were still holding Sean to the stern deck rail.

Mac turned to Jonathan and winked. "Standard MI5 issue." Sean rubbed his wrists.

Now, Sean," said Mac. "Are you going to cooperate or do we wake up these likely lads?"

"Mr. Fergus, sir, I'll come quietly. Those spooks were going to shoot me and throw me overboard. There's gratitude for doing their dirty work!"

"We'll need to do something with these guys," said Mac. He took the handcuffs and used them to cuff the two unconscious spooks. He cuffed them right hand to right hand, which would make it more difficult for them to move about if they woke up. He then searched both of the unconscious bodies and found another pair of handcuffs, which he used to cuff one of the spooks to the deck rail.

"That should keep them out of trouble for a few minutes," said Mac. "Jonathan, how long will they be out for?"

"I haven't a clue. I've never done that before."

"Well, they are going to make a hell of a racket when they wake up."

"Excuse me gentlemen, what is going on here?" A voice from behind Mac surprised him. He looked around and was confronted by a crew member who was wearing blue jeans, a heavy blue sweater with the ship's company logo across the chest, and a baseball cap with the same logo.

He was clearly a deckhand or some other lowly rank of crew. Mac thought quickly. He pulled out his old expired MI5 identification card and showed it to the deckhand.

"This is an MI5 operation," said Mac, "and I really don't want to kick up a fuss." Mac leaned in a bit closer to the deckhand and lowered his voice. "This poor chap here works for us and these two pieces of scum on the floor are heavies working for a drug dealer. This was a sting operation that I am afraid went horribly wrong."

The deckhand pointed at the two spooks still lying unconscious on the floor. "Are these two men dead?" he asked.

"No, they're just out for the count. But they are going to wake up in a minute and start making a hell of a racket and I really don't want anyone else to find out there are potential murderers on board. There's no danger to other passengers if we can just keep these guys quiet. Can you help us? You'd be helping your country as well." Mac showed his MI5 badge again.

The deckhand looked uncertainly at the three men standing, then down at the two spooks lying on the deck.

Mac looked at Jonathan and winked, then pulled out his wallet and produced a wad of £50 notes. If you could help us and not tell anyone about this mission, I am authorized by Her Majesty's Government to offer you a reward of £300."

"I'll get some duct tape from down below," said the deckhand. "Put a strip across their mouths. That'll keep them quiet."

"Do you mind if my colleague here comes down below with you?" said Mac, nodding towards Jonathan.

"No problem," said the deckhand.

Jonathan followed the deckhand and they disappeared behind a door leading to the lower decks of the ship.

Mac turned to Sean, who was shivering in the cold wind. "When we've got these two sorted out, I'll take you to the bar and buy you a large Jameson's Irish Whiskey," said Mac. "That'll get the cockles of your heart warm again. We can catch up on what we've been doing, and I think I can offer you a much better deal than these guys would."

One of the spooks started to wake up and he grabbed Mac's ankle and twisted. Mac fell heavily to the deck. Sean stamped on the spook's arm with his shoe. There was a sickening crack as the spook's forearm fractured and he was forced to let go of Mac's ankle. Then Sean rammed the spook's head back against the deck, knocking him unconscious again. The other spook started to wake up and Sean repeated the procedure.

Sean stood up. Mac was looking a little stunned. Sean held out his right hand and Mac gave him a firm handshake. "I'll make that two large Jameson's," said Mac.

Jonathan and the deckhand returned with a roll of silver duct tape, which they handed to Sean, who tore off a strip and stuck it over the mouths of the two spooks.

"That'll keep 'em quiet for a while," said Sean.

"I knew I had a job for you in our organization!" said Mac.

"Well, with my record Mr. Fergus, a good employer is hard to find," said Sean, "so I'd be prepared to consider any reasonable offer."

"We need to hide these two," said Jonathan. He turned to the deckhand. "Any ideas?"

Mac produced the wad of £50 notes again and presented the reward of £300 to the deckhand. This seemed to spark the deckhand's imagination.

The deckhand nodded towards the cluster of machinery on the deck. "If we lift up one of those hatch covers, there's a chain locker down there. It's not used these days unless we have to anchor offshore, and we haven't done that in the three years I've been working on this ship."

He walked over and lifted up a hatch cover about six feet square. He used a metal stay in the cover to prop it open. "Let's do it then," said the deckhand, and the four of them dragged the unconscious handcuffed pair to the edge of the chain locker.

"I am so sorry to have to do this," said Mac as he heaved the spooks over the edge of the locker. They landed on the bottom of the locker with a sickening, echoing thud. The deckhand closed the hatch cover.

"I'd better get back to work," said the deckhand.

"Perhaps you could discover these guys on the way back to Newcastle? They'll probably be happy to be alive and they'll probably have no idea how they ended up in the chain locker."

"I've got no idea how they ended up there either, sir," said the deckhand. "I'll be seeing you." He patted his pocket containing the money.

With that, the deckhand walked off towards the forward end of the ship.

Mac turned to Sean and Jonathan. "Right, I think we all deserve a drink for tonight's work."

Chapter 34

The trio found some comfortable seats in the ship's bar and Mac gave Jonathan his debit card and asked him to get the drinks. While Jonathan went on his mission, Mac and Sean settled into the armchairs.

"We go back quite a few years, you and me, Mr. Fergus," said Sean in a soft Irish lilt.

"We certainly do, Sean," said Mac. "What do you think about joining our little organization? I think we could use some of your skills. You seem very good with electronics and communications."

"I suppose it means coming over to the good side," said Sean.

"All sides think they are doing the Lord's work!"

Sean gave a hearty laugh. Jonathan returned to the group carrying two large single malts, two large Irish whiskeys and a pint of beer. He placed the glasses on the table, put the tray on the floor next to his chair and sat down.

Holding up his glass, Jonathan said, "Here's health to us."

While Jonathan took a sip of his beer and Mac took a sip of his single malt scotch, Sean raised his glass, saying "To us all!" and drained his first glass of whiskey in one gulp.

"Sean is thinking of joining us, Jonathan," said Mac.

"Really? That is good news. Sometimes my little tricks need a good pair of knuckles as a backup!"

Jonathan reached out at shook Sean's hand.

"But there is the little matter of Kings Cross," said Sean.

"Don't worry, Sean" said Mac. "That little matter has been sorted out."

"Now how in the hell did you manage to do that, Mr. Fergus?"

"I'll explain that a bit later, Sean, but I've got a couple of housekeeping duties to look after before this ship docks. Give me your mobile phone."

Sean reached in his pocket, pulled out his mobile phone and handed it to Mac, who dialled a number.

After a few seconds, Mac spoke into the phone "BBC newsroom? I want to tell you there is a bomb in the northbound tunnel at Kings Cross station. It has been made perfectly safe. It was placed there by an MI5 Special Forces Unit under the specific instructions of the Prime Minister."

Mac gave a codeword that was used by the IRA whenever they called in a bomb warning to verify that the warning was not a hoax. Then he ended the call.

"I think this phone needs to end up at the bottom of the North Sea," said Mac.

"That was my plan," said Sean.

"Would you do the honours, Jonathan?" said Mac.

Jonathan picked up the phone from the table and walked out of the bar with it. He threw it over the deck rail and watched it fall into the grey, turbulent waters of the North Sea.

He returned to the bar. "Job done!" he said, and he sat down.

"Right," said Mac, looking at his watch, "we will be docking in Bergen in a few hours. We need to get organized. Sean, I think you ought to come with us and we can spend a couple of days talking things over."

"That's a fair deal, Mr. Fergus."

"Thinking about those two spooks in the chain locker, I think it would be advisable to fly back to the UK, so we'll get a shuttle bus to the airport and get a flight back. We will get a flight to London, then a connecting flight to Glasgow. I'll get Karen to meet us at Glasgow with the Land Rover and we can go up to the castle."

Mac looked at Sean, then at Jonathan. "Does that work for everybody?"

"Works for me," said Jonathan.

"I'm with you," said Sean.

"Can I use your phone, Jonathan?" said Mac. Jonathan passed over his phone. Mac called Karen's number.

"Hello Karen!" said Mac, "Mission accomplished. We'll be on our way back to Scotland in a few hours. Can you get up to the castle and bring the Land Rover to Glasgow Airport? Roger will have a spare set of keys for the Land Rover and for the castle."

"Of course," said Karen.

"I think you'll need to fly up to Glasgow and get a train on to Fort William. I'll call you when I know what time we will land at Glasgow. We will need to connect through London, so I think you should have plenty of time.

"Call me when you are changing planes in London."

"Will do. See you soon." Mac ended the call.

"We need to clear our stuff out of the cabin," said Mac. "I'll go and do that if you two want to stay here."

Mac left the bar.

Sean turned to Jonathan and said, "Jonathan, how long have you been working for Mr. Fergus?"

"Actually working for him? About two days. But I met him just after Christmas."

"Mr. Fergus and I go back a very long way."

"Yes, he gave me a bit of background on you while we were chasing you around the country."

"He did, did he? How do you come to be working for him?"

"Well, look at that table." Jonathan put Sean into a seizure and took the empty glasses back to the bar and returned to his seat. He brought Sean out of the seizure. "That's how come I'm working for Mac."

"Now that's the cleverest trick I ever did see," said Sean. "I'd love to know how you did that."

"Trade secret," said Jonathan, tapping the side of his nose with his index finger. "I'll show you a few more tricks when we get back to the castle."

"I can see why Mr. Fergus would like to have you on his side."

Mac returned carrying the two suitcases.

"How are you two getting along?" said Mac as he sat down.

"Like a house afire, Mr. Fergus," said Sean.

Jonathan smiled.

"Do you have a suitcase, Sean?" said Mac.

"It's in the baggage rack, just down there," said Sean, pointing towards a corridor that led from the bar towards the stern of the ship. "I'll go and get it in a few minutes."

The beat of the ship's engines changed, indicating that the vessel was about to enter the port of Bergen. Sean went off to collect his bag and to the visible relief of both Mac and Jonathan, he returned to his seat. After a few minutes, an announcement on the public address system asked passengers to proceed to the exits.

"Which of your passports will you are using today, Sean?" said Mac as the three left the bar.

"To be sure, Mr. Fergus, you're a funny man," said Sean.

They proceeded off the ship and they passed through the immigration and customs formalities without incident. MI5 had given Sean a new identity when they pulled him out of jail and his British passport now identified him as Matthew McConnell, a business man from Belfast. He had business cards and papers in his briefcase showing that he represented an engineering company making parts for the car industry. Once outside the port terminal building, they caught the shuttle bus, which would take them to the airport.

Mac bought three one-way tickets from Bergen to Glasgow. As he had expected, there was no direct flight, and so they flew first to London Gatwick and then changed aircraft for the short flight to Glasgow. As they waited in the Gatwick baggage hall to reclaim their suitcases, Mac called Karen and gave her the flight number and arrival time of the Glasgow flight.

"I put the heat on in the castle and I started out about an hour ago. I should be at Glasgow airport in another hour," said Karen. "I'll park and meet you in the terminal."

"Karen, you are an angel," said Mac. "See you there" and he ended the call.

Once through UK customs and immigration, they had about twenty minutes to wait before their flight to Glasgow, so they went on through security to wait near the boarding gate. Jonathan walked over to a shop and bought a collection of sandwiches, which he shared with the others. "I don't expect we'll get anything on the aircraft," he said as he bit into a sandwich of smoked salmon and cream cheese.

The flight left on time and just over an hour later, they were greeting Karen in the terminal at Glasgow airport.

"Karen, this is Sean," said Mac. "He will probably be joining our team."

Karen shook Sean's hand. "I'm pleased to meet you, Sean."

Sean smiled. "The pleasure is mine."

Karen led the way out of the terminal and over to the car park. They loaded their cases into the back of the Land Rover.

"Do you want me to drive, Karen?" said Mac. "I slept pretty well on the plane."

"Sure," said Karen, and she tossed the keys over to Mac.

Karen got in beside Jonathan in the back seat. Sean got into the front passenger seat beside Mac and Mac started off.

"It's about two hours drive to the castle, Sean," said Mac.

"That's just fine, Mr. Fergus," said Sean.

Within half an hour, Mac found that all three of his passengers had fallen asleep as he drove through the beautiful West Highland scenery. The weather was cloudy but clear and there was no rain. Mac was happy to be driving through his beloved Scotland with a successful mission behind him. He looked in his rear view mirror and saw that Karen was awake, but Jonathan had fallen asleep with his head in her lap and she was quietly stroking his hair.

"I hope you put a bottle of champagne into the refrigerator, Karen," said Mac quietly.

"Two bottles, actually, and I put a joint of beef into the slow cooker as well."

"You are beyond an angel!"

Just two hours after leaving Glasgow airport, Mac pulled the Land Rover into the driveway of McKinnon Castle.

"Wake up you guys," said Mac as he stopped the engine outside the front door

They all got out of the car and Mac opened the front door of the castle and led them all inside.

"I think us three all need showers and a change of clothes," said Mac. "Karen, if you could throw some potatoes in the oven to roast, I'll show Sean to his room and we'll all meet you down here in half an hour."

Karen disappeared into the kitchen while Mac led Sean and Jonathan upstairs to their bedrooms. "Usual room for you, Jonathan? Your room is the third door down on the right, Sean. I'll see you down in the Great Hall in about half an hour."

Half an hour later, Mac was popping the cork from a bottle of champagne and pouring four glasses.

"Ladies and gentlemen, to a successful mission and a safe return home!"

All four drained their glasses and Mac re-filled them. "What's news on dinner, Karen? Need any help?"

"No, it's all under control. Should be ready in about half an hour."

"Good! Let's all sit down and we'll tell you all about our adventures."

They walked over to the armchairs around the fireplace. Karen had got a log fire going while they boys had been showering, and it was now burning brightly in the huge fireplace. When they had all taken their seats, Mac produced three envelopes and passed them round to Karen, Jonathan and Sean.

"These are your wages for the mission."

Inside each envelope was a bundle of fifty-pound notes amounting in total to ten thousand pounds in cash in each envelope.

"With my profound thanks for a job well done," said Mac.

Once again, Mac topped up their champagne glasses. He was just about to speak again, when the telephone rang. Mac got out of his chair and walked over to the phone. He looked at the screen showing the caller ID.

"It's Roger," said Mac. "I think I will call him back in the morning."

Mac returned to his seat. "Now, Karen, where do we start?"

THE END